MW00895819

TEMPT THE COUGAR
COUGAR CHALLENGE

SAMANTHA KANE
LYNNE CONNOLLY
DALTON DIAZ

ELLORA'S CAVE
ROMANTICA PUBLISHING

PLAY IT AGAIN, SAM
Samantha Kane

Monica Allen has always been attracted to younger men. She even married one. But after the divorce, she thought she was through with them for good. Then she meets a group of ladies at RomantiCon, and they form a blog celebrating younger men, Tempt the Cougar.

After another lonely Friday night, Monica challenges her friends to each find a younger man to make their fantasies come true. She doesn't have to marry him—been there, done that, threw away the t-shirt. But for a night of hot sex? Hell yes.

But Sam Lincoln refuses to be just a fantasy. He's a graduate student with a yen for older women and he may have just found the one to make his own fantasies come true. With a little help from his roommate Josh, Sam fulfills Monica's deepest desires. Can he convince this sexy cougar to give him a chance at happily ever after?

BEAUTY OF SUNSET
Lynne Connolly

When Edie Howard meets cosmetic surgeon John Sung, she can't think of anything except getting the younger man naked. Her friends on the Tempt the Cougar blog remind Edie of her promise—to seduce a younger man. It's time for Edie to take action.

Dr. John Sung takes one look at Edie and knows he can't operate on her. He signs off as her doctor and makes her a bet—if he can make her love her body as it is, she won't have any surgery.

John's bet involves close examinations—and torrid, sleepless nights. Their passion is far more than either expects, and John begins to wonder if he'll ever get enough of this woman. Edie just counts her blessings and hopes their age difference won't drive John away.

WINTERS' THAW
Dalton Diaz

OR nurse Elizabeth Winters is forty-one, divorced and determined to figure out what all the fuss is about sex. Her ex spent over twenty years crushing her sensuality and it is long past time for release. Literally, dammit! In her quest, she befriends a group of women her age who admit having a passion for younger men—and thus begins a challenge...

Thirty-year-old engineer Kevin Springer loves solving puzzles and "Elle" has him aching to fit the pieces. The more he gets to know her, the more intrigued he becomes, especially in bed. He quickly realizes he wants more than her offered no-strings-attached, wild sex, but convincing her to take a chance on a relationship isn't going to be easy.

An Ellora's Cave Romantica Publication

www.ellorascave.com

Tempt the Cougar

ISBN 9781419961175
ALL RIGHTS RESERVED.
Play It Again, Sam Copyright © 2009 Samantha Kane
Beauty of Sunset Copyright © 2009 Lynne Connolly
Winters' Thaw Copyright © 2009 Dalton Diaz
Edited by Raelene Gorlinsky, Briana St. James and Helen
Woodall.
Cover art by Syneca.

This book printed in the U.S.A. by Jasmine-Jade Enterprises, LLC.

Trade paperback publication September 2010

The terms Romantica® and Quickies® are registered trademarks
of Ellora's Cave Publishing.

With the exception of quotes used in reviews, this book may
not be reproduced or used in whole or in part by any means
existing without written permission from the publisher, Ellora's
Cave Publishing, Inc.® 1056 Home Avenue, Akron OH 44310-
3502.

Warning: The unauthorized reproduction or distribution of this
copyrighted work is illegal. Criminal copyright infringement,
including infringement without monetary gain, is investigated
by the FBI and is punishable by up to 5 years in federal prison
and a fine of $250,000.
(http://www.fbi.gov/ipr/)

This book is a work of fiction and any resemblance to persons,
living or dead, or places, events or locales is purely coincidental.
The characters are productions of the author's imagination and
used fictitiously.

TEMPT THE COUGAR

๛

PLAY IT AGAIN, SAM
Samantha Kane

BEAUTY OF SUNSET
Lynne Connolly

WINTERS' THAW
Dalton Diaz

PLAY IT AGAIN, SAM

Samantha Kane

഼

Dedication

ॐ

*These days I like my men with a little mileage on them.
This story forced me to remember what it was that I liked
so much about all those young men in my past. I really
enjoyed that. And this book is, of course, for the one who
didn't get away. In the interest of research I had to ask
him some rather personal questions about men and sex, to
which he replied, "I love you."*

Acknowledgements

ॐ

*To the ladies of the cougar club, I salute you. I'd like to
thank Ciana Stone for the series premise, the invitation to
join the series and the blog design. She has been the
driving force behind this collaborative effort. Mari
Freeman came up with the blog title, Tempt the Cougar,
which was inspired. Mari Carr, Lynne Connolly, Dalton
Diaz and Desiree Holt have been a wonderful group of
friends and professionals to work with. Thank you all for
the opportunity and the support.*

Trademarks Acknowledgement
ഇ

The author acknowledges the trademarked status and trademark owners of the following wordmarks mentioned in this work of fiction:

AARP: AARP Non-Profit Corporation

Armani: GA Modefine S.A. Corporation

Barbie: Mattel, Inc.

BMW: Bayerische Motoren Werke

Glenlivet: The Glenlivet Distillers Limited

Heineken: Heineken Brouwerijen B.V.

Author Note

You'll find the women of *Cougar Challenge* and the Tempt the Cougar blog at www.temptthecougar.blogspot.com.

Chapter One
ഇ

Monica Allen stumbled into her house after another very long workday, nearly drunk with exhaustion. She'd been pulling ten or twelve hour days as Assistant Director of Human Resources at Blake and Howell Pharmaceuticals. They'd had to let so many people go in the last year, the paperwork was killing her. Unfortunately, several of the eliminated positions at the company were in HR and that meant she was working overtime to handle jobs that used to be someone else's responsibility. The economy sucked. So did her job. And these days, so did her life.

Well, maybe not that last one, she reluctantly admitted to herself as she threw her briefcase on the sofa and headed to the refrigerator for a beer. And, okay, if she were brutally honest she'd have to say not her job, either. As an administrator at one of the largest pharmaceutical research companies in Research Triangle Park in Durham, North Carolina, she had it pretty sweet. Nestled in an area that claimed four major universities, it was the largest research and development park in the United States. Everyone wanted a job at RTP. They were on the cutting edge of high-tech and pharmaceutical research. And Monica loved being a part of it. She might not have a doctorate like most of the employees she dealt with, but companies that size needed someone who could handle people and not just research and statistics. And Monica was the go-to gal. At least she used to be.

She was pretty sure they had her picture up on the dartboard in the staff lounge. People had started running for cover when she stepped off the elevator. It seemed the only friends she had these days were online. Thank God for the *Tempt the Cougar* blog she shared with her friends.

Monica and her friends also shared a love of reading. and romance novels were their favorite books. Not just romance, but erotic romance. Steamy, no-holds-barred, anything goes, she-didn't-even-know-a-human-being-could-do-that sexy romances. Strong, smart, funny, sexy heroes doing incredibly naughty things to the lucky heroines. Just the thought of some of those things made Monica sigh as she raised the bottle of beer and took a sip of the cold brew. It did nothing to take the edge off. She was horny. She'd been horny since 1995 it felt like. And she had no man. Nope. Not a one. Zippo.

Monica kicked off her shoes in the hallway as she made her way to the office in the back of the house. She stopped as soon as she entered the room and put her beer down to undo her skirt and shimmy out of it. The next thing to go was the damn pantyhose. Geez, she hated those. She stomped on the evil things where they lay on the carpet like a crushed sea slug.

Wearing nothing but her silky blouse, she picked up her beer and sat down in her computer chair. She needed some cougar time. She clicked the bookmark under favorites and there was the blog, a sexy young man staring back at her with a come-hither look, inviting her to come in and play. Oh, how she wished! She'd nicknamed him Rico, and many of her fantasies involved playing with him. She clicked past the adult content warning page and hit the latest blog entry.

Autumn had posted some very sexy cowboy pictures again. God, she loved Autumn, and she loved those cowboys. She scrolled down and had to laugh. The cougars had been busy today. At least three had posted new pictures. Oh, man, Edie put up some more Asian hunks. Sweet. Cam had her usual mixed group, this time a black firefighter, an Hispanic underwear model, and, good lord, a bald bodybuilder whose slicked-up skin glistened in some sort of artful light. Monica sighed. Why was it the only men she was attracted to these days were the impossibly perfect younger men she and her friends posted on the blog?

She remembered when they'd all met at the bar at RomantiCon, an erotic romance readers convention. Monica had been so busy ogling one of the sexy male cover models that she'd walked right into Rachel and spilled her wine all over herself. Her best friend Stevie had laughed so hard she had to sit down, and Elizabeth just happened to be at the table she picked. And then Autumn was there with a tiny little napkin trying to help her clean up and Cam, who'd been at the bar buying herself a drink, bought another wine for Monica. Edie was the only one who hadn't been there. The new friends had spent the remainder of the weekend staring at the cover models, talking about their love of erotic romance, and confessing their attraction to younger men. She couldn't remember now who had suggested starting the blog, but as soon as they'd all gotten home Cam had set up the blog and they'd been in constant contact ever since. It had become her lifeline the last few months.

Monica stared at the bald bodybuilder for a few minutes, contemplating her earlier question. Why was she only attracted to these out-of-reach hotties on the blog? She thought hard, trying to remember the last good-looking man she'd met in person. There were a few that she could assess almost clinically and say, yes, he was attractive. But there had been no spark, no carnal interest on her part. Why? Gary Martinez was built, with a shy smile, but his gray hair made him seem so old. And Phil Sampson was a tall, funny, sexy older man. They were both doctors in the research department. But, oh boy, the young UPS deliveryman was seriously hot. He was muscular, tan, with blond hair streaked by the sun, and every time he came into the office Monica got tongue-tied. There! Someone she'd been attracted to. But her administrative assistant had told her he was gay. Just her luck.

Monica put her elbow on the desk and thunked her forehead down on her palm. Why couldn't she get over her obsession with younger men? Her ex-husband had been younger, and look where that had gotten her. He'd dumped her after she helped pay his way through law school and supported him until he made junior partner in his firm. Once he was ready to have kids he'd told her she was too old for the family he wanted and left her to marry his much younger paralegal. Bastard. She was only thirty-eight, for fuck's sake. She wasn't ready to join that organization for retired people—what the hell was it? Oh yeah, AARP. Well, she wasn't sending in her dues yet.

Monica sat back in the chair and contemplated the beautiful body on her computer screen. There was just something about younger men. They were gorgeous, of course, and their stamina was second to none. But it was the excitement they still felt about life and the future. Everything was possible for them and they knew it. They had an ingrained arrogance and confidence that so many men lost as life beat them down. Well, maybe not beat them down. But they became complacent. They settled for the status quo. She loved younger men who wanted to break through the status quo like a quarterback through the pep rally banner at a Friday night football game. Wham! And she was the cheerleader, starry-eyed and gullible enough to believe nothing could stop them. When would she learn?

Wow, that bodybuilder really was hot. Monica tilted her head to the side. What would she do with him if she had him? First thing she'd do is roll all over him until she was as slick as he was. They could wrestle like two greased pigs. She giggled. She was just perverted enough that the idea made her warm and tingly. He was wearing a tiny pair of briefs that resembled swim trunks. They were so tight they hugged his package, which contrary to the popular belief about bodybuilders, seemed to be more than ample. She could actually see a heavy vein running down the back of his hard cock, which was pressed up against his stomach by the briefs. The photo was black and white, but in the shades of gray she could just make out the head of his cock peeking over the edge of the briefs. *Just sayin' hello*, she thought with a grin. If he said hello like that to her she'd just have to greet him with a big, wet kiss right on that head.

She slid down in the chair, hot and bothered. The tingle had become an insistent pulse in her pussy. She could actually feel herself getting wet at the thought of sucking this young stud off. She closed her eyes and licked her lips at the image. Mmm, she missed that. And she'd learned a lot of new and wonderful things from her erotic romances that she'd like to try, too. Could a woman really take a man so far in her mouth she could caress him with her throat as she swallowed? Monica gulped, trying to imagine a dick there. It was so hot she moaned.

She sat up and hurriedly clicked back to Rico. But she was assailed by thoughts of Rico and the bodybuilder both, Rico fucking her deep while she sucked their new friend off. She was depraved. But, honestly, those were some of her favorite books. With an almost morbid fascination she clicked back to the bodybuilder. She didn't really go for the muscle guys in real life. She liked the boy-next-door types. Nicely built, leanly muscular, the kind who looked like they'd mow your lawn and then fuck you in the kitchen with the same lopsided grin.

She wanted one of those so bad right now she was ready to cry in frustration. She gave in to temptation and slid her hand down her stomach, through her short pubic hair and zeroed in on her clit. At the first touch her whole body jerked. She gasped and then bit her lip. She pressed and circled the hard pebble for a minute, staring at the computer screen. But he wasn't doing it for her anymore. She used her free hand to scroll down to her own post from last week. And there he was. He was young, way too young, but she loved his blond, curly hair blowing in the wind, his bruised-looking lips, the big shoulders and small waist and hips. And there, another pair of tight, white underwear outlining a huge, hard cock. What was he thinking about? What had made him hard? She slid her finger down and gathered some moisture from her pussy and then brought it back to her clit. God, that felt good. She let her eyes slide closed and imagined him pushing her down onto her hands and knees, roughly spreading her legs and then fucking that big cock into her hard and fast. She fucked herself with her finger and rubbed her clit with her palm as she fantasized. He'd be so big, and his skin so soft over hard muscle. She could almost hear him grunt each time he rammed that cock into her.

Monica tried to imagine what he'd think of her soft, swollen inner walls, slick and hot on his finger and his cock. She was so worked up it only took a few short minutes before she climaxed. She thoroughly enjoyed the buildup. She loved the tingling feeling, the ache in her pussy as her muscles clenched tighter and tighter before she broke. She kept rubbing her clit as long as she could before it became too sensitive. She pulled her hand away and sat there panting. Her eyes fluttered open to gaze at her newest boyfriend on the screen.

She was so pathetic. It was Friday night and she was sitting here masturbating to pictures of younger men on the computer. It wasn't only pathetic, but kind of creepy. It felt better when it was the real deal. Not nearly so sad or weird. In the past, when she was with her younger husband, it had felt natural. She was just a woman with a guy who happened to be younger. No big deal. So why was she making it into such a big deal?

She sat up so fast the movable back of the chair popped up and hit her, nearly toppling her to the floor. She braced a hand on her desk while she stared at the computer with wide eyes. She was making it into a big deal. She could get a younger man. She'd done it before hadn't she? Her husband had been twenty-four to her thirty-two when they'd gotten married. He certainly hadn't objected to her age at the time. And she knew there were a lot of younger man-older woman pairs out there. Look at Demi Moore and Ashton Kutcher, for heaven's sake. It was fashionable now. So what was holding her back? Nothing, that's what.

With a shaking hand Monica reached for her beer. It was warm now, but she didn't care. Her mouth was suddenly dry with nervousness. Could she do it? She wasn't exactly the party girl type. She'd met her ex at work. Clearly she wasn't going to meet anyone new the same way. She had to be proactive. She bit her lip again, frowning. She wasn't sure she wanted to get involved with a younger man again, at least not that much younger. It was a risk that she really didn't want to take again. But for some fun and games? Hell, yes.

The computer keys clicked furiously as Monica typed in a new blog entry. She didn't give herself time to think about it too much.

Another Friday Night and I Ain't Got Nobody

This is it. Another Friday night in front of the computer staring at younger men has convinced me it's time. No more fantasies. I want the real deal. So, put your money where your mouth is, ladies. Or where your blog is. ☺ Let's do this! I challenge each of you, and me, too, to go out there and find a younger man to make our fantasies come true. No more dreaming. Let's live, live, live!

She hit Send without even reading over the message. Within moments an answer came back from Edie.

I never realized—I've never actually dated a younger man, not more than a dinner date, anyway. Never been involved with one. But do we go out and hunt them down, or wait for them to come to us? I'm definitely there with you, but I'm not sure where to start. But then, you girls know I'm in the fashion industry, so I should be able to find someone! Maybe it's time I took advantage of those hunky men in Armani underwear!

Hmm. Edie had a good point. Where did one find younger men? Edie may be able to take advantage of hunky underwear models, but Monica didn't have that kind of luck. The computer beeped and another comment came through. It was Rachel. Monica laughed out loud. Apparently she wasn't the only one spending her Friday night staring at younger men on the computer.

You want us to REALLY hook up with a younger guy? Shit, where's my notebook? I need to make a list of yummy potentials. This is gonna be fun!

Monica snorted with laughter. Rachel and her lists. She had a list for everything. Monica already knew she didn't have enough potential younger men to make a decent list. She was starting from scratch. Elizabeth's reply came next.

Oh geez. Seriously? Ok, ok, I know my ex did the younger woman thing, but me with a younger man? It's one thing to think about it...

You know what? Screw it. I haven't had sex in over two years, and it wasn't all that great to begin with. Bring on the hot young hunk, but stick around, ladies. I have a feeling I'll need you.

Well, this was not looking promising. Edie had never done it. Rachel had to make a list first, and Elizabeth needed someone to hold her hand. It was Cam's response, however, that pushed Monica into a decision.

You first. *grin*

Chapter Two
❧

"Stevie, you're overreacting," Monica said patiently into her cell phone while she searched for a place to park.

"Monica, listen to me," her best friend said earnestly, "this is a bad, bad idea."

Honestly, she sounded as if she were talking Monica off the ledge as opposed to trying to discourage her from having a sexual adventure.

"You know why I'm doing this," Monica said again. "This is for me, for fun. This is what I want. What we all want. I issued the challenge, it's up to me to get the party started. I really don't see a downside here, Stevie."

"Fine. Have some fun. But do you have to be so impulsive? Couldn't you think about this a little more? You only issued the challenge last night."

Monica laughed and then yelled in triumph as she zipped her sporty little red BMW into a space on the street moments after another car pulled out.

"What?" Stevie screeched into the phone. Monica rolled her eyes. If only the guys in Stevie's research department could hear her now. At work she was notoriously calm and kind of ruthless, a regular ballbuster. They'd be shocked to hear her sound so girly.

"I found a parking space. What did you think? I just picked up some hustler on the street and got lucky while we were talking?"

"Very funny," Stevie replied dryly. "I thought the hustler was slitting your throat for your Beemer and cell."

"Ha, ha," Monica told her as she checked her lipstick in the rearview mirror. She grabbed her purse and opened the door.

"Exactly which bar are you at?" Stevie demanded.

"Nope," Monica calmly replied. "I'm not falling for that. If I tell you, you'll ride in here like the cavalry and totally ruin this whole sexy cougar thing I've got going on."

"Okay," Stevie said after taking an audible, deep breath. "Let's think this through."

"You sound like a police negotiator," Monica teased.

"Monica, you told me it's a college bar! It might very well be illegal."

"It's not a college bar," Monica clarified. "It's a grad student bar. My ex used to hang out here when we met. They're younger than me, but not that young."

"Coo, coo, ca-choo, Mrs. Robinson. While you're at it advise them all to go into plastics."

Monica burst out in genuine laughter. "I doubt any of them have seen that movie."

"Exactly! You have nothing in common. What are you going to talk about?"

Monica actually pulled the phone away from her ear and stared at it incredulously for a moment before she put it back to her ear and snorted. "I have no intention of saying much more than 'right there and harder'."

Stevie laughed but Monica could tell it was reluctant. "Fine," Stevie said. "But it doesn't matter, you know. I am not going to go on a cougar hunt just because you double dog dared me."

Monica sighed. She'd known Stevie would be the hardest to convince. She was so entrenched in her life and set in her ways. She might fantasize about younger men, but she'd compartmentalized it as "Not Going To Happen", and she just couldn't think outside the box about it. "That's your decision,

Stevie. But you need to do something. You're petrifying in that life of yours. Some archeologist will dig you up in a few thousand years and say, "Well, this one certainly didn't do much with her life. No tattoos, no piercings, and clearly no sex. Just computer ass and carpal tunnel from masturbating so much."

Stevie roared with laughter. "You know very well I have no ass. And your juvenile taunts will not sway me."

Monica's steps slowed. She'd just rounded the corner and she watched a group of guys go into the bar that was her destination. They looked alarmingly young. She gulped silently.

"Mon?" Stevie asked quietly.

"They look awfully young," she said quietly.

"You don't have to do this," Stevie assured her. "No one will think less of you. We'll put our heads together and think of another plan. There must be some other way to find available, younger men. We could go to the gym."

That shook Monica out of her momentary loss of confidence. "And sweat? Are you crazy? I am not a good sweater, Steve."

Stevie knew better than to disagree. She'd forced Monica to go to the gym a couple of times before. "Good point."

"And I'd think less of myself if I backed out now," Monica admitted. "This is something I really want. I realized I've put my life, well my personal life, on hold since that asshole walked out. I almost had myself convinced that he was right. And that is just wrong. I'm only thirty-eight, Stevie. My life could truly begin tonight if I let it. All that shit that came before could be nothing more than practice. This is it. This is my second chance to be and have all that I can. Does that make sense?"

"I thought this was just for fun?" Her best friend gently reminded her.

23

Monica blew out a breath. "It is. At least, whoever the guy is tonight is strictly for fun. But I haven't had this kind of fun since my jerk of an ex left, and you know it. The fun is one part of my life I want back."

"Understood." Stevie was supportive, as usual, but tempered by her characteristic caution. "But I still say it's unnecessary to jump right from the icebox into the fire."

Monica laughed a little desperately. "Exactly. I've been on ice for the last year, and I'm freezing. And I know just what I need to warm up. I'm going to play tonight, Steve, and play hard. I've earned it."

"Don't play too hard," Stevie said with resignation. "You need enough strength to call me tomorrow morning and tell me all about it."

"Make that tomorrow afternoon," Monica answered gratefully. "I'm too old to stay up all night without any sleep." She ended the call as she listened to Stevie laugh.

When she tried to put her cell phone back in her purse she saw that her hand was shaking. She shoved the phone in and then put her shaking hand against her somersaulting stomach. Okay, so she was nervous. Of course she was nervous. It was natural. That didn't mean she couldn't do it. She could. She had to. She took one step, and then another. Isn't that what they said? One step at a time?

By the time she reached the door she'd regained her confidence. It was only a bar, after all. If she didn't meet someone the worst-case scenario was that she had a drink, listened to some music, maybe danced a little and went home. It was still better than sitting home alone all night. She yanked open the door as if she were storming enemy lines and marched into the bar.

Sam couldn't say whether he'd heard the bell over the door ring as it opened, but something made him look up. He caught a glimpse of dark wavy hair and a gorgeous pair of tits in a low-cut top. The crowd moved then and came between him and the newest customer.

"Hey, two beers," some frat boy demanded impatiently as he slapped some money on the bar.

Sam raised an eyebrow. "Any beer?" he asked with an insincere smile.

The guy scowled. "Yeah, really funny. Two Heinekens."

Now why wasn't Sam surprised? But wouldn't the joke have been on him if the kid had said yes? Sam had no idea what he would have given him. Probably Heineken. Sam laughed to himself as he turned to pull a couple of cold bottles out of the cooler. He turned around and placed them on the bar, grabbed the money and looked down while he made change. When he looked up to give it to the kid, she was there.

Whoa. He blinked a couple of times. Women like her just didn't walk into this bar. She was a tiny thing. If there was a god then her ass was more than a match for that chest. Her pretty blue eyes met his across the bar and it was as if a live current of electricity shot straight down to his dick.

"Hey, aren't you Drew Jenkins' mom?" the frat boy asked.

Blue Eyes turned to him with a horrified look. "What?" she asked in a matching tone.

The guy had the grace to blush a little as Sam shook his head. Even an idiot could see she wasn't old enough to be some college kid's mom. How many beers had this guy had already? Sam made a mental note to cut him off after this round.

"S-sorry," the frat boy stuttered. "For a minute you looked like someone I knew. But I guess I was wrong."

"You think?" she answered sarcastically. Sam didn't bother to hide his smile as the kid turned and hurried off. Blue Eyes turned back to him. "Hit me," she said flatly.

Sam blinked. "What?"

She closed her eyes for a minute and sighed. Then she looked at him again. "Hit me? With a drink? Something liquid and alcoholic? Quick?"

Sam could feel his face heat with embarrassment. "Oh yeah, sorry. What'll you have?"

"What has the highest alcohol content behind your little bar there?" she asked, clearly standing on her tiptoes as she craned her neck to see behind the bar.

Sam grinned. "That bad, huh?"

She looked around the bar with an exaggerated grimace. "Yep, that bad."

Sam nodded. "Yep, that bad." He definitely knew what she meant. He had to face this crowd several nights a week. But it helped pay the bills until he got out of grad school.

"I'll have one for the road," she told him, leaning forward to put her elbows on the bar. She almost put her arm in a puddle of beer and Sam stopped her with a hand under her elbow. He lifted her arm and grabbed a bar towel and wiped it clean before gently placing her arm back down on the bar. Oh, yeah. He wanted her. Just touching her elbow had him worked up. How sad was that?

She stared at him for a couple of seconds and then said in a husky voice, "Scotch, please. Glenlivet."

Sam was impressed. "On the rocks?"

She nodded and then she licked her lips. And that was when he decided that he was not going to let her walk out of the bar tonight without him.

When the bartender returned with her drink he put it down in front of her, but when she tried to pay he pushed her money away.

"On me," he said with a smile. "And my name's Sam. Sam Lincoln."

Monica had an almost irresistible urge to toss the drink in her face as if she was Harpo Marx with her hair on fire, this bartender was so hot.

"What?" she said stupidly. It couldn't be this easy. It couldn't.

She reached for the drink but he moved it out of her reach. She gave him a confused look.

"Stay," was all he said.

"Stay?" Oh, yeah, she was totally going to impress him with her witty conversation. She could see his feet being swept out from under him right now.

He laughed. Christ on a crutch. She nearly came in her new slinky black cougar panties. "Stay as in don't leave. Without me."

Monica was so far under his spell she almost said yes without even thinking about it. Then some college kid fell against her, knocking her in the shoulder and she stumbled. The kid laughed and turned to her, obviously drunk.

"Oh, hey!" he exclaimed. "Aren't you a little old for this place? Looking for some young meat, huh?" he winked broadly. "I'm your man, little lady." He scrunched up his face and raised his hands like they were claws. "Rawrrrr," he said, and then he and his friends nearly pissed themselves laughing.

It was so farcical Monica couldn't even be offended, much less embarrassed. She just put her forehead in her palm and reached blindly for her drink. This time the bartender gently pushed it into her hand. "Thank you," she mumbled before she took a drink.

She could feel the bartender's eyes on her and she peeked around her hand to see him with his arms crossed on the bar and his chin resting on his fist, staring at her. He smiled slowly.

"I'm your man," he told her in a voice with a heat index of about 110.

Monica's jaw just dropped open and he laughed. She gulped and managed to squeak out her name. "Monica."

"Monica," he repeated slowly. Then he smiled and straightened up, tapping the bar with a fist. "Oh, yeah, Blue Eyes. You just sit right there. I'll be back."

Did he think she was going to walk away from his blond hair, blue eyes, impressive muscles displayed in a tight tee-shirt, and his low-slung jeans that she was sure were hugging a world-class ass? Last time she checked she may have been old, ahem, older, but she wasn't senile yet.

She grinned as she watched him walk away. Yep, world-class ass.

Chapter Three
ಏ

Josh looked around the bar as he came in the door. He dropped in a couple of times a week to visit Sam, but always during the week and never on weekends. This place was a zoo on the weekends with college brats. He shuddered. If Sam hadn't called in a panic and pulled in a favor he sure as hell wouldn't be here now. He knew Sam made good money here, but it was Josh's version of hell. He had to teach them all week. He didn't want to spend his weekends with them.

He saw Sam waving at him over the crowd and he waded through the gyrating bodies and loud conversation to the bar.

"What's up?" he asked. "Where is she?"

Sam grinned and pointed to the end of the bar. Whoa. Josh whistled low and Sam's grin grew bigger. Josh waggled his eyebrows. "What do you need me to do?"

Sam huffed out a laugh. "Not that. I just need you to entertain her until closing time. These assholes won't leave her alone, and she's getting ready to bolt." Even as he spoke Josh watched some puffed-up football player approach her. He smiled and said something and then he raised his arm and flexed his muscle—actually flexed his muscle—as if he was outlining his selling points. Josh watched the gorgeous little brunette shake her head. The kid frowned and lowered his arm and said something else. She shook her head again and the guy looked pissed.

Josh started to walk over there but Sam was already moving.

"Problem?" Sam asked quietly as he put his arms on the bar. It was casual and yet threatening somehow.

"No," the football player said. Josh remembered him. His name was Matt Taylor. He made the All-Conference team last year, and he'd been in Josh's Chem class. He was a tool.

"Yes," Sam's brunette said. "Tell this Neanderthal that I'm not interested. He apparently doesn't speak English."

"Hey, Neanderthal, she's not interested." Josh answered for Sam because he knew Sam couldn't mouth off to the customers, but Josh sure as hell could.

Taylor turned to him with a frown. His eyes widened in surprise and then his lip curled in dislike. The feeling was mutual.

"Why, if it isn't Mr. Taylor, All-Conference tool," Josh said with a smile. "Who's doing your homework this semester, Taylor?"

"You know the conduct committee threw out your complaint," Taylor said with a smug grin. "You couldn't prove a thing."

And that's what really pissed Josh off. He admitted it. Taylor had won their little war and it really, really bothered Josh. "May you blow out a knee and be passed over in the draft," Josh said, flipping him the bird. "How much did it cost to get Evan Mitchell to switch schools so he wouldn't testify against you?"

"Fuck you," Taylor said as a parting shot and stomped off. At least he was smart enough to realize that he now had less than no chance with the brunette.

Sam sighed. "Josh, don't piss off Taylor and his buddies."

Josh shrugged. "Who cares? He won and he knows it. He doesn't need to do a thing to me."

The brunette laughed and Josh was surprised at the husky quality of it. It made all of his parts want to get closer to hers. He'd never been interested in any of Sam's older women before. But this one was hot as hell.

"Thanks," she said, sticking her hand out. "I'm Monica, and I'm grateful. Not only was he a Neanderthal, but he was also apparently a tool. Good riddance."

Josh shook her hand with a grin and Sam made the introductions. "Monica, this is my roommate Josh Vann. He's agreed to keep you company until I get off."

Josh laughed. "Poor choice of words, dude."

Sam blushed and Monica laughed again. Oh, yeah. Josh was going to make her do that a lot. Sexy didn't describe it.

"You know what I mean," Sam said. He looked at Monica and the heat between them almost peeled the varnish off the bar. "He's going to keep you here until I get off work. Because you are definitely going home with me."

Monica raised an eyebrow. "Don't I have anything to say about it?"

Sam shook his head with an insincere expression of regret. "Nope. Sorry."

Well, Josh had known Sam was interested. He hopped up on the barstool next to Monica with a real sigh of regret. At least he could enjoy her company for a few hours.

Monica turned to him with a rueful smile. "Sorry to ruin your Saturday night."

Josh gave her an exaggerated, shocked glance. "Are you kidding? You've made my Saturday night. I get to spend the night in Sam-approved flirting and ogling with a gorgeous woman instead of doing laundry. Win-win situation."

Sam narrowed his eyes at Josh. "Remember what I said. She's going home with me."

"Dude, we live at the same address. That means she's going home with me, too." As he said it the thought struck Josh that what he'd said could be true in more ways than one. And that would really make his Saturday night. He chanced a glance at Monica and she looked intrigued. But Sam had a frown on his face. Josh just grinned and pointed behind Sam.

"The beer line is getting pretty long. Don't worry, I've got everything under control here."

"So, Sam's roommate Josh, what do you do?" Monica asked as she sipped her scotch. Josh was almost as cute as Sam, but in a brown-haired, wholesome boy-next-door way. He was quite tall and would have been thin if not for the muscles evident under his too-small, dark blue tee shirt. It read, "Don't Worry About What People Think. They Don't Do It Very Often." Amen to that.

The shirt barely covered his hard stomach and she was catching glimpses of an intriguing line of dark hair that arrowed down to his jeans. She licked her lips. Okay, it was official. She was a cougar tramp.

"I'm a grad student in Chemistry. I teach undergrad classes, too."

Wow. That pretty much meant he was way smarter than Monica, and probably just like one of the PhDs she worked with. Maybe they'd be able to find a conversational middle ground.

"Ah, that explains the exchange with Mr. Taylor the tool."

Josh laughed. "I actually like athletes as a general rule. Most of the players are good kids and they try hard. They've got a big load, trying to take classes and play what amounts to pro ball at the same time."

"I'm glad to hear that. I'm a big college ball fan, and I'd hate to think all the players are like him."

Josh shook his head. "Nope. He's the unfortunate exception to the rule."

"How did you meet Sam?" Monica asked, keeping the conversation personal but light. She could not seem to take her eyes off that strip of hair on his stomach. It was getting ridiculous. She forced her eyes up and met Josh's amused ones.

Josh's smile was delighted and far too knowing. "Sam and I met in undergrad. Same class load. We became roommates when we moved out of the dorm. Now that we're in grad school, it works out even better."

Wonderful. Monica's heart sank. "Just how long have you been out of the dorm?" She nearly choked on the words. She'd thought the two of them were older.

"Hey, don't freak. We're big boys."

"What are you talking about now?" Sam's exasperated voice interrupted whatever Josh had been about to say. Sam turned Monica. "I'm big. He's, shall we say, size-challenged."

Monica sputtered on the drink she'd just taken and grabbed the tiny napkin her glass had been sitting on. She wiped her chin as she coughed and laughed at the same time.

"You are so jealous you can't see straight." Josh's comeback was amused rather than angry. "Go get a ruler. I'll prove it."

"No rulers," Monica said, still laughing. "Seriously, how old are you?" she asked Sam.

Sam gave her that melting smile again. Between the two of them she was so wet she was surprised she hadn't slid off the barstool. "I'm twenty-six," he told her. He shrugged. "Not that it matters. Does it?" The look he gave her was curious and she got the impression that he was prepared to convince her it didn't matter if it did. But he was right. She could work with twenty-six. She gave a relieved sigh and Sam grinned again.

Josh took the beer Sam held out for him. Monica waited for them to ask her age but they both just stared at her. "I'm—"

Sam cut her off. "Hot as hell."

Josh nodded. "Burning down the house."

Monica blushed. "Actually, that's not what my birth certificate says, but thank you."

Sam looked over his shoulder as someone shouted behind him. He turned back to Monica and tapped the bar with his fist again. "I'll be back, Gorgeous. Gotta work."

She watched him go and almost sighed like a love-struck teenager. She cleared her throat and saw Josh watching her with those knowing eyes.

"Wait," she said, thinking about their earlier conversation. "Sam's in graduate school, too?"

Josh gave her a funny look. "Yeah, didn't he tell you that? He's in pharmacy school. Next year he'll do his field work and then he'll be Dr. Lincoln."

Monica closed her eyes with a painful grimace.

"You don't like pharmacists?" Josh asked, clearly confused.

Monica opened her eyes and smiled at him. "It's not that. I just don't actually have much to talk to them about."

"Talk to a lot of them, do you?" he replied, amused.

"Yep." He was surprised by her answer. "I work in Human Resources at Blake and Howell Pharmaceuticals."

"Okay," Josh said with a laugh. "You got me. You really do talk to a lot of pharmacists. Chemists, too, I'll bet." He leaned in close as if getting ready to tell her a secret and Monica couldn't resist moving towards him. "That must be why I'm so attracted to you," he said softly. "You understand me."

Monica laughed. "Hardly. That is, not if you start talking chemist-speak."

Josh nodded emphatically. "Got it. No chemist-speak tonight."

"Hi, Josh," a feminine voice purred next to them, and Monica turned to see a Barbie look-alike rubbing her breast on Josh's arm as she smiled coquettishly at him. "Long time, no see."

34

Josh looked distinctly uncomfortable. "Oh, hi, um, Marcie, right?"

The blonde looked momentarily pissed that he'd forgotten her name, but covered it quickly. "Darcie." She smiled at him in a way that said, "I could blow you all night long until you lose your freaking mind."

He turned away from her. "I have to go to the bathroom, Monica. Can I get you another drink on the way back?"

Monica shook her head. "No thanks. I'm sure as soon as this one is done Sam will swoop in and give me a refill."

Josh laughed. "Is he trying to get you drunk and take advantage of you? Good plan." He winked as he climbed off the barstool. Darcie was so close he was forced to slide sideways between her and the stool, and Darcie maneuvered even closer as he tried to dodge a full body press. "It was nice to see you again, Darcie," he said insincerely. He took off as fast as he could.

As soon as he was gone Darcie turned to Monica, all pretenses of sweetness gone. "He won't go home with you," she told Monica coldly.

Monica took a sip of her drink while she studied Darcie. She was pretty enough, she supposed, in a plastic sort of way. Most men liked that. Josh got points for seeing beyond it. She put her drink down on the bar.

"He won't be going home with you, either," she told Darcie sympathetically. "Trust me. When they run away, it's never a good sign."

Darcie's face grew tight with anger. "Is that your experience talking? It's clear you've had quite a bit."

Ouch. Darcie went up a notch in her estimation. Girl could duke it out. Monica just smiled, however. "Looks like I'm about to get some more."

Before Darcie could answer, Sam's voice came quietly over Monica's shoulder. "Beat it, kid. She's right. You're not his type."

Darcie glared at Sam. "Ha. As if you'd know. Everyone knows you're cougar-bait. Any old grandma walks in here and winks at you and you take her home."

Monica turned wide eyes to Sam. He shrugged. "I like older women."

She laughed and raised her glass in a toast to him. "They like you back." She stopped right before she took a drink. "But just FYI, I'm not a grandma."

Sam pretended to consider it for a minute, then shrugged again. "You'll do anyway." They both burst out laughing as Darcie turned and stomped off in a huff.

Sam's expression turned serious as he absently rubbed down the bar in front of Monica. He peeked up at her from under a lock of hair that had fallen across his forehead. Her hand itched to brush it off his face, to feel how soft it really was. She got chills as she realized she'd be doing a lot more than that in a little while. "Did you mean that? That you were about to get some more experience with Josh?"

Monica was taken aback. "No, not with Josh. But I made it sound that way so she'd leave." Monica wrinkled her nose. "Okay, and because she was a bitch and that's the sort of thing you say in a catfight."

Sam laughed. "Good. Because I already told you, tonight I'*m* your man."

Monica smiled and took a drink as Sam turned away to speak to the other bartender. "You sure are," she murmured happily.

Sam turned back and caught her comment. His grin was cocky as he leaned on the bar in front of her again. "I am, huh?" he asked. "Glad to hear it." He dipped the tip of his little finger in her scotch and she watched curiously to see what he was going to do. He brought his finger up and painted her lips with the liquor. Her lips tingled, and she wasn't sure if it was the scotch or his touch. "How's the Glenlivet?" he asked suggestively.

She cleared her throat. "Good." It came out as a squeak when he sucked the tip of his finger clean.

"I can't really tell," he said thoughtfully. Then he slowly reached for the back of her head and pulled her mouth to his. He stopped just before it became a kiss. "Do you mind?" he asked, and she felt his mouth move and his warm breath flutter against her lips, he was so close. She nearly came on the spot.

"Nope," she said stupidly. She would have slapped herself upside the head if he hadn't kissed the bejesus out of her just then.

Holy crap, she thought as she fell into his kiss like Alice down the rabbit hole. She was so far over her head with this young stud she was drowning. And she didn't give a damn. He tasted so good. Better than scotch. Better than chocolate. And the way he felt—it was amazing. His lips were soft and full and hot, and his tongue was slick and rough as it danced around hers, enticing her to play with him. She rubbed her tongue against his and his breathing hitched. Up until that moment he'd been in complete control of the kiss. His loss of composure was the sexiest thing she'd ever heard.

He broke the kiss abruptly and she nearly fell on top of the bar. Okay, that was embarrassing.

His pupils were so dilated she could barely see a rim of blue around them. His chest was rising and falling rapidly and his cheeks were flushed. She'd done that to him? Wow. Then she realized she was just as bad. And she was half on top of the bar.

"Get a room!" someone shouted from behind her and people around them laughed.

She blushed but Sam grinned. "The scotch *is* good," Sam said roughly.

She nodded lamely, and he laughed and tapped the bar again as he walked off. He was practically strutting. What a man. Her man. For tonight.

A few minutes later she watched Josh make his way back to her across the bar, and she thought about what she'd said to Darcie. Suddenly she remembered the fantasy she'd had the night before, but this time it was Sam and Josh fucking her instead of Rico and the bodybuilder. She shivered in arousal at the thought and took a gulp of her scotch.

Three hours flew by. Monica and Josh traded made-up stories about the kids in the bar. They speculated which one was the son of a sheik, or the love child of a Hollywood star and their plumber. They had a long conversation about what kind of super powers they wished they had. Sam came over every couple of minutes and interjected his own comments, all of which were hilarious. Monica hadn't laughed this hard since she'd met her online friends.

"So," Josh finally asked as the bar was emptying out after last call, "what are you really doing here? You didn't actually come here on a cougar hunt, did you?"

Sam was wiping off the bar and loading the dirty glasses into trays that busboys carried into the back. He looked over at Monica with the question in his eyes, too.

She could have lied. But she'd had one too many drinks, and she wasn't a good liar anyway. "Yep, I actually did."

Josh laughed. "No shit?"

Monica shook her head. "No shit."

Sam had walked over and he leaned on the bar in front of her. "Why?"

Monica leaned on the bar in an imitation of Sam's position, their noses almost touching. "Because I like younger men."

Sam grinned and gave her a light, teasing kiss. She moaned out loud at how soft his lips were and how much she wanted him. "They like you back," he whispered.

"So, how often do you do this sort of thing?" Josh asked. He took a sip of his beer as he watched her and Sam.

Monica laughed and sat back. "Including tonight? Oh, once in my life."

Josh's eyes grew wide and Sam laughed. "Decided to live the dream, huh?" Josh asked with a wag of his eyebrows.

Monica frowned. "Sort of. You see, I was married before. To a younger man."

Josh put his beer down and Sam gave her his undivided attention. "What happened?" Sam asked quietly.

"Oh, nothing too dramatic," Monica said. "He left me for a younger woman. Told me I was too old to have a family. At least, to have his family."

Sam winced and reached out to take her hand. "Ouch," Josh said.

Monica shrugged. "I was starting to believe him. Then I met a group of ladies at a conference and we've become great friends." She grinned. "We have something in common, you see. We all fantasize about younger men. We even have a blog about it."

Both men laughed. "That I'd like to see," Sam said, rubbing his thumb along the back of her hand.

"*Tempt the Cougar*," Monica told him. "Google it." She laughed with them. The next part took liquid courage and luckily she'd already imbibed her fair share. "Last night I issued a challenge to my friends. I said it was time to stop dreaming and to live out our fantasies instead. And since I issued the challenge, I figured I'd be the first one to do it." She looked around the bar. "This used to be more of a grad student hangout. That's why I came here. Not for those younger guys."

"Lucky for you," Josh told her as he put his arm around her chair and kissed her cheek, "you found two grad students."

Sam glanced at him sharply. "What does that mean?"

Josh ignored him and focused on Monica. "Is that what tonight is about? Living out your fantasies?"

Monica nodded, her heart in her throat. "Yes. I told my friend Stevie, tonight I was going to play, and play hard."

She could see Josh's eyes dilate he was so close to her. "Does everyone get to play? Or is it only your fantasies?"

Monica's breath hitched and Sam's hand tightened on hers. She couldn't look at him, but clutched his hand in response. "Not just mine," she whispered.

Josh slid off his barstool and stood very close to her. He nuzzled the hair above her ear, then he whispered loud enough for Sam to hear, "Good, because I have a fantasy. Would you like to hear it?"

Monica nodded. Sam's grip was so tight her fingers were going numb.

Josh looked in her eyes for a minute and apparently was satisfied with what he found there. Then he looked at Sam. "I want to have a threesome. I want to know what that's like."

If Monica hadn't been sitting she'd have fallen over. Oh, yes, that was a favorite fantasy. As a matter of fact, she'd just had it, starring these two. Heaven help her. She found herself nodding without realizing she was doing it.

"Sam?" Josh asked. There was something about the way he said it that made Monica think that if Sam said no he'd accept it and walk away.

Sam tugged on her hand and she finally looked at him. "Is that what you want?" His face gave nothing away.

Monica licked her lips and watched Sam's eyes follow the unconscious gesture. His cheeks were flushed. Was it the heat of the bar or something else? "Yes," she answered in a rush.

A slow, hot, wicked grin slowly spread across his face. "If that's what you want, that's what I want. Because I want to watch you live out your fantasies, Monica. That's *my* fantasy."

Chapter Four
℘

When they walked into the apartment it was obvious that Monica was nervous. She'd been quiet on the walk to their apartment. One of the things Sam liked about working at the bar was that it was only three blocks from his apartment. He'd been worried about Monica walking the distance, she was wearing some pretty high heels. He shook his head, amazed again at how short she was. Even in those shoes she barely reached his shoulder. He must be a freak because he really, really liked it.

"Mi casa, su casa," Josh murmured as he closed the door behind them. Monica jerked a little as if his voice had startled her. Sam put a steadying hand on her elbow and she leaned into him a little. He liked that, too.

Sam looked around and tried to see the place through her eyes. Overall it wasn't that bad. They had actual furniture instead of the usual hand-me-down collection you saw in most grad student apartments. Sam had a credit card and he knew how to use it. He refused to live like a transient student. Josh was always telling him he was a pretentious prima donna, but he didn't care. He noticed Josh didn't complain when he sat on Sam's couch with his feet on Sam's coffee table.

And now he was going to fuck Sam's woman.

The thought should have disturbed him. Well, it did, but in a way that was more disturbing than the thought. It actually turned Sam on. How weird was that?

And Monica was clearly Sam's. She and Josh hadn't so much as touched since they left the bar. She'd looked to Sam for guidance since they'd made the decision to do this. She'd held his hand on the walk back—the hand she was currently

41

clinging to, actually. In some strange way he felt that he was giving her pleasure by sharing her with Josh. He was helping her to live her fantasies and making her happy, and wasn't that what a man did for his woman? And Sam was so going to need therapy after this.

"It's very nice," Monica said nervously. "Much better than I expected." She looked horrified after she said it, and blushed.

Sam and Josh laughed. "That's Sam's doing," Josh admitted, tossing his keys on the table near the door. "He likes pretty things."

"Yes, he does," Sam murmured, looking at Monica, letting her see how turned-on he was. Monica blushed even more. Her cheeks were fire-engine red. He wondered if she got that flushed when she had sex, and his cock jerked in his suddenly too-tight jeans.

Fuck this awkward conversation. He wanted to kiss her again. "Let's play," Sam said. He pulled Monica close, wrapped his arms around her and practically lifted her off the floor as he lowered his mouth down on hers.

Monica gave as good as she got. She got a hold on him with a hand in his hair and it felt like it might take a crowbar to get her loose. He growled into her mouth and was so surprised at the sound, a sound he'd never made before in his life, that he nearly dropped her. Monica held him tighter and groaned into his mouth while she humped his leg and Sam nearly embarrassed himself by coming right then and there, his arousal was so intense. His heartbeat had taken up permanent residence in his cock, and the heat of the pre-cum leaking out was driving him crazy.

"Damn," he heard Josh mutter, partly amused but also clearly turned on. The sound of the other man's voice, the knowledge that he was watching them and obviously enjoying it gave Sam a shiver of desire. He humped Monica back and slid a hand down to cup that gorgeous ass of hers in a pair of jeans that ought to be illegal they were so damn sexy.

God she tasted good. Like scotch and heat and wet woman. Her lips were soft and slick. He could taste the shiny gloss he'd watched her apply several times at the bar. It was thick and sticky and made him think of other thick and sticky things he'd like to taste. Suddenly both hands were on her ass and he was hauling her up against him hard, until she wrapped a leg around his waist and his dick was rubbing on the seam in the crotch of her jeans.

He loved everything about having her like this. The feel of her, the taste of her, the smell of her, the desperate heat of her. She clung to him like honey, her fingers running through his hair and then down his back and over his shoulders to clutch his biceps. He wanted to inhale her — to eat her, fuck her, kiss her, love her. He broke the kiss and pulled his head back, putting some distance between them. He had to slow things down. This wasn't meant to be a quick fuck. They had all night and he wanted to use every second of it to savor her.

Their breathing was harsh, and suddenly Sam realized it wasn't only him and Monica panting in the stillness of the apartment. The thought of Josh hot and bothered by them was making Sam crazy. He wanted to show Monica off, to fuck her for Josh and say, *Look how fucking sexy my woman is. Look how good I can make her feel.* And he knew he could, too. He could make her feel so damn good she'd forget that before they left the bar she'd made a point of telling them this was a one-time-only fulfill-a-fantasy fuck, and she'd want him for more.

Whoa. Where had that come from? But as he gazed into Monica's flushed face and dazed expression he knew that's what he'd wanted from the start. Not just a night. He didn't know all the rules, but Sam was pretty sure there was one that said don't start a meaningful relationship with a woman by sharing her with your friends. And yet, he knew that's what she wanted. And he was so far gone he'd admit that he wanted it too.

"What should Josh do, Monica? Tell me what you want Josh to do." Sam didn't ask so much as command. He was so

43

totally getting off on being in charge and that had never been a turn-on for him before. But he wanted to orchestrate everything that happened here tonight. Everything that happened to Monica, anyway.

But Monica just looked at him helplessly and shook her head. "I don't know," she whispered. A frown line appeared between her brows and she looked unhappy. "You'd think I might have researched this a bit more."

He laughed softly. "Shh," he whispered, kissing her cheek. He gave her a little smile. "We'll figure out how to play, Monica. I'll think up games that you'll like. Do you trust me?"

She nodded.

"Good." Sam looked over her shoulder at Josh. Josh was so hot for what they were doing he looked closer to coming than Sam had been a minute ago.

Sam maneuvered Monica over to the big leather armchair. He sat down and then he pulled Monica down to sit between his legs, her back to his front. He pulled her in nice and tight and then cupped one of her large breasts in his palm. She melted back against him with a sigh.

"Would you like to see what you're going to get, Monica?" he whispered suggestively in her ear. "Would you like Josh to show you?"

Josh tilted his head, giving Sam a questioning look.

"Yes," Monica moaned. "Please, Sam."

Sam grinned at Josh. "How about a good old-fashioned striptease, Josh?"

Josh's jaw dropped and Sam laughed. Wow. Was Sam like this with all his lovers? Josh had never seen him so in control. He was clearly the boss tonight, and Josh was along for the ride. Since it was a ride Josh had wanted to go on forever he didn't much care who was in charge as long as he got to have fun.

Monica was completely under Sam's spell. It was so incredibly sexy Josh thought he could come from just watching them together. She'd practically climbed Sam like a monkey up a tree when he'd first kissed her. She was probably so wet it was soaking through her jeans. Josh licked his lips. *Let's get this party started*, he thought. He smiled back at Sam. "Music?" he asked teasingly.

Sam began to hum ACDC's *You Shook Me All Night Long* and Josh laughed. "Good choice."

He didn't dance so much as slowly take his clothes off. He rubbed his hands over his stomach, pulling up the tee shirt a little more each time. Monica's eyes never left him and he could see the pulse racing in her throat.

"You like this, don't you?" Josh asked, running his hand down the strip of hair that went from his stomach to his pubes. "You couldn't take your eyes off it in the bar."

Sam squeezed Monica's breast as his other arm slid around her waist and held her tight. "Is that right, Monica?"

She nodded. "Yes, yes I…I like it," she said breathlessly, pressing her breast into Sam's hand.

"Show her more," Sam ordered Josh. Josh was a little disconcerted at the shiver of excitement that raced down his spine at Sam's tone. While he unbuttoned his fly with excruciating slowness he contemplated it. Was it because it was Sam? He didn't think so. Surprisingly, he thought it was the tone. It could have been anyone ordering him around like that and he'd have gotten excited. Jesus, who knew? He grinned and shimmied his hips a little to make the jeans slide down to his ankles. Monica groaned.

"That's good, Josh," Sam said. "Kick them away."

And there it was. That shiver again. Josh laughed and did as he was told. He was so turned on his dick was aching.

"What?" Sam asked. "What's so funny?"

"Me," Josh told him as he looked up at the two of them sitting so cozy in the chair, watching Josh perform for them. Sam frowned in confusion.

"Trust me, there is nothing funny about *that*," Monica said, pointing at his crotch, his dick hard and long, outlined by the tight material of his dark blue boxer briefs. He thanked the sex gods that he'd put on clean underwear after his shower this afternoon. Not that it mattered. There was a wet stain on the material already, and it was growing as Sam and Monica both looked at him.

Josh laughed again. "No. I mean I like it. I like Sam ordering me around." Sam looked a little alarmed. "Not Sam. I meant I just like being ordered around. And I didn't know that until just now."

Sam grinned. "It would seem we're all learning things about ourselves tonight. Monica, what are you learning?" Sam whispered provocatively in her ear as he rubbed his open palm on her thigh, stopping just short of her cunt. Her hips gave a little thrust and Sam laughed. Josh just groaned.

"I'm learning that two men can be just as frustrating as one." Her voice was disgruntled. "If we're going to play sex therapy, I want a pair of nerdy black glasses and a pen and pad of paper." She pointed to the couch opposite. "I'll sit over there and take notes while you two play."

Sam and Josh laughed. "New fantasy," Josh joked.

"Yep," Monica told them with that wicked grin. "Number six hundred and thirty-two."

Sam whistled. "It's going to be a busy night."

"Well, that one involves you two having sex with each other," Monica teased.

"Cross it off the list," Sam said firmly.

Monica sighed. "A girl can dream, can't she?"

Sam gathered her shoulder-length hair in one hand, pulling it aside to kiss her neck. "You don't have to dream about this anymore, at least," he told her quietly. She tipped her head to the side to give him access and he slid his mouth to her shoulder and bit her through her shirt. She gasped and then licked her lips, sucking a little on the lower one as if holding in her response. When Sam let go of her shoulder he rubbed his nose on the spot. "Show her," he told Josh quietly, never looking up.

It was then that Josh realized it wasn't about him for Sam. It was all about Monica. He was getting off on giving Monica what she wanted. Josh was like a present for her, a toy. And, oh boy, he shouldn't like that so much. But he did.

"Shirt or shorts?" he asked obediently.

"Shorts," Monica said.

"Shirt," Sam corrected her. Monica groaned in frustration, but Josh knew who was in charge. He reached behind him and grabbed the back of his shirt, pulling it over his head.

"Oh, my," Monica breathed. "Look how tall he is." She reached out a hand tentatively, as if she wanted to touch his stomach, touch the hair that fascinated her so much. She hesitated. Sam looked up at Josh from the corner of his eye and nodded, moving his head a little to indicate that Josh should come closer. He took two steps and came up against Monica's hand. She flattened her palm on his stomach and Josh groaned at the heat of her touch.

"Do you like the way it feels?" Sam asked her. Monica rubbed her fingertips from his navel to the waistband of his underwear.

"Yes," she said with a hot little grin. "It feels silky, just like I imagined."

"Do you want to feel more?" Sam's voice was getting deeper, slower, and his cheeks were flushed. Josh could tell Monica's playing with him was turning Sam on.

Monica nodded, looking up at Josh. "If he wants to show it to me."

"You mean if I want him to show you," Sam told her, tucking her hair behind her ears.

"I mean if you want him to," Monica responded breathlessly.

"Josh," Sam said. That was all he had to say.

Josh slipped his fingers under the elastic of his shorts and slowly pushed them down. They snagged on the head of his dick and he sucked in a breath. He pulled the waistband out and over it, and then pushed them over his hips and they fell to his ankles. He started to kick them away.

"Did I tell you to do that?" Sam said sharply.

Josh's dick actually jerked it liked that so much. "No, sir," Josh replied. He just stood there, shorts around his ankles, cock hard and leaking pre-cum, while Monica looked at him. Sam was rubbing both her thighs now, and Josh watched as Sam's hips thrust against her.

"Touch him," Sam told her.

Monica seemed to be having a hard time catching her breath. "Are you telling me what to do?"

"Do you want me to?" Sam asked sincerely.

Monica thought about it a minute, a minute of Josh standing there nude before them, on display, aching, so hot he was afraid he might spontaneously combust. Finally, she nodded. "Yes. But just for now. I don't know if I want to play like that all night long."

"All right," Sam agreed. "We can take it one game at a time. Fair?" He looked up at Josh.

Josh nodded. "You know I'm up for anything." He laughed at his own double entendre, and closed his eyes to savor Monica's throaty laugh. He opened them again to see Sam fighting a smile. "I can't wait to see what other surprises you've got in store for us."

"I can't, either," Sam said ruefully. "I'm winging it here."

Monica reached a hand behind her head and ran it through Sam's hair before pulling his head down next to her to whisper in his ear loud enough for Josh to hear. "You're doing a fine job, Sam. I'm wet, I'm so aroused I can barely think straight, and I want to touch Josh's cock so much my hands are shaking. Part of that is just because I want to touch him, and part of it is because I want to do what you told me to do."

Sam rewarded her by sliding his hands up her thighs and cupping her mound in one of them. She moaned loudly and thrust against his hand. "Then touch him, while I touch you."

Josh had to grit his teeth when Monica reached out both hands and wrapped them around his cock. She slid her thumb over his wet head, rubbing his slit a little, and Josh groaned and had to lock his knees to keep from falling at her feet.

She moaned and her hands tightened on him, and Josh saw Sam rubbing the base of his palm in circles. He must be right on her clit, Josh thought, and he wanted to watch it. He wanted to see Sam's hand on Monica's bare cunt.

Monica had the same idea. "I want to be naked. I want you naked." It was clear she was talking about Sam.

Sam stopped rubbing but left his hand there, pressing into her. Monica's breath hiccupped and she thrust into his hand.

"We can do naked," Sam said, and he nibbled her earlobe a little. He smiled at her. "Naked sounds really good right now."

Monica slid one hand off Josh's cock and cupped his balls and Josh was almost ashamed at the hoarse shout that broke from him. Almost.

"Naked is good," Josh said breathlessly. "Trust me, Sam, naked is good."

Chapter Five
∞

It didn't take long to get undressed. Monica sighed with regret at how little attention was paid to her new black, cougar lingerie in comparison to how much it cost. All Josh and Sam seemed to care about was getting her naked. Okay, maybe that wasn't so bad. As Sam crawled toward her on the bed with a determined glint in his eye, she was actually sure that was pretty darn good.

"Mine," Sam said in a voice that defied anyone to argue with him. Monica gulped. She had absolutely no intention of arguing. She was so his. So totally, absolutely, embarrassingly his that she was a little worried. This was all for fun, right? She shook off her unease. It was part of the game. She was into what they were playing. She'd had no idea at the bar that Sam would be like this. That he'd be so dominant when it came to sex. Or that Josh apparently had a submissive streak.

She smiled at Sam like a cat at the canary. "Yours," she said, adding slyly, "first."

"Yes," Josh murmured triumphantly from his corner of the bed. He smiled back at Monica.

Sam watched the exchange. Without saying a word he reached out and pressed his hand against her cunt, one finger gliding through the moisture there. Monica moaned and clutched the sheets as her hips bucked into his touch. Sam just rubbed that finger on her until they could all hear how wet she was. "For me," he said.

Monica couldn't deny it. "For you," she gasped.

Sam's smile was predatory and made Monica shiver with desire. God, she had no idea she'd like a man like this so much—a take-charge, take-no-prisoners, fuck-you-blind kind of man. She felt her feminist side blush guiltily as her slutty side rolled around in her submission like a cat in catnip.

Sam pushed his finger inside her and Monica met the breach with a thrust of her hips, driving him deeper. Her back arched. "Oh, that feels so good," she purred. "It's been so long since I've had something that doesn't run on batteries in there."

Josh laughed and moved closer to them as Sam lay down next her, draping his leg over one of hers, preventing her from spreading her legs wider. "Keep them close," he whispered. "It makes you tighter."

She clenched on his finger inside her. "Mmm," he murmured nuzzling from her ear to her mouth. "Yeah, Blue Eyes, just like that."

He kissed her then. It was a good thing, because she'd been about to demand that he kiss her. All right, she admitted to herself, beg him. She'd been about to beg him to kiss her. And it was worth begging for. He ate at her mouth as if it were a delicacy. She'd never had anyone kiss her like that, as if her taste, texture, everything was the most delectable thing they'd ever had. She just about melted into the bed when he tenderly licked the corners of her mouth. It was crazy, but for some reason it made her weak and wild at the same time. As if he knew how much she liked it, he did it again.

And that was it. That was why she liked this game so much. Because it was all about her. All about what she wanted, what she liked, what she needed. Sam was attuned to every nuance of her reactions, somehow anticipating what she'd need before she even realized it. He hadn't been lying earlier when he'd said that watching her live out her fantasies was his fantasy, not if his actions were to be believed. She could tell he liked ordering them around. But so far all that he'd asked had been for her pleasure. Oh, yes, she liked this game a lot.

He was fucking her so deliciously with that finger. She fucked it back, fucked him back, the anticipation of fucking his cock burning her up inside. Suddenly she felt fuller, a pinch of stretch and it burned a little. She broke the kiss on an indrawn breath, one knee pulling up as the other remained trapped under Sam's leg.

Sam's fingers stopped moving in her and he just lay there pressing them inside. He'd added another, that was what she'd felt. "Are you okay?" he asked quietly, his mouth still so close to hers she felt the words on her lips.

She nodded. "I…it just surprised me a bit."

He began to move his fingers again. It felt good again, the burn gone. "You're tight, sweet thing. How long has it been?"

She bit her lip as he thrust a little harder, a little deeper.

"Answer me." His voice had gone all deep and sharp again. She shivered, anticipation and arousal building.

"Over a year. Since before he left." She hated to admit that. Hated to admit that no one had wanted to fuck her for over a year.

"He was a moron." That was Josh.

Monica huffed out a laugh. "His new wife doesn't think so." She turned to look at Josh and smiled. "But you're right. He is a moron. Because he never, ever made me feel like this."

"That's all I want," Sam growled into her neck, "to make you feel like this. Better than this." His fingers drove into her again and she moaned as her back arched again. "Good?" he rasped in her ear.

"So good," she said in a voice that sounded suspiciously like she might cry. But only because it felt so good. So amazing.

"Don't ever waste your time on morons, again, Monica," Josh told her, leaning down and kissing her shoulder. "Not when we can make you feel so good."

Monica caressed his cheek. "What do you want, Josh?" she asked him quietly. Sam had gentled his motions, and she hovered on the edge of slow arousal and reckless passion. She liked it. Liked the way he played her body.

Josh blushed and pulled away. He hesitated until Sam said, "Tell her."

"I want to watch."

He couldn't look away from Sam's fingers in her cunt. She moved her leg so he could see better and she saw his breath catch. Sam had insisted they leave the bedside light on, and she was glad now although she'd been very nervous about it when he'd told her. She was even happier for the light when Josh reached out and traced her hip bone with his index finger. Just one finger, but it was Josh's finger, and as she watched two men touching her at once, the heat of it pulsed in her cunt around Sam's fingers.

Sam chuckled, and she felt it in his chest pressed against her. "She liked that. Her cunt just closed around my fingers."

"Oh, God," Monica moaned, turned on by the talk and the language, but embarrassed that she was so easily aroused.

"I like porn."

Josh's statement jerked Monica out of her embarrassment. "What?" She looked at him, confused.

Josh was blushing harder now and he shrugged. "I really like porn. I like watching two other people fuck. This is one of my fantasies. To have two people fuck for me, live and in person—the full monty of reality." His eyes were glued to her pussy. "The sight of Sam's fingers fucking you is so damn hot I can't believe I haven't come."

"You'll come when I tell you, and when Monica is ready for it." Sam's voice was silky smooth but unrelenting just the same.

Josh just grinned. "And thank you, Sam, for just making the whole experience that much better." He shook his head. "No, sir. I will not come until you both say I can."

"Good boy," Monica murmured, and she ran her hand lightly up Josh's thigh. His muscles trembled and his hands fisted. "Now watch." She pulled her hand away and wrapped her arms around Sam's neck. "Fuck me, Sam," she whispered in his ear. "Please. I need you to fuck me."

She moaned in frustration when Sam shook his head. "Nope. I'm not done playing yet."

"Fucking is playing," Monica argued, trying to sound seductive as she ran a finger around the rim of his ear.

Sam shook his head and grinned wickedly. "Who's in charge?"

Monica sighed. "You are."

Sam rewarded her with another hot kiss. "That's right," he murmured when he broke the kiss. "And I know what's best for you, Monica."

"You do?" God, she sounded so weak and pathetic she inwardly cringed, but Sam seemed very, very happy with her response. He nodded.

"Yes, I do." He looked over at Josh. "Both of you."

"What do we need?" Monica's mind was racing with the images in her head. If he only knew how much she really needed.

"You need me to eat this luscious pussy and Josh needs to watch me do it."

"Holy shit," Josh whispered. "Are you crawling around inside my brain?"

Sam didn't answer. Instead he began kissing his way down her body. He stopped to give her breasts some attention. Monica had never really liked men to play with her breasts. She was a D-cup, which was ridiculously large for a woman as short as she was. But watching Sam lick and suck her nipples until they were cherry red and glistening was the sexiest thing she'd ever seen.

Sam kneaded her breasts while he looked at his handiwork. "These are the most amazing tits I've ever seen," he whispered reverently. He winced and looked up at Monica. "I mean breasts. Sorry."

Monica laughed. "I don't care if you call them tits. Especially when you say it like that."

Sam leaned back down and sucked a nipple back into his mouth, flicking it with his tongue before he sucked hard a couple of times. She moaned and grabbed a fistful of his hair. He let go with an audible pop. "When you walked in the door tonight at the bar, I caught a glimpse of dark hair and gorgeous tits. If you hadn't come up to the bar right away, I was going to go search for you."

Monica laughed. "Well, I've had men obsessed with my boobs before. I mean, comparatively speaking, they're at least half of my total body weight."

Sam laughed and gave her breast one last kiss. "I'll be back here later."

"I'd like to fuck those later." Josh had been so quiet that Monica jerked a little when she heard his voice. "Sorry," he said, "but I thought you ought to know."

Monica laughed. "I've never had anyone do that."

"You have got to be kidding me." Josh sounded incredulous, and Sam gave her a shocked look.

"Was your ex-husband crazy?" Sam asked. Then he shook his head. "Sorry, that's already been established. This just confirms it. Never mind."

He sank down between her legs, nudging them open. "Oh, I can open them now?" she asked teasingly.

"The better to eat you," Sam told her, playfully biting her thigh.

She sighed at the sight of his shiny, bright curls contrasting so erotically against her dark pubic hair, and then he put his mouth on her cunt and kissed her, just like he'd kissed her mouth, and her head fell back into the pillow as she cried out.

"Tell me what he's doing," Josh whispered. "In detail."

Monica shook her head, but Sam stopped kissing her and she whimpered.

"Tell him."

She couldn't disobey Sam. Not now, not tonight, not when she loved this game so much.

"Well, then, if you want me to tell him about it you better get back to it," she replied tartly, the effect not diminished by her breathlessness.

Sam just chuckled and licked a path from the sensitive skin of her perineum to her clit. She gasped.

"He just licked me," she panted.

"A little more detail, please," Josh told her, amusement in his voice. "That much I could see. I want to know where, and how it felt."

Sam did it again, slower this time. "He just licked from right past my..." she hesitated, not sure what word to use, "my vagina all the way to my clit. And it felt fantastic." She couldn't believe she was doing this. Sleeping with a younger man, a virtual stranger, wasn't enough. No sir, not for her. She had to have sex with two of them, and then she had to talk dirty the whole time. God, how perfect was this?

"How does his tongue feel?" Josh asked.

"Wet." She licked her lips. Sam licked her cunt. She moaned. "Hot. God, he's so hot."

Sam thrust his tongue inside her and wiggled it around and she thrust against his mouth.

"Monica, please," Josh begged.

"He just fucked me with his tongue," she moaned. "It's still inside me, moving around, and, God, Josh, I don't know how to describe it. It feels so good." She shook her head. "It's like being fucked, but not. It's so amazing because I know it's his mouth on me, his tongue in me. Does that make sense?"

Sam began to eat her in earnest. His tongue was everywhere, inside, on her clit, licking the wetness from her pussy lips. And it was obvious how much he enjoyed it. His hands slid under her ass and lifted her higher against his face, and she felt the rasp of his beard on her sensitive skin, making her shiver.

"You smell so fucking good," Josh whispered. "I can tell you taste good, too. Sam is eating that cunt like it's the dessert buffet."

Sam laughed against her and Monica grabbed the pillow next to her head. "Sam, please," she begged.

Sam pulled back with a long lick from bottom to top again. "Please, what?"

"I want to come with you inside me," she told him. She was shaking, and she tried to hide it. But she knew Sam saw it, and Josh too, probably.

"I want you to come on my face, Monica, and then again on my cock. Is that too much?"

Sam's question was serious, but it made Monica laugh. "In terms of how good that would be? No, it's not too much. But I haven't done this in a while. I don't know how many times I can come."

"That's my job, Monica. You don't have to try or think about it. It's my job to make you come as many times as you want."

"Where have you been all my life?" she joked, raising her head from the pillow.

He winked at her. "Learning how to do this," Sam answered. "I had to do some serious studying before I was ready for a woman like you."

"Like me?" Monica asked, wondering what he meant.

He smiled. "A woman as sexy, beautiful, and adventurous as you," he told her. "You're the trifecta of lovers."

Monica burst out laughing. "Wait a minute. I thought I was the one who won tonight."

"You did," Josh said from beside her. She turned to see him grinning. "Now let's get to the payoff."

Sam was still laughing when he kissed her cunt again, and Monica was thrown right back into the maelstrom of desire she'd been fighting when he stopped. She'd been trying not to come too soon, but they'd made her realize there was no such thing for her tonight. They wanted her to come as much, and as often, as she could. Well, then, so be it. With determination she dropped all her barriers and let the pleasure wash over her, moving her hips, fucking Sam's mouth, moaning when it felt good, doing what felt good.

"Jesus, Monica," Josh whispered in a reverent tone. "You are so fucking hot. Don't hold back anymore."

Sam speared two fingers into her while he focused his mouth on her clit, biting it softly, and it didn't take but a couple of minutes before Monica had an orgasm the likes of nothing she'd felt before. Stars burst behind her eyelids as she rode Sam's mouth and cried out at the pleasure. She cupped her breasts in her hands and squeezed as she pressed her thighs closer together, trapping Sam's mouth on her. He just laughed quietly and swirled those fingers around inside her, making her tremble and pant as intense sensations tumbled through her.

When it was over her legs dropped open and her arms fell to the bed beside her. She felt drained, and yet oddly unfulfilled, which she couldn't explain since she'd just had the best orgasm ever.

"Give me a condom, Josh," Sam growled. "I've got to fuck her. I've got to fuck this juicy, hot little cunt right now."

Okay, that was what was missing. Monica moaned. "Hell yes, you do."

Chapter Six
ॐ

Sam was desperate. And there weren't many times in his life he'd ever said that. His first time, and then the first time with an older woman, the young divorcee next door when he was nineteen. That was about it. And those were different kinds of desperate. He'd wanted to fuck more than he'd wanted to fuck *them*. But now? It was all about Monica. Sam had to get inside her or die. Period. No one else would do. Nothing else would do. His hands were shaking as he tried to put the condom on.

"I want to fuck you so bad I'm shaking," he told Monica, completely unashamed of it. Let her see what she did to him.

Josh moaned and Sam looked over to where he was kneeling beside them to see Josh cover his face with his hands. "Sam, you're killing me," Josh told him dramatically.

Sam laughed, his voice a little shaky, too. "You? I'm the one who's dying here."

"Here, let me," Monica said in a rough voice that Sam loved. It was rough now from her cries and moans. Sam put the rough there. He got a little lightheaded as more blood seemed to pound in his dick.

"Please," was all he said, letting go and watching Monica's hands take over.

"Oh, now it's please," Monica teased. "Aren't you going to order me to do it?"

"Put the fucking condom on and lie down," Sam said, although his heart wasn't in it.

"Too much," Monica told him, pulling her hands away.

"Put it on, Monica. Please." He let the desperation creep back into his voice.

Without a word she rolled it onto his cock. Before she was even done he could see pre-cum slicking up the tip. Her hands were so hot, literally, and soft, and her touch delicate. "Wrap your fist around it," he told her roughly. "I want to feel your tiny hand holding it."

"You make me sound like a munchkin," she complained, but she did as he told her.

He groaned as she held it tightly. She started to move her hand, jerking him, but he grabbed her wrist and held her still. "No," he said sharply. He took a couple of deep breaths. "I don't want to come until I fuck you. Okay?"

She looked up at him with those melting blue eyes wide. "Okay," she whispered. She let go of him one finger at a time. Then she lay back with her arms over her head, one knee raised, and she looked like a fucking pinup in Playboy.

"She looks like a Penthouse model, fuck-me look and all," Josh said appreciatively.

Sam grinned. "Now you're crawling around inside *my* brain," he said, "except I was thinking Playboy."

Monica raised a brow. "Is that good? Or does it mean I'm a slut?"

"You're my fucking slut," Sam growled and he fell over her, stopping himself with his hands next to her shoulders just before he would have crashed down into her.

Monica squeaked and then laughed. "I like the sound of that. But don't tell anyone."

"As long as you like it, what does it matter?" Josh asked the question Sam was thinking.

Monica thought about it a second or two and then shrugged. "Damned if I know. Sam's fucking slut it is."

Sam had to laugh. "You are so funny, Monica. I love that about you."

She got a strange look on her face. "Some people don't like it so much. I have a hard time being serious for any length of time."

"Life is short," Sam told her. "Live it or lose it." The smile she bestowed on him for that pearl of inane wisdom knocked just about every thought from his head.

"Now you're talking," she whispered. She ran her hands up his arms and rubbed his biceps. They were bulging as he held himself up, and he wasn't above a little pride over her obvious appreciation. "That's exactly what I'm doing. Living. Now fuck me, Sam. Make me scream it feels so good."

Sam lowered his forearms to the bed and bent to kiss her. God, she was unbelievable. "No pressure, huh?" he whispered against her lips. As she laughed he kissed her. Swallowing her laugher like that nearly made him come. And how fucking weird was that?

She wrapped her arms and legs around him and pressed her wet pussy against him. She rocked up into him and moaned. Oh, she wanted it all right. She wasn't done, not nearly. He'd make her come at least twice more before he let himself go. Could he do it? He smiled against her mouth.

He sucked her lower lip between his teeth and nibbled it a little. He really loved to bite on her. She was just so plump and juicy everywhere. He fucking loved it. Then he licked the corner of her mouth and she made a breathy sound that was so girly and hot he wished he could record it. "I'm going to make you come twice more before I let myself come, Monica. Okay?" He rubbed his nose on hers while she tightened her legs around him.

"Okay," she said, and there was so much trust and absolute conviction in her response that Sam knew he'd do it. He'd do it because he'd promised her he would.

"You've got to ease up a little so I can get my cock into that tight little cunt, Blue Eyes," Sam whispered.

"Oh, God," Monica moaned, and Sam laughed. That was the response he wanted.

"Are you watching, Josh?" he asked, not forgetting his best friend kneeling next to them. And that was the truly weird part. Sam loved it. He loved putting on this show for Josh. He loved fucking Monica like this in front of someone, loved showing her off, and showing how good he was. It was arrogant, vain, and the wildest thing he'd ever done in bed. He was damn glad it was Josh. If it was some stranger Sam would really be freaking.

"I'm watching," Josh said in a strangled voice.

"I may want you to do more than watch in a little bit," Sam told him, surprising himself. "If I think Monica wants it."

Monica moaned and Sam knew that the second time she came it would be because both he and Josh were doing something to her.

"Yes, sir," Josh said quietly.

Sam reached behind him and grabbed Monica's leg behind her knee. Then he pulled it forward, opening her up. Without a word he pulled his hips back, lined his cock up and thrust into her all the way.

"Sam," she cried out, and her pussy sort of trembled around his dick.

"Damn," he whispered. "You are so tight, sweetheart, and so fucking hot in here. Are you okay?" He had to grit his teeth to keep from fucking her like a wild man she felt so damn good.

"Sam," she cried out again, clutching him in her arms. "It's so good." She gave a little sob that made Sam feel like a man. That was the only way to describe it. It made him feel like this was why he'd been given a dick in the first place. Just for this moment.

"You know," he said conversationally, although his voice was rough and kind of breathless, "I have some seriously stupid shit going through my brain right now."

Monica gave a breathy little laugh. "Don't we all."

And with that she made everything he was thinking legit. He stopped worrying about it and let himself ride that puffed-up, big fucking man feeling. He liked it. A lot. "Am I making you feel good? Tell me. I like to hear it."

"Mmm," she murmured, and her hot little cunt clenched on him. "So good. You're kind of wide, aren't you? Thick and stretching my pussy just right."

Sam choked out a laugh. "Boy, you really got the hang of the dirty talk pretty quick, didn't you?"

"Fuck me, fuck me, fuck me," she chanted. "How's that work for you?"

Sam didn't need another "fuck me". He pulled out and drove back in, kind of rough but he got the feeling that's what she meant when she said it. From her enthusiastic reaction he was right.

She was so wet that each stroke sounded juicy and loud. Another thing Sam hadn't known he liked, but damn that was making him nuts, sending shivers down his back with each move. He let go of Monica's leg and she wrapped it back around him and then she gasped.

"Am I hitting it now, honey?" he murmured. "Just like that?" He gave a hard thrust right into the same place the last one had gone and Monica tried to crawl inside his skin with a whimper. "Oh, yeah," he said smugly. "I got you now."

"You had me at 'I'm your man'," Monica gasped.

Sam laughed and fucked her harder. God! She was fucking strangling his cock in that cunt, she was so tight. It was making him crazy to know he was the first one in here since her asshole husband. The only one to make her feel this good. The only one who knew what she needed and gave it to her. He couldn't help himself. He was practically fucking her through the mattress she felt so good and liked it so much.

Suddenly she gave a strangled scream and her nails dug into his back and then she arched her back and he felt it. He felt her orgasm shaking her like a little earthquake, her pussy getting tighter and hotter and wetter. He rammed his cock in there and let her have what she wanted, grinding his hips against her, rubbing on her clit.

"Sam," she moaned, her voice raspy and thick as she shook in his arms.

Sam tried to let his mind sort of take a vacation so he wouldn't come. And it was damn hard not to come watching her. She was so fucking pretty when she came like that.

She lay there beneath him when it was over, and he felt her muscles relax. She was panting hard and he let her catch her breath.

"That sounded like a good one," Josh commented, and Sam could hear the admiration and amusement in his voice.

"You have no idea." Monica sighed happily. "The best. Ever. In the history of the world."

"Thanks," Sam said sincerely.

Monica shook her head with a smug little grin. "No, thank you. May I have another, please?"

"That's the plan," Sam told her with a deliberate leer. "Any specific requests?'

"More fucking," she promptly answered.

Josh laughed. "God, yes, more fucking."

Sam turned to his best friend. If anyone had told him even yesterday that he'd be in bed with Josh today he would have told them they were crazy. But here he was, and he was planning on making Josh come. Well, not him personally. But he knew just what Monica needed. And Josh needed it, too. Bad. His dick was hard and leaking and bright red. And Sam was sort of freaked out that the sight of it wasn't freaking him out. Instead, the thought of what he was going to make Monica do turned him on even more, if that were possible. It was twisted, but he liked using Josh like a sex toy for Monica to play with.

Sam turned back to Monica. He slid his hands up to hold hers over her head and then he nuzzled her ear. "Josh looks like he's in a bad way, Monica. Don't you think?" he whispered in her ear. Her heart, which had slowed somewhat, began to beat a fast rhythm against his chest. "I hate to see him this way. Don't you? Wouldn't you like to help him out?"

Monica's legs tightened around him. He felt a surge of possessive male pride. It was as if her body was acknowledging that this pussy was his. She didn't want to let Sam go. He didn't even think she realized what she was doing.

"He can't have my pussy, Monica," he told her sternly, loving this game more every second. He thrust into her and she whimpered. "Remember? This is mine." He fucked in and out a few more times while he kissed the shit out of her. He'd always liked kissing, but it had really just been part of the process. Kissing Monica was something else. It was as if she just opened up and gave him her soul through those sexy lips when he kissed her. When he let her up for air Monica looked drunk.

"I want you to suck Josh off for me, Monica. He needs it bad. And so do you. Don't you?"

Josh actually groaned next to them, but Sam didn't look at him. This wasn't really about Josh, although Sam was inexplicably proud that his woman got his best friend so horny.

Yep, first thing tomorrow he was calling a therapist.

He kept his gaze on Monica's, watching for her reaction, for any sign that she didn't want what he was offering her. But he knew her, better than he should, really, considering they'd just met tonight. Deep inside he knew she was going to say yes.

"Yes," Monica whispered.

Oh, my God, she thought, blinking hard, *did I just say that? What the hell am I doing? And I thought I was a cougar tramp earlier. Hello, my name is Monica and I'm cougar trash.*

She was glad Sam couldn't hear the thoughts in her head. He nodded, acting very serious. "I thought so. I'd fuck your mouth and your pussy if I could, Monica. But if I'm going to keep fucking you I've got to give Josh your mouth, okay? It's what I want, Monica. And you're so perfect, to give that to me."

Monica bit her lower lip and nodded. She suddenly, desperately, wanted to suck Josh off for Sam. Anything for Sam. Anything to make him happy.

She was such an idiot. Such a well-fucked, greedy idiot in bed with two incredibly sexy younger men who wanted nothing more than to fuck her, she amended, which didn't sound quite so bad. And she was living the dream, wasn't she?

"Josh," Sam said. That was it. That was all he had to say. She had to give Josh credit, the man knew how to play this game.

Josh scooted over, and when he lowered his dick right over Monica's mouth Sam groaned. "I want to see that dick in your mouth almost as much as I need to fuck you. And that's pretty messed up," he said. He actually looked a little upset.

"But very, *very* fun." Monica figured at this point honesty could only help.

Sam grinned widely. "Open up, baby."

Monica licked her lips, never breaking eye contact with Sam. Then she opened her mouth.

"Good girl," Sam whispered. He moved back until he was on his knees, supported on one hand and holding on to Monica's hip with the other.

"How do I do this so she's comfortable?" Josh asked, sounding a little panicked. "She can't do this with her head turned to the side like that."

Sam paused. Josh was right.

"On all fours, your cock over my mouth," Monica whispered in a husky voice.

Sam smiled at her approvingly. "Have you done this before?"

She shook her head. She could feel herself blushing. "I've read a lot of books." She cleared her throat. "And um, maybe, you know, fantasized a time or two. Or fifteen. Hundred."

"I've got to read some of those books," Sam told her, "if I plan to keep up with you."

Josh took her advice, his hands on one side of her head and his knees on the other, his dick right over her face. Monica reached for him with her mouth and Josh lowered his hips until she sucked the head of his cock between her lips.

"Okay, Josh, now I get the watching thing." Sam watched them a minute in silence. "It's like my own personal sex show," he added with wonder when she took Josh to the back of her throat.

Wow, she really could do that. But then, Josh was a lot longer than her ex-husband. Monica could feel Sam's dick twitching in her cunt as he watched.

Josh groaned. "Oh, yeah, watching you two was hot. But this? This is amazing."

Sam started moving in Monica again, and he set a pace that was in counterpoint to Josh. When Josh fucked gently into her mouth, Sam pulled back. When Josh pulled out, Sam fucked in. Within moments Monica was moaning around Josh's dick.

"Suck hard, please, Monica," Josh begged. Monica pulled her head back slightly.

"Pull out, Josh," Sam ordered him, stopping. Josh obeyed immediately.

Monica licked her lips. "Sorry. I just wanted to say, um, I like you, Josh, but please don't come in my mouth."

Josh laughed. "I'm not offended. And I won't. Where can I come?"

"On her breasts," Sam told him. "Come on those gorgeous tits." He watched Monica carefully to see if that was okay with her. She caught his look and smiled a secret little wicked smile just for him. It didn't matter that Josh could see it, too. It was for Sam and they all knew it.

"Yes," was all she said. Actually she didn't care where he came, as long as it wasn't in her mouth. She sighed. It was all about making Sam happy. If that's what he wanted, that's what she wanted. That was the game, right?

"Sweet." Josh got back in position and Monica sucked him in with a happy little hum.

They fucked her like that for several minutes, and Monica was beginning to wonder if Sam was going to make it. He'd promised her another orgasm before he came, but he was getting wild watching her suck cock. And Monica wasn't even sure she could get off again. She'd already come more than she ever had in one night in her life. Monica let her hand glide over and slide down her belly until she could rub her clit with her finger, just to help him out. Her inner walls shimmied deliciously around him.

"Are you close, Blue Eyes?" he whispered. "Keep rubbing your clit. I like to watch that. I like to watch you being such a dirty girl, baby. Sucking Josh's cock, fucking my dick, rubbing your clit." He was really pouring it on, and it was obvious he was making himself crazier, but the words were pushing Monica closer. "You suck cock so well, Monica. I can tell you love a cock in your mouth. I'm going to have mine there soon, baby. I'm going to eat you out again while you suck my dick."

Monica moaned and her hips were thrusting frantically back at him. Just the thought of sucking Sam off made her crazy.

"Sam," Josh said in a strangled voice. "I can't wait, man. I've got to come. This is too much. I've got to. Please."

"Do it."

As soon as Sam spoke, Josh jerked out of Monica's mouth and rose to his knees again. He fisted his cock and jerked two or three times and then he was coming all over Monica's breasts. Sam groaned at the sight.

Monica gasped as the hot liquid hit her nipples, and then she thrust against Sam wildly. Something about the whole thing just suddenly set her off. Her body was on fire. It almost didn't feel like hers anymore. "Sam," she said in a breathless, scared voice. "Sam."

"Shh, baby," he said. "Come for me. I need to see you do it one more time, and then I'm going to come so hard for you."

Josh fell to the bed beside them and Sam crawled up over Monica again. She pulled her hand away from her clit and Sam slammed into her while she grabbed him and held him close. He didn't even care about Josh's spunk all over her. He pressed her down into the mattress and fucked her hard and she went off like a rocket. She sobbed his name and then he came. He came so hard, just like he'd promised, and all Monica could do was hold him as he trembled and gasped, his face buried in her neck.

Chapter Seven
🔊

Monica woke slowly to a pleasurable pressure between her legs. Suddenly something slick and smooth slid in and filled her and she moaned at how good it felt. She was a little disoriented. The last thing she remembered was falling back into bed between Sam and Josh after she washed up. She'd snuggled up to Sam, Josh curled around her back, and she'd fallen asleep. She took a deep breath as the cock fucking her pulled slowly out and then pushed back in. She spread her legs and lifted her ass, taking it deeper. It was then she realized that she still lay half-pillowed on Sam. That meant it was Josh fucking her.

The thought brought her up short. She was instantly awake and jerked her head up to see Sam watching her, his expression enigmatic. What was he thinking? Was this what he wanted?

Monica shook her head at the thought and frowned. It was what she wanted, wasn't it? It was part of the fantasy.

"Move up, Monica," Josh told her, "onto your hands and knees."

She didn't want to. But she did want to. She was so confused she didn't know which way was up. The cock in her pussy moved again and her body didn't care who it was, it grew wetter and she had to bite back her moan of pleasure.

She rose to her hands and knees, pulling away from Sam. Her front felt cold. He'd been so warm against her she hadn't needed a blanket. Josh put his hands on her hips and then slid them up her sides to brush against her breasts. Josh pressed deep inside her. He felt good, but different than Sam—longer and thinner. And his hands weren't as rough.

Sam had turned his head and was watching them, but he still didn't say anything. She could make out his hard cock in the moonlight. It was still night, then.

"You feel so good, Monica," Josh said, panting a little. "Hot and tight and so fucking wet."

She bit her lip and took his cock as he fucked her. It felt good, but something was wrong. It wasn't like the first time with them. Sam was so quiet, and there was no joking. Did they feel it, too? She chewed on her lip, her pleasure waning. She shook her head and looked up at Sam helplessly.

"Stop, Josh," Sam said quietly. He moved over and Monica lifted up her hand to let him slide under her. "Pull her up a bit, Josh." Josh helped her to rise onto her knees, his cock still inside her. She gasped as the angle changed. Sam was beneath them now, his legs spread so she and Josh were between them. "Come here, baby," he whispered, pulling Monica down on top of him. She snuggled into his chest, her nose buried in the soft skin under his ear. He smelled so delicious. Sam stuffed his hand between them and adjusted his cock until Monica felt it against her clit and lower stomach. She pressed into him and he pulled his hand out and groaned. The tip of his cock was leaking against her, hot and slick.

Sam grabbed a handful of her hair and pulled her face around, his lips hovering just below hers. They stayed like that for a minute, Josh still buried inside her, his hands running over the cheeks of her ass, warming them. Her pussy began to throb with excitement. Was Sam going to have Josh fuck her like this? On top of him?

"Let's play again," Sam whispered to her. "Go, Josh." Monica's eyes widened in surprise. She hadn't expected it, truthfully. She'd thought Sam would take over and fuck her.

Josh pulled out and thrust back in, rocking her against Sam. They both gasped, their mouths so close together it seemed as if they inhaled the same breath. Before she could say anything Sam pressed her lips to his. She fell into his kiss, into the thrill of their two big, male bodies cocooning her in the

71

heat and scent of sex. And suddenly it felt so good, just like last night. And she wasn't going to question it. She wasn't.

She rubbed on Sam's cock while Josh fucked her. And kissed Sam. Endless, drugging kisses, slow and deep and sexy. As her pleasure and excitement built, their almost leisurely kisses became wilder, ravenous. She craved the taste of him. She wanted to devour him. She wanted him to come all over her. Sam was holding her hips now, moving her cunt back onto Josh, controlling her. It was kinky and wild and so hot. He knew just how far to push her back, how hard, and then he pulled her back down onto his cock pressed between them.

"So sweet, Blue Eyes," Sam murmured against her cheek, pressing kisses to her face. He licked the corners of her mouth and Monica's breath trembled between them. "I want you to feel good, Monica," he whispered. He nipped at her chin. "Is this all right? Is this what you want? I only want to give you what you need. Tell me what you need."

"You," she gasped. "This." He fucked her back onto Josh. "Sam," she cried out.

"He wanted you so much, Monica," Sam told her, "and I wanted to give him to you." He was at her neck now, and she had her head arched back to give him room. He licked the pulse pounding in her throat and then moved on to her shoulder and bit her gently, holding her with his teeth and lips as Josh fucked her.

"Oh God," she moaned. Her fingers dug into Sam's shoulders. She could feel her orgasm coming, the heat and shivery pleasure of it racing up her spine to where his mouth was locked on her.

"Come on me, Sam," she begged him. "I want to feel it."

Sam had to let go of her to laugh roughly. "Believe me, I'm going to do just that."

He couldn't believe how sexy this was, to not just watch but feel Monica being fucked by Josh. With every thrust Josh made Sam felt Monica move on him, rubbing and sliding on his cock. Every emotion she was feeling, every spike in pleasure, showed on her face. He could watch her fuck for hours. Or maybe not, he thought ruefully as he felt his balls pull up and begin to burn with his impeding climax. The sight, the sounds, the scent, the feel of Monica and Josh fucking, not to mention the fantastic friction of her pussy and stomach against his cock, was going to make him come.

"Right now," Sam groaned. Monica seemed to know what he meant and she pressed into him, her hips rolling gently, massaging his cock. That was all it took. He bit his lip as his cock jerked between them, and the wet heat of his cum glued their bodies together. His hands were gripping her hips tightly, and he fought the urge to roll up in a tiny little ball and ride out the almost painful pleasure.

"Oh, Sam," Monica cried out, and suddenly she froze against him, the grip of her hands on his shoulders nearly as tight as his.

"Yes," Josh shouted, and Monica rocked roughly against Sam as Josh came.

Monica collapsed against him a moment later and Josh had to lean over on one hand. Sam was suddenly so tired he could barely keep his eyes open. But he made himself watch as Josh pulled slowly out of Monica and then got up to get rid of the condom. In spite of everything, Sam had expected some jealousy. But there was none. Because he knew that even though Josh had been the one fucking her, Monica had done it for Sam. Well, not for him, but with him. It was about the two of them enjoying the...well, the kink factor together. But he knew without a doubt that he couldn't let anyone other than Josh do that to her. If it had been any other guy Sam would be ripping his head off right now.

Ordinarily he was a laid-back, peace-loving kind of guy. Apparently Monica brought out the animal in him. He closed his eyes and smiled to himself as he palmed one of Monica's ass cheeks and squeezed softly.

"Sam." Josh's voice woke him up from a light doze. He opened his eyes to see Josh standing beside the bed with a damp washcloth. "You need to clean her up."

Sam nodded. Monica gave a little snore from atop his chest and he and Josh exchanged amused smiles. Sam gently rolled Monica onto her back on the bed. She opened her eyes and blinked blearily. "Shh, baby," Sam whispered. "I'm just gonna clean you up."

"'Kay," she mumbled. "Sam."

"Yeah, it's me," he told her quietly. She smiled and a moment later she was snoring again.

Sam reached up to take the cloth from Josh and saw immediately that Josh had lost his smile.

"I'm sorry," Josh said sincerely.

Sam didn't try to hide his confusion. "What are you talking about?"

"I shouldn't have fucked her."

Sam shook his head. "What?"

Josh sighed and ran his hand through his hair, leaving it standing up comically, but Sam didn't laugh.

"I knew from the minute I walked into the bar that you and she had a connection. I should have left it alone. I'm sorry."

Sam wiped Monica's stomach off gently. Josh had thoughtfully used warm water on the cloth so it didn't wake her. He ran the cloth softly along the crease under each breast, using his other hand to lift each heavy mound so he could get all his cum off her. Part of him wanted to leave it as a sort of territorial mark, but another part wanted to take care of her and make sure she was comfortable when she woke up. Since that was the sane, commonsense part he was familiar with he went with that inclination.

"I liked it." He didn't look at Josh when he said it. They were close, probably as close as brothers in a lot of ways, but still theirs was not a "share intimate secrets with one another in the dark of night" friendship. They were guys, after all.

"No shit. I may not be Sherlock, but I figured that out."

Josh's sarcastic reply had Sam snorting with suppressed laughter. He shook his head, feeling as if they were back on solid ground. "No, I mean I really liked it. In a seriously kinky, twisted, this is crazy and so fucking hot kind of way."

"No shit?" Josh asked skeptically.

"No shit," Sam told him. "What we did tonight totally did it for me." He shrugged. "I thought it was going to be all about Monica's and your fantasies tonight. I guess I had a few repressed ones of my own. Who knew?" He was done cleaning Monica off, and he looked around for a place to put the cloth.

"Just throw it on the floor," Josh told him.

"Are you nuts?" Sam asked. "It'll stink up the carpet for weeks."

Josh just shook his head and held his hand out. When Sam gave it to him Josh held it by two fingers as if it were radioactive.

"Nice," Sam said. "I let you fuck my woman and this is the respect I get?"

Josh gave him a penetrating look. "So she's your woman already?"

Sam nodded decisively. "Oh, yeah. She may not know it yet, but she is definitely my woman."

"Got it," Josh said nodding. "You don't have to beat me over the head with it."

He turned and Sam watched him toss the washcloth into the bathroom. Sam winced, briefly wondering where it had landed. In the sink or tub, he hoped. Josh started walking out of the room. "Where are you going?" Sam demanded in a hushed voice.

Josh stopped and pointed to the hallway. "To my room."

"No way, man," Sam said, settling down onto his pillow and pulling Monica back over to lie against him. "She may want to get seriously kinky and twisted again in the morning."

"I really, *really* like your woman," Josh told him as he climbed into bed and curled up behind Monica.

"Me, too," Sam said right before a huge yawn nearly cracked his jaw. "Me, too." He closed his eyes and breathed in the scent of her and was very glad to be him.

Chapter Eight
𝕤𝕠

The first thing Monica noticed when she woke up was the unfamiliar smell. Not unpleasant, just...strong. And earthy. Like sex. It smelled like sex. And sweat. Then the pillow beneath her moved and she realized it was a body and she remembered what she'd done last night and where she was.

She was afraid to open her eyes to see if Sam and Josh were awake. She knew she was no beauty queen in the morning, and that was when she'd had enough sleep and hadn't spent the better part of the night getting herself fucked silly. She experimentally ran her hand over the hairy chest it lay on. Suddenly a large, rough palm covered the back of her hand. She stopped moving immediately, feigning sleep.

"I know you're awake," Sam whispered. "Your breathing changed and your eyes are moving behind your eyelids."

She cracked her eyes open and wrinkled her nose. "That's kind of gross. It always creeps me out when I see that."

Sam laughed quietly. "Nothing about you creeps me out." He was still whispering. Monica glanced over her shoulder and saw Josh sprawled across the bed behind her, sound asleep. She looked back at Sam and he held a finger to his lips. "Shh," he told her.

She nodded. "I need to get up," she whispered.

"Why?"

She pursed her lips. "I have to pee."

Sam laughed again. "Oops, sorry. Just climb over me. Josh can sleep through just about anything."

Monica self-consciously crawled over Sam's big chest and slid her feet down to the floor. Before she could stand up, Sam grabbed her arm. "Come back," he said simply. It was so much like his "Stay" from last night that Monica was struck for a moment by déjà vu.

"All right," she assured him, and he let her go.

She didn't turn the bathroom light on. If she had she would have seen herself in the mirror and then she would have been forced to try to repair her appearance. Then she would have been stuck in the bathroom for half an hour. She forced herself to just pee, wash her hands, and go back out. If Sam didn't like her morning look, well too bad. He didn't have to see her this way again, anyway. One time wouldn't kill him.

When she wandered back out to the bedroom she felt awkward and embarrassed. This man had watched her suck another guy off while he fucked her. She bit her lip in mortification. What must he think of her?

Sam was watching her closely. "You found the washcloth, didn't you?" He sighed and rubbed a hand through his hair. "Sorry. Did you step on it?"

Monica didn't know what he was talking about. "What?"

Sam's eyes widened. "Uh, nothing." He motioned her over. "Come back to bed. It's early."

Monica hesitated. She should just go. Leave and not look back.

Sam frowned at her. "What's wrong?"

"Nothing." She could tell she'd spoken too quickly when his eyes narrowed.

"Get over here." He was using that irresistible voice and she shivered with immediate arousal. Sam smiled in satisfaction when he saw it. "Please." His please did not sound as if he were asking. It sounded more like a command.

This was where she should say, thanks, it's been great, have a nice life. Instead she walked over and took the hand he was holding out to her.

"Climb on," he said suggestively, and Monica laughed. "That's more like it," he said, tugging her down on top of him.

She tried to be careful so as not to wake Josh. "I can go if you want me to." It was a token offer. She could clearly tell from the hard bulge under her that Sam didn't want her going anywhere. She wiggled her hips, rubbing on his cock.

He groaned. "I want you to go, but only in the best possible way."

Monica kissed his neck and nibbled his earlobe. He was so gorgeous in the light of day. His skin was a beautiful golden color all over. It wasn't a tan, either. Where on earth had he gotten that skin from? And the curly blond hair that covered his chest was a shade darker than the hair on his head. She hadn't noticed that last night. And he had laugh lines. Faint, but they were there. She could picture him in ten years, those lines more deeply etched, framing his sexy blue eyes.

"I have a fantasy." Sam sounded as if he were confessing a great sin.

"Hmm, have you?" Monica murmured, her head on his shoulder, just enjoying the feel of his skin on hers, his warmth and the sheer size of him. "I was pretty sure we hit a few of your highlights last night."

His chuckle traveled from his chest to hers and then down to her toes, which curled against his hairy legs in pleasure. "Noticed that, did you?"

"You were so shocked at how much you liked what we were doing it was almost funny. It didn't take much to figure out you hadn't done anything so kinky before."

"And hot. Don't forget hot. Because it was. Hot."

"Got it." Monica nodded against his shoulder. "Hot."

"Did you like it?" His question was tentative, as if he really wasn't sure.

"Hello, weren't you in the same bed as me last night? I thought it was obvious, but apparently not." She pushed up, her forearms on his chest and looked into his face. "I liked it. A lot. Thank you." She leaned down and kissed his cheek. "You really did make my fantasies a reality last night, and I'll always be very grateful."

Sam frowned. Well, that wasn't the reaction she'd expected. "Don't you want to know what my fantasy is?" he asked.

"Well, all right," she told him, wondering what on earth they still hadn't done.

Sam wrapped his arms around her and pressed her down until she moved her arms and lay full against him again. He put both hands on her head and guided her mouth to his. "Just you and me," he whispered against her lips. "That's the fantasy I had the minute you walked in the door at the bar."

She loved it when he did that, talked right against her mouth. It was so sexy. "Just you and me?" she repeated, falling back on brilliant conversation to hide her astonishment.

He nodded. "Mmm hmm. Just you and me." Then he played dirty by kissing her, morning breath and all. She tried to pull away, but he wouldn't let her. Instead he kissed her more thoroughly than she thought she'd ever been kissed in all her thirty-eight years.

When he finally let her up for air before her scrambled brains became permanent, Monica was a great big puddle of desire melting on top of him.

"How about it?" he whispered. "Will you help me make my fantasy a reality?" He licked the corners of her mouth, setting her pussy trembling.

"Just you and me," she told him, thrusting down against his cock. He made a delicious, low sound deep in the back of his throat and his muscles shifted beneath her as he pressed up against her.

"Top or bottom?" he asked.

"Both," she answered and he laughed. But she was serious. She wanted him in every way.

His eyes grew hooded when he realized she meant it. "Which one first?" He reached over to the nightstand and grabbed a condom, ripping open the package. Then he stopped, about to pull the condom out of the wrapper. "Um, do you want some foreplay first?"

Monica couldn't help it, she laughed at his comment and his rueful expression. She shook her head. "To be honest, I just want to fuck you," she said. "I just want you inside me right now, no preliminaries. But thanks for asking."

"It's almost scary how much we're on the same page," he murmured. He handed her the condom. "You get the honors."

Monica sat up, straddling him, and took the condom. She scooted back and slid the condom on. Then she rose up on her knees and adjusted herself over him, aiming his cock at her already wet entrance. "Since I'm already here," she told him with a grin.

He grinned right back. "Go for it," he told her. "It's your playground."

Monica notched his cock against her and the first inch slid right in. It felt so good. She was a little sore, but it was a good sore, an ache that his cock soothed. She set both hands flat on his hard stomach and settled down on him, taking him deep. She was panting by the time he was sheathed fully inside her.

"Were you this big last night?" she asked breathlessly.

Sam laughed. She was happy to note he was a little breathless too. "Were you this tight?" He cupped his hands around her ass and lifted her just a fraction of an inch and then let her fall gently back down. It could hardly be called a move but it set off little explosions of heat and pleasure inside her.

"Kiss me, Monica," he whispered. "Kiss me like you mean it."

His words didn't make sense. "I meant all of them," she told him. It was the right thing to say. He slid his big, rough hand up her back and buried it in her hair, then pulled her down to him. When he put her lips against his, he didn't move. He just waited.

Something made Monica hesitate. What was he really asking? What was she really doing? What was this really about? Her head grew dizzy as she tried to figure it all out. And still he waited.

"Are you going to kiss him?" Josh spoke from the other side of the bed in a sleepy voice. "Is this just for the two of you, or do you want to get twisted and kinky again? Give me a minute to wake up, and I can do that."

Panic seized Monica. She didn't know what to do. Keeping this just between her and Sam...that was crazy thinking. Hadn't she just told Stevie yesterday that she was only looking for fun? Sam and Josh were fun. But Sam alone? Sam was trouble. With a capital T. Well, not really. It really began with S, but then that wouldn't make any sense. And she was actually babbling in her own head now. Nice.

Josh ran his hand over her ass. Suddenly she knew she didn't want Josh's hand on her ass. She wanted Sam's there, and only Sam's. *Well, I guess that's that,* she thought. *I'm in over my head and sinking fast.*

"We never did have a real threesome," she said thoughtfully. Sam stopped breathing underneath her and Josh's hand froze. "You know, double penetration and all."

"What?" Josh sat up and stared at her, wide awake now.

"But I'm really not into that," she continued. Beneath her Sam's muscles, which had turned rock hard with tension, relaxed.

Josh flopped back down on the bed. "That was just cruel."

Monica laughed softly. "It was. I'm sorry." She turned and looked into Sam's eyes. "I'm sorry," she whispered. "I'm sorry I hesitated," she clarified. His expression grew hopeful.

"This is my fantasy, Josh," Sam told him without looking away from Monica. "Just me and Blue Eyes."

"But it's going to be just the two of you from now on, for years and years," Josh complained.

Monica's heart began to pound. Okay, that sounded a little scary. Years and years? So that when he was in his prime she'd be on Social Security? Oh, wait, probably not. There wouldn't be any left by the time she retired. But she'd be old. That was the point. Old.

"Calm down, Monica," Sam told her. He shifted beneath her and she realized he was still inside her. And still hard. Apparently the thought of years with Monica didn't faze him.

"What's the deal, Monica?" Josh asked. "Don't you want to try with Sam?"

"I...I..." She didn't know what to say. Try what? Try getting her heart broken again?

"You owe me a chance," Sam said quietly. "I'm not him. Granted, I'm no prize." He smoothed a hand down her back. "I'm still in school and I've got the debt to prove it. And my schedule is crazy, what with work and school. And, well, I am a bit of a neat freak."

"I sort of figured that out last night when you folded my clothes and put them on the chair as I took them off," Monica said wryly.

Sam laughed self-consciously. "I tried to be surreptitious about that."

"A career in espionage is not for you."

Sam smiled ruefully. "Well, you're no prize either. You retreat into jokes and sarcasm when the emotional going gets tough."

"Ouch," Monica said, but he was right. That had been her ex-husband's complaint, too. It was close enough to the truth to sting. "Don't forget I'm old, too."

Sam sighed in frustration. "In case you've forgotten, Grandma, I like 'em old." He turned serious. "But I can handle all that, Monica. I think we could be really good together."

"I can't make any promises," she said. Her voice was shaking. This was why she hadn't tried in the last year. Because she was afraid. The truth was she was scared silly.

Josh puffed out a breath and climbed out of bed. "He's not asking you to marry him, Monica. Just to give him a chance." He turned to face her from beside the bed, his arms crossed, his face disappointed. "From the minute he saw you, this meant something to Sam. Don't make it less than it could be. Don't make me regret last night."

Monica made a face. "Isn't that supposed to be my line?"

Josh turned and made an impatient gesture as he walked toward the door. "Why should women get all the good lines? I've never understood that."

"What about, 'Frankly, my dear, I don't give a damn'?" Monica called after him.

"'Of all the gin joints in all the world, she walks into mine'," Sam added.

"Thank you," Monica said with dignity. "You've helped to prove my point."

"Actually, I meant that one," Sam told her, pushing her hair over her shoulder and then tucking it behind her ear.

"I'm going to make breakfast," Josh told them. "Before you come out of this room you two had better learn to play nice." He closed the door behind him as he walked out.

They lay there quietly for a minute or two. Monica grew increasingly aware of Sam's cock still buried inside her.

"How do you do that?" she asked. "How do you stay so hard when we're having a fight?"

"That was a fight?" Sam asked incredulously. "You are going to be unbelievably easy if you think that was a fight."

Monica laughed a little. "I don't know if I can do it, Sam."

Sam suddenly slid his cock out of her. "Roll over," he said.

Monica missed the heat and hardness of him. She rolled over onto her back, and Sam crawled on top of her. He pushed his cock back into her and she moaned and arched her back.

"It's easy," Sam told her. "See?" He thrust into her softly again and she gasped. Then he nuzzled her neck and lay still.

He felt so good. He *was* so good. Okay, the neat freak thing they'd have to work on. He was going to have a fit when he saw her house. But for now, he wasn't really asking for more than this, was he? He wasn't asking her to risk it all. He was asking for a chance. A chance to see if they fit together outside of bed as well as they fit together in it.

"How often are you going to want to live out those fantasies of yours?" she asked.

"Which ones?" he asked suspiciously.

She looked at him then. "The sharing me with Josh ones," she clarified. She kept her face as neutral as she could.

Sam's expression was pretty closed, too. Another thing they'd have to work on, apparently. Opening up was not easy for either of them. "Not often," he answered finally. Then he sighed in frustration. "Maybe not ever. It was hot as hell last night, but I pretty much wanted to bite his hand off this morning when he touched you."

Monica laughed. "Good. It *was* hot last night. But I wasn't kidding at the bar. Last night was a once-in-a-lifetime thing for me."

"Good." He paused, a look of consternation on his face. "What about the, you know, ordering you around part?"

"Oh, yeah, that part." She watched him seriously. "That part was also hot."

He looked so disgruntled she almost laughed. "Once in a lifetime?" he asked, obviously disappointed.

Monica shook her head. "At least once a night."

At her answer, Sam's eyes lit up. "I can do that."

"You certainly can," Monica told him, playfully biting his shoulder. He growled and a shiver raced down her spine.

"And maybe I'll let Josh watch once in a while," Sam added roughly.

"Oh, you will?" she teased. He sucked on her lower lip a bit and pulled on it before letting go. "Okay," she said meekly, "Josh can watch." Sam laughed.

"Sam," she whispered in his ear as he kissed his way down her neck.

"What?" he whispered back.

"Did you really mean it? 'Of all the gin joints…'" she let words trail off.

He nodded, rubbing his nose along her collarbone. "Umm hmm," he murmured, "but in a good way."

Monica wrapped her arms and legs around him and he slid deeper into her with a groan. "In that case," she said with a smile, "play it again, Sam."

Chapter Nine
✂

So then I agreed to give Sam a chance and we made love all day. By Friday I should be recuperated enough to see him again. Well, I am going to see him Friday. What I really meant was to have sex again. Because I really, really want to have sex with Sam again. And again. And then, if possible, again.

Monica stopped typing her blog post, thinking about what she was going to say. She'd been the first, and it had turned out great for her. But she didn't want to set up unrealistic expectations in her friends. She began typing again.

Honestly, last night was the best thing I ever did for myself. Even if Sam and I hadn't connected like we did, I still wouldn't regret it. For the first time in years I feel alive and sexy and self-confident. I could take on the world! I am cougar, hear me roar!

She laughed to herself.

I think even if I'd only found Josh last night, I'd still be pretty happy about the whole thing. He was sweet and hot and sexy and helped make the night unforgettable. But he's not interested in me romantically. For Josh and for me it was a once-in-a-lifetime thing. A chance to live out our fantasies. I think a lot of younger guys out there fall into this category. And yes, a threesome is indeed as hot as the books make it sound. Even more so. Two guys completely absorbed in making you come as many times as possible? As Josh says, win-win situation.

So eat your hearts out, ladies. I am now an experienced cougar! Cam, do you want a picture of me so you can put me at the top of the blog with Rico? *grin*

Monica laughed as she sipped her coffee. She absolutely could not wait to see what the others had to say. Maybe this would make them all stop fantasizing and start living. With a happy little grin, she hit Publish Post.

BEAUTY OF SUNSET

Lynne Connolly

ॐ

Dedication

ဆာ

To all the ladies of the Tempt the Cougar blog and their creators. To Sam, Dalton, Desiree, Mari F and Mari C. And last, but by no means least, Ciana, for bringing us together. This is the most fun ever!

Trademarks Acknowledgement

ဆာ

The author acknowledges the trademarked status and trademark owners of the following wordmarks mentioned in this work of fiction:

Barbie: Mattel, Inc. Corporation

Calvin Klein: Calvin Klein Trademark Trust Business Trust

Dior: Christian Dior Société anonyme France

Gaultier: Gaulme, Société anonyme

Google: Google Inc.

Ralph Lauren: PRL USA Holdings, Inc.

Victoria's Secret: Victoria's Secret Stores Brand Management, Inc.

Author Note

You'll find the women of *Cougar Challenge* and the Tempt the Cougar blog at www.temptthecougar.blogspot.com.

Chapter One
ஐ

Tempt the Cougar Blog:

We've been talking about younger men for a while now. I've known a few, from male models who can't see further than their own beautiful asses to photographers who demand favors for good pictures. But I've never been to bed with one. They prefer the young vulnerable wannabes, the ones who can't fight back. I've always despised younger men.

But you girls have given me a new way of looking at it. I think you're right. There are some great younger men out there. You know that a few years back my husband traded me in for a younger model. I know, I know, some of you have the same experience but this bastard keeps waving her in my face.

Time I did something about it. I'm seeing a plastic surgeon next week. It's taken me a long time to get to this point but I'm taking the plunge. Then watch me.

Comments

Cam: Are you sure you want to do this, honey? Being in the fashion industry makes you super-conscious, I know that, but you've held your own for this long why change it now? I'll call you.

Edie had faced many mirrors in her time, especially naked, but this one was different. This time it was all about her instead of the clothes she wore—or didn't wear. That made a change.

People didn't understand that essential difference—they weren't looking at her, they were looking at Sunset, supermodel, and the Dior or the Calvin Klein or the Gaultier she was wearing, not at Edie Howard. She didn't even use her first name professionally. She was Sunset or Adelaide, not Edie the little girl from Coventry, England, scared of her own shadow.

So here she was facing another mirror in another large bare room with white walls and large mirrors. The décor had been like this in the designer ateliers so that the master and his acolytes could see the toiles and the gorgeous fabrics clearly. Here it was to see the patient. Her.

She stripped out of the surgical gown and kicked it aside as she took a step closer to the mirror. Time to see herself clearly. Maybe for the last time.

Time had etched lines next to her eyes and between her nose and mouth. Until recently she'd regarded them as well-earned trophies. Her breasts still held up well, though, and despite two children having nestled inside it her stomach remained firm and only slightly rounded.

At least they were allowed curves in her day.

She twisted to view her ass. Not bad for an old broad. It could still do with some refining though. She doubted Victoria's Secret would want her in its spectacular. Once they would have paid her a shipload of cash and bestowed as many freebies as she wanted on her but these days she bought her own underwear.

She preferred it that way. The modeling profession had been dirty enough in her day but she'd remained in control of her career.

Until this. Maybe she was wrong, maybe she shouldn't do this. Doubt assailed her again as she looked at the body in the mirror, a body most women her age would be proud of, but used to assessing her body as if it were a separate entity, Sunset rather than Edie, she could see the flaws. And maybe just maybe she could shove it to the man she'd thought she'd loved who hadn't hesitated to trade her in when a younger more amenable Sunset clone walked by. A shame the bastard seemed to get more handsome with age. The suave cool features, the dark hair which she suspected owed as much to the bottle as her autumn-tinted locks and every line added character instead of age.

Fuck him. He wasn't worth it. But as much as she knew that, she couldn't block the raw hurt that nobody but she knew about. Not her first two husbands, still her friends, not her family. Nobody except Cam and now the other women on the blog. They said she should be what she was, not turn herself into a Stepford Wife.

She wished she had half Cam's confidence. A makeup artist and friend of many years' standing she'd been the only one horrified when Edie had mentioned the possibility of plastic surgery. Everybody else had been all for it, encouraging her to take the plunge.

Except Cam and the other women on the Tempt the Cougar blog.

She turned back to the mirror and only then saw the man who'd silently appeared in the open doorway. She didn't even pretend to be startled. Why should she? After the chaos of changing rooms at big runway shows, she could hardly pretend to be shocked by one man staring at her naked body. However gorgeous that man was.

She'd seen photographs of John Sung, plastic surgeon extraordinaire, but she'd never knowingly been the recipient of that dark intense stare emphasized by his heavy black-framed glasses. No one had ever looked at her like that with a hunger she could almost touch. She'd seen desire before; she'd even seen possession but not starvation.

Not for her surely. John Sung had to be significantly younger than she.

This man reminded her of nobody she'd known before. This was something new. A shudder passed through her and, strangely, embarrassment. He was looking at *her*, Edie, not Adelaide nor even Sunset. And Edie was embarrassed.

She snatched up the robe and shrugged into it, pulling the belt tight around her waist and turned to face him, tilting up her chin. Only then did he speak.

"You are the most beautiful creature I have ever seen in my life. I can't do this to you. Wait here."

He spun around and left the room.

Chapter Two
ॐ

Dr. Sung refused to treat Edie and referred her to the man with whom he shared a business, but not a medical list. Just as well really because after that zing between them she'd felt even worse about the procedure. Procedures.

So after an hour with the efficient but clinical Dr. Roubiere, Edie was unaccountably distracted and exhausted. She went home and stood in the shower for half an hour, washing away the lines Roubiere had made on her body telling her what he'd do if she went ahead, where he'd operate.

She traced one of the blue lines just under her breast. He wanted to lift them, maybe remove some of the bulk as he put it. She touched her legs at the lines he'd put there to show her where she'd have minimal marks for a while if she had liposuction on her thighs. Return her to the pre-baby model shape. She'd always regarded her body as her income, an instrument she used to get what she wanted, never part of her. So why did this latest effort feel like a personal criticism, a step too far?

Maybe she was just depressed today. It happened.

A little cheering up. That was what she needed. She reached across to the glass shelves and opened the plastic box labeled "cotton" that didn't actually hold anything of the kind. It was just the convenient holder for her waterproof toy.

She held the silver marvel in her hand, enjoying the way the smooth oval fit so well there. With a twist she turned it on and it pulsed slowly. Another twist took it to three-quarters strength, a buzz she sometimes used to ease aching muscles after a day in high heels.

That wasn't what she had in mind today. She eased it over the lines now at last fading under the relentless beat of the overhead fitting. If she went ahead with the procedure, she wouldn't feel much there anymore. The surgery would destroy nerve-endings but Dr. Roubiere had assured her he'd minimize the damage inside and out and he was good. That was why she'd chosen them.

But she didn't think about Roubiere now. She let her mind pass on to the tall devastating figure of his partner, the surgeon who'd refused to take her as his patient. What was his first name? It didn't matter, not for this. Sung would do. She had no idea what had caused his outburst but that didn't matter now. He'd help her ease her tension now although he'd never have any idea that he did. Sung would sing for her.

She smiled at her stupid pun, feeling her tension ease further. She slid the small vibrator down her body over her stomach, slightly rounded these days, not hollow as it once had been. It shook a little. Tummy tuck planned, she eased the bullet over the line Roubiere had drawn and watched it melt and disappear down the drain.

Sliding the sleek silver cylinder further down, she teased herself with a slow advance, going further still until she nudged her clit, that peeked through the curls she allowed herself these days. In her model days she'd shaved it all off but now she allowed herself the indulgence of a neatly trimmed bikini-waxed thatch. Now it nestled sweetly between her thighs, honey blonde, hiding secrets she'd never shown to the public. She'd always drawn the line at full nudity. Expensive lingerie had cupped her, revealing evening dresses threatened to expose her but she'd kept her cunt to herself, always. And her husbands, lovers and doctors.

The reminder sent her back to Sung although he'd never be her doctor now. He stood behind her clad in nothing—no make that tight boxers, lovingly revealing a long hard cock, the water drenching the underwear so it was almost transparent. She licked her lips. She'd love to take that treat into her mouth, suck it right down and make him come, refuse to release him, taste the reward he'd give her. But not today. Today he took the bullet from her hand, eased it down between her folds, now wet with more than water, slick with her arousal. Her clit was throbbing, begging for attention but Sung wouldn't touch it not yet. His body pressed close behind hers, his strong mobile hands working her teasing her.

He pushed ever closer to her opening, sliding the vibrator up one side of her labia and down the other. It wasn't her holding the bullet now it was him. He moved it past her opening along, around, setting up a circular route until with a vicious twist that drove the bullet up to full capacity he pushed it right inside her.

Her hand went to her clit, unable to stand his teasing anymore but in her mind, he pushed it away and took over himself. She could almost hear his voice telling her to hold on, to let him do it all. So she did. Her fingers became his.

The vibrator had worked its way up to her sweet spot deep inside. She'd always been afraid to let it go that far before, worried she might not get it out but she was so wet now she had difficulty keeping it in. It was barely two inches long but it reached spots few other devices could.

Sung's fingers flicked and tweaked but orgasm remained frustratingly distant just out of reach. If she didn't come now she'd burst.

She reached forward keeping her eyes closed. She didn't need to see to flick the switch that changed the water stream from directly overhead to body wash. If she bent her knees and moved slightly forward—like that—the hard rain drummed over her clit.

"Fuck, oh fuck!" Her cry came from somewhere deep inside as everything exploded. Her clit sent pulses deep inside her body her cunt throbbed and clenched around the bullet sending her into overdrive turning her restless body into pounding waves of orgasm.

Edie stood shaking with one hand against the tiled wall to steady herself, the other fishing inside her pussy for the bullet. It came out easily, nestled in her hand as she held it under the water to clean it.

She rinsed off and exited the shower wrapping herself in thick fluffy towels. She lingered in the bathroom letting her imagination wander again. Now she wanted to slide into bed next to someone, let him hold her and talk over the events of the day before she explored him, maybe fuck him again.

Yeah like that was going to happen.

Chapter Three

ಚಿ

Tempt the Cougar blog:

I walked away but I can't stop thinking about him. I'm like a lovesick teenager and I can't help wondering if I did the right thing.

Camille: Honey if you're still wondering then there's business between you. He's not your doctor anymore so anything you do is up to you. Maybe he's wondering the same who knows?

Edie: I think I'll leave it like it is. Probably ships passing in the night or something like that.

A week later Edie stood contemplating a splash of paint on canvas. She usually liked modern art but this exhibition had left her cold. Even though the splash was a particularly bright blue. Maybe she was getting old or something. She'd felt enervated for a while now.

Then a sense a feeling of warmth swept through her and a voice deep and somehow intimate came from behind her. "Good evening."

She caught her breath, breathed out slowly and turned around. "Hi."

John Sung, mouthwatering in a charcoal gray dress shirt unbuttoned at the neck and black pants that she knew had to be designer, probably Ralph Lauren from the cut. His coal-black hair was cut short to shadow the shape of his skull and his clean-cut cheekbones pushed against the gleaming olive skin just below the almond-shaped eyes.

As before, he watched her with a single-minded intensity. She shuddered and resisted clasping her arms around her body in a protective gesture. She hadn't felt this vulnerable for years. Forever.

Stupid. She shook her hair back off her face and held out her hand. "Nice to see you again."

A brief touch of his fingers then he was gone but she felt the tingle of the contact and wondered at it.

"Do you like them?"

She glanced around and gave a small shake of her head. "They're perfectly fine but not precisely my thing."

"Me too."

She couldn't walk away again. Remembering the advice the blog girls had given her she decided to take the plunge. Business between them was far from over she knew that now. "I live fairly close. Come back for coffee?"

"I'd be glad to."

An old invitation but sometimes it meant just that. She could throw him out if she chickened out but at least she'd know him better, get him out of her system. Or they might just take things a bit further. She'd play it by ear.

Once outside the gallery they passed the inevitable gamut of photographers who were more interested in the young heiress who'd just entered the gallery, and walked away from the event where John lifted his hand and hailed a passing cab. "Dreadful weren't they?"

She laughed. "Yes but it wouldn't have been good to say it there. That artist is the latest sensation."

He shrugged. "I couldn't live with one of those daubs for long. They'll be decorating some swish offices downtown before too long."

That was so much what she was thinking she had to suppress her laugh. He helped her into the cab and she gave her address and leaned back. "Not your offices though."

"What?" She turned her head to see him staring at her. "Oh yes. Not fucking likely. Pure crap. Pretty colored crap but if I had to look at it every day I'd probably go insane."

She laughed knowing what he meant. She kept her apartment clean and filled with only the things she needed or she liked. Only a few people saw it these days so she kept it exactly as she wanted it.

The taxi dropped them at her building and she let Sung—John—pay. Fighting over a few dollars didn't seem worth it especially with her stomach tying itself in knots. The night she'd allowed her fantasy to win played through her again sending thrills through her. And he hadn't even touched her. Probably wouldn't.

They stood either side of the elevator as if avoiding touch and he stood back and let her exit first when they reached her floor. She unlocked the door and passed through turning on the floor lights and touching the dimmer. Not too intimate just lower than full-on.

"Nice." He stood in the center of the large room and turned around. She'd left the mezzanine in shadow but its depths added richness to the effect. She'd kept colors muted and cool, comfortable and soothing rather than challenging. This was her home now.

"Thanks. My last husband liked the French Empire style. Fussy, lots of gold, you know the type."

He laughed. "Yeah. I've visited places like that. This is more to my taste. Understated. Classy."

She smiled as she walked through to the kitchen area and found the coffeemaker. "Do you want something fancy, cappuccino or latte?" Her huge machine did it all.

"No just coffee, black, no sugar."

Typical. Most men asked for it like that but she'd bet a few secretly went for double shot Americano when nobody was looking. Somehow this man seemed the black coffee type. "Make yourself at home."

She wasn't. She took hers with cream. Plenty of it. She put the cups on a tray and carried them through.

He'd settled on a wide sofa facing the window. Lights twinkled in a cityscape she'd dreamed about as a little girl in small-town England. Now she was here. Having that view reminded her every day how lucky she was. It helped. Sometimes.

She put the tray down on the glass coffee table and sat next to him. They didn't have to touch on this wide sofa but somehow she ended closer than she'd planned. He sat, his arms spread over the back and arm, more relaxed than she'd imagined him.

"Do you want to know why I wouldn't take you as a patient?"

Yes. She swallowed and touched her throat. "Why?"

His glasses glinted as he turned away from the view to look at her. Behind the lenses his eyes gleamed with truth. "Because I can't take a scalpel to you. You're too perfect to be touched. I can't do it."

She frowned squinting at him. "Are you sure you were looking at the right woman? Maybe one time I might have agreed with you but you have to know that I'm forty-five years old. My years of perfection are behind me."

"I don't think so. You carry your life with you and you'll only grow better with age. Your bone structure is awesome."

"Is that a medical term?"

"Abso-fucking-lutely." He huffed a laugh but didn't sound amused. "Operating on you would be like smoothing the statue of the Venus de Milo back to a blurry approximation of what it should be."

"You're dissing plastic surgery? Don't you make your living at it?"

His lips twisted in a wry smile. "Sure. But we don't just do vanity stuff. And even then, it isn't always about vanity. Some women make their living from keeping their beauty. Actresses over forty have difficulty getting good leading roles or they did before the cosmetic surgeon got to work. Pop stars need to be honed and buffed weeks after giving birth or leaving rehab." He shrugged. "You know how it goes."

"None better." Although she'd never gone under the knife before she didn't condemn people who made that choice. "But now it's my turn. I take it the confidential doctor-patient relationship between us is no more?"

"You take it right. It was there for about five minutes. I'd still like to know why you want it done but you're not talking to a doctor here. Just me, John, a man."

She loved that voice the way it purred over her skin like a caress. Suppressing her shudder she concentrating on what he was saying. It wasn't as if she were about to give him her deepest secrets after all. "I've written my autobiography and I have a promotional tour coming up. TV personal appearances. I got a new manager, Randy Norwood, and he put me in touch with a great ghostwriter who helped me turn my book into something else rather than just another exposé."

His eyes widened. Despite his sangfroid that name impressed him. "Doesn't Norwood manage Pure Wildfire?"

"'The hottest rock band on the planet'. Yes. And Scott Evans, one of the most literate writers on the planet. Randy picks people he's interested in."

He watched her, his stare almost unnerving. "And does Norwood say you have to have cosmetic surgery?"

She hesitated not wanting to lie to this man. His tall leanness intrigued her and his cologne-free male scent reminded her of heat between the sheets. "Not exactly. He says I should do what I feel most comfortable doing."

"Wise man. So will you let me help you?"

She arched a brow. "You think I need help?"

He smiled. "You're nervous about the surgery. I don't have to be a doctor to spot that. So I want you to take a bet." He leaned forward, picked up his coffee and sipped. Used to reading and using body language she sensed his tenseness, his need for something to do rather than look at her. This bet was important to him.

"What kind of bet?"

He stared into the midnight depths of his cup. "If I make you feel good about your body will you cancel the work?"

She shook her head not understanding. "What do you mean?"

"I'll pay attention to any part of your body you want to have altered. I'll prove to you that it's perfect as it is."

"How?"

He came around to her front and faced her again. "You need to take the bet first." His voice had lowered to a purr.

"And what's the bet?"

"If I can't persuade you I'll pay for all the surgery."

"Is this an excuse to get into my panties?"

"Totally." He looked up meeting her gaze and his intensity took her breath away. She felt that stare as if he was touching her and the hairs on the back of her neck rose. This was more than a quick fuck. For both of them.

"How old are you?" she said suddenly her senses jolted by his low words. She needed to think.

"Thirty-five."

"Ten years younger than me. Are you kidding me, John Sung? Or is this some kind of sick wish fulfillment? When you were a kid, I was the star of the runways, rushing from show to show in July in Paris, in the pop videos, my picture on billboards all over the world in satin underwear. Is that it? Did you want me then?" She was used to that, men wanting her without knowing who she was. She wouldn't take offence though she would be disappointed.

He put down his cup half drunk. "When I was a child I hardly ever looked up. I never noticed billboards, I didn't watch pop videos. I was a boring fat kid and I grew into a studious teenager. I didn't lose the weight until I started running every day in my late teens. So no. I want you now as you are not as you were ten or twenty years ago."

The air between them stirred, tightened. The women on the blog had encouraged each other to get out of their ruts find someone younger less hidebound. So was this her younger man? Could she crow on the blog tonight?

Oh yeah. What the fuck was she waiting for? John Sung would be her first younger male.

"Yes."

He stared at her as if she'd grown a spare head before he laughed. "I didn't think you would but, fuck, I hoped for it. Are you sure? You want to go on this trip with me?"

"Maybe you'll take me further than I've ever been before. Maybe you'll only take me to the end of the street. I have no idea but it's worth a try." And maybe he'd jolt her out of this uncharacteristic doubt and help her see where the next part of her life would lead her.

"Go upstairs take off your clothes and find a robe. I'm betting you have a full length mirror somewhere. I'll give you ten minutes. Five."

When she got to her feet, she was surprised to find how shaky she felt. As if this was her first time. Okay, first time in a while but she was far from a virgin. About twenty men away from one if she counted. Which considering her age and profession wasn't bad at all.

She crossed the room and climbed the stairs, feeling his avid stare all the way up the open-plan pale blue glass steps. She watched every one, careful with her steps. The almost untouched brushed steel handrail was a welcome aid now.

Her feet sank into the soft carpet on the mezzanine and she walked through to her bedroom.

He was as good as his word. Five minutes and she heard a soft knock on her bedroom door and called, "Come in!"

He entered. He'd discarded his jacket and now stood in dark immaculately tailored pants and a charcoal-gray shirt unbuttoned at the neck. He crossed the room. She'd changed into a white fluffy bathrobe and stood in front of her mirror, a full-length one with wings either side that she could tilt. "I'm not that vain but it's easier to check how I look that way. If I don't do it, paparazzi will." She glanced at her closets. Edie was cursed with a neatnik personality that abhorred mess. She kept her closets tightly closed, like her life.

He circled her. She didn't follow his movements but let him walk around her examining her like a designer studying his latest creation.

Despite her utilitarian robe he made her feel as if she were queen of Dior again, pampered, feted. Wanted.

Right now he was staring at her, his look as far from the professional as she could imagine.

The silence tensed her. She broke it. "So what now?"

He took off his glasses and tucked them in his pants pocket "This." He leaned forward.

She didn't press back but she held steady for their first kiss. His mouth touched hers briefly and he withdrew. "You want to alter your lips?"

"Botox is an option."

"Collagen actually. Or implants." He touched her top lip, traced his finger over the contour. "You'd lose some sensation. Let me show you what you'd lose." He removed his hand and instead traced the outline of her lips with his tongue touching only that part of her. She shivered deliciously in response but held steady under his examination. Then he flicked his tongue over the seam and she gasped.

106

He took her gasp and moved closer, licking his way into her mouth, exploring the planes and textures and she responded. He tasted wonderful, of a spice she couldn't identify, something she'd never come across before. She loved it. The taste was all him all John Sung.

She lifted her arms to hold him but immediately he withdrew. A smile curved his lips. "Not until you say it."

"One kiss and you want me to give up lip implants?" Although he'd tempted her to say yes the moment their lips met. The instantaneous connection between them stunned her, made her wonder why she hadn't felt this complete before with anyone else. Every man was different but this was out of her experience. She felt newborn. Maybe it was because she hadn't had sex in a couple of years. No, it couldn't be that. She hadn't missed it at all until now.

Excitement rocketed through her at the thought that she might be having sex with this man soon even if it was on a temporary basis. Temporary worked for her at this point in her life though she wanted enough time to explore and enjoy him. But at the expense of the surgery. She wouldn't cheat, she wouldn't go elsewhere but her unaccustomed uncertainty about her looks had haunted her since she'd turned forty. Since Peter had divorced her in favor of a younger clone of herself.

"Don't think," he said now his voice more husky than before. He glanced at her shoulders.

"Maybe I'd get rid of the bat wings," she said. But she was lying. Her constant regime of weight training had kept the sagging at bay and she hadn't had to wash any lines away when she'd showered.

He lifted his hand touched her arm. Even through the robe, the contact tingled, all her senses centered where he cupped her shoulder. "So I have these to play with too. But you haven't promised not to have lip implants yet." He drew closer and kissed her again.

The bare inch of space between their bodies heated and she scrabbled at her belt to strip the garment off her sensitized body. His hand covered hers, preventing her but he kept his lips on hers and explored her mouth at his leisure. He used his tongue to devastating effect rimming her lips before venturing inside to stroke her tongue and then the roof of her mouth. And all the time his lips played on hers urging her to go deeper faster harder.

But every time she tried, when she twisted her tongue around his, pushed it into his mouth, he pulled back and slowed what they were doing. It tantalized her and eventually infuriated her.

Because she wanted more. She wanted to fuck him, pin him down on her bed and ride. With his kisses he evoked sensations she'd never felt or had forgotten.

John kissed her as if nothing else mattered nothing in the world. He curled his hands around her upper arms his fingers spread to encompass her biceps. She reached for him and this time he let her put her hands on his waist but he kept the rest of his body separate from her. When she tugged, he resisted with a strength in his lean body that surprised her. But there was no mistaking the tightening of honed muscles when he stopped her drawing him closer or when he held her off. And still he kissed her, alternating deep probing kisses with tiny gentle ones.

When he eventually drew away, it was with such smoothness that she remained, her eyes closed, her lips slightly parted. "Can you feel that?" he murmured, his voice smooth as silk. "That awareness the knowledge that you've connected with someone else. Your body full of tingling nerves each one attuned—to me. All centering down there in that exquisite pussy."

His hands on her shoulders renewed the feelings. Every part of her body turned toward his hands, became aware of them, waited for his next move. Taking her time, she opened her eyes and gazed into his face.

This close she could see the difference between the dark iris and the darker pupil. A touch of warmth edged the iris a slightly lighter brown than the intense depths within. She could drown in those eyes and count herself lucky.

He was saying something. Still drugged with kisses she had to concentrate. "Turn around."

She found herself facing the mirror again. When his hands left her shoulders, she felt bereft but he went to the mirror and tilted the wings so she could see herself reflected three times. He came back and stood behind her touching her shoulders once more. "Look at your lips."

She looked. The kisses had plumped them, filled them.

"You don't need artificial aids."

"You tell that to your patients?"

A ghost of a smile drifted across his mouth and then was gone. "Only you. I could go bankrupt if they all thought they could look this good."

"You won't be here all the time. I can't pull you out of my purse like a lipstick whenever I want to look like this."

"Maybe remembering will do the trick." She appreciated that he didn't make any false promises. Thinking about it made her lips moist and her pussy flooded with liquid, eager for him and unashamed. But she refused to clench her thighs together or tighten her muscles. He'd see it through the fabric of the garment, feel her muscles tense and he'd know how much she wanted him right this minute.

As if he didn't. But he might not know just how much.

"Look at your eyes."

Light glared down on them. Edie was so used to bright lights she hardly noticed but it made her hair gleam and her eyes glisten. She knew the tricks. Closing the eyes tight for a minute to make them wider, tilting the chin down and looking up but this time her eyes glinted promise and desire honestly with no tricks.

She'd never seen them quite like that before. She had blue eyes, bright true blue, one of her trademarks and every tear and sadly, every flaw showed. Photographers airbrushed the flaws out. A single drugs binge early in her career scared her enough to make her stop and although she loved wine and cocktails, she rarely drank more than a couple at a time. So her eyes remained clear for the most part, although fatigue did awful things to them.

Like put shadows underneath and add light veins of blood. Just like today.

"You've not been sleeping well have you? But they're beautiful. Your eyes are famous. Change the shape one tiny bit and the public will notice. Surgery on the eye is particularly tricky. And of course if you have a facelift the eye area will be affected."

"I have lines."

He bent and kissed the fine lines at the corner of her left eye. "I love them. They give you character."

She snorted. "I've heard that before."

He kissed her temple. "In your case it's true. You're lovelier than you ever were." He smiled at her reflection, meeting her mirrored gaze. "Tell me which part of you needs surgery in your opinion and I'll persuade you that it's better as it is. Have I won anything yet?"

"The lips." She couldn't bear to give up that kind of sensation and in any case, she'd always had full lips. If they thinned a little with age that wouldn't be a problem. "But my eyes need some help."

He touched the corner of one eye then pulled up the skin so the eye slanted and the laughter lines disappeared. "You want that?"

She met his gaze with the one eye that could still see. "What do I say to that? Do I resort to cliché?"

"Contrary to popular opinion the oriental eye doesn't bear much relation to that."

She could see that for herself. His heavy-lidded oriental eyes gleamed back at her, gentle humor in them. But he wasn't wearing his glasses. "Can you see that far?"

He smiled. "I'm mildly shortsighted. Enough to use glasses when I drive and for a few other activities. I wear them all day for convenience—easier to put them on and forget it. So yes I can see that far." He released her eye. "If you have a facelift it will stretch and lift your skin. You'll have tiny scars at your hairline and behind your ears." He bent and kissed her earlobe, softly nibbling at the edge around the gold studs she wore then licked up and just inside the rim. The delicate caresses made her shudder. She didn't try to hide it. "The thought of it makes me shudder. You'll have a lift every five years or so and you'll look slightly different each time. It will erase your character."

"In that case why do you do cosmetic surgery?"

He smiled. She loved that smile it seemed to hold secrets hidden inside. "Because I'm good at it, because it pays well and it's a challenge. I'd rather see someone like me do it than someone who can't. I've seen some botched jobs that make me want to hit something, preferably the surgeon who committed the atrocity. We redo procedures when we can and I do a lot of corrective surgery for people who actually need it. Harelips, burn scars, birthmarks that kind of thing." He gave a short laugh. "I'm telling you all my secrets. You're too easy to talk to."

"Nobody told me that before."

"Not your previous husbands?" He seemed mildly curious not jealous or possessive. She liked that. Her previous husbands had wanted to own her. Perhaps finally she'd met a man strong enough to meet her on her own terms.

Who was she kidding? This sense of bone-deep rightness couldn't be anything but an illusion. He was ten years younger than she was, they hardly knew each other although she liked what she did know. *Idiot. Just enjoy this for what it is.*

Though she wasn't sure what it was yet.

He curved his hands around her waist to touch the knot on the belt. "I know you thought of a breast lift."

"You read my notes."

"No I didn't. Most women want a boob job it's one of the most common procedure around."

He touched the knot and his hands stilled. "Can I see?"

She jerked her head in a quick nod. "You think men haven't seen them before? Don't you remember the Quick Nails campaign?"

He shook his head.

"Billboards all over the country had it. It caused quite a stir. I was naked but on the poster, I didn't show anything. Except the fingernails that were the whole point of the ad. It sold millions of fake nails." She huffed a laugh. "Randy Norwood would have negotiated me a percentage but in those days I was happy to get the work and I took the flat fee. It made my name in the wider world, outside high fashion that is. But enough men saw everything I had to offer then and I did topless shoots, the see-through, the 'let's get them to look at the boobs instead of the dress' clothes. I didn't realize I could have the studio emptied and rather than that, it filled. The photographer insisted on a closed session after my first one and came on to me. I kicked him in the balls so it was just as well the photos turned out well or he wouldn't have used me again. Sometimes the full studio is the safer one."

"There's only me and you here." His hands tightened on the knot, the knuckles showing white. "I don't intend to lose this bet."

She felt the smile start deep inside her and she didn't stop its release. "That poor are you? Can't afford to lose?"

"It has nothing to do with money."

He loosened the knot and the belt eased. She let the robe open. It caught on her nipples. No hiding now that his attention had made them crinkle into tight peaks. He hadn't even touched them. But he did now. He cupped her breasts, lifted them and she sighed at the contact, her flesh aching for his touch. "You don't want augmentation or reduction?"

"What do you think? What would you do?"

His eyes burned into the reflection of hers. "I can't imagine them any more perfect. That's why I didn't know what you wanted."

"A lift and a reduction. I can't do the pencil test anymore."

He chuckled and nuzzled his mouth against her temple. "That doesn't mean a thing. If you have a lift, you'll lose sensation and have a few discreet scars under your breasts. A reduction would help you fight gravity but if you had it done I'd mourn the loss. You have beautiful breasts Adelaide."

"Edie."

He frowned.

"My first name's Edith. My friends and family call me Edie. I've always been Edie. Adelaide and Sunset came later."

"Edie." He tried it again. "Edie. It's good. It suits you."

She leaned her head against him. "I'm glad you think that."

His slender fingers spread. The darker skin of his hands against her pale skin looked stunning and again that unaccountable feeling of rightness swept over her. Her garment was open down the front but she still wore her delicate lace panties so she wasn't completely naked. Nerves had stopped her stripping completely.

He took the weight of her breasts in his hands, lifted them and touched her areolas with his long forefingers. Just touched them and watched the way she responded as her nipples tightened even more leaving little beads of flesh at the tips. "You might not respond as well as this afterward. Does it feel good?"

"Yes. Yes it does." She suppressed her shiver of reaction.

"Close your eyes." She obeyed. "Just feel. Concentrate on feeling."

He lifted his hands away before he put the tips of his fingers back onto her skin. He stroked her breasts from the base to the nipple, just stroked and didn't linger. When he reached the nipple, he lifted away and did it again. Base to tip over and over again. His voice heated her ear when he murmured to her. "Feel that? If you have work done it will affect some of those nerve endings. Small numb patches, tiny areas you won't notice. Unless someone does this."

His fingers left her and he stood away from her making her feel bereft. Before she could check where he was, he said, "Keep your eyes closed." He was still close.

Then she felt a soft damp kiss on her nipple. She caught her breath, made a small sound of wanting. "Fuck!"

He kissed the other and touched it with the tip of his tongue. She couldn't tell if he was kneeling or bending to her until she felt his hands on her waist steadying her. Kneeling then. She so wanted to see that sleek dark head against her flesh but he'd told her to keep her eyes closed and she was too afraid he might stop if she opened them. He circled her nipple with tiny laps then increased his licks to long sweeping caresses until he was curling his tongue around it and then, *then* he sucked it in.

Wonderful so good.

If he hadn't been holding her she would have jerked right out of his hold. She'd never felt such intensity from having her breasts sucked before. Pleasure sure but not this. He made her feel as if all her senses centered at the tip of her nipple, now held in his mouth between his teeth as he delivered a nip that made her shudder. He suckled drew hard and before she had time to draw breath had moved to the other nipple. He didn't build up the sensation here but drew it right in and because he'd built up her expectations it drove her to more and harder sensation.

He released her nipple long enough to say, "Open your eyes," and he returned to her.

She glanced to the side and saw their profiles reflected in one wing of the triple mirror. His cheeks were hollowed where he sucked, his eyes closed. The sight of his lips curled around the tip of her breast was for a moment a separate entity until he curled his tongue around her nipple and she saw the movement reflected in the mirror.

She sobbed and her pussy pulsed, convulsed and she came.

Incredulous she gripped his shoulders for balance and rode it out. John released her nipple and leaned his forehead in the cleft between her breasts, breathing heavily. Heated air crested her stomach and pussy. She must have soaked her panties. She felt dampness seep over her thighs, too much for the tiny scrap of lace to contain.

He firmed his hold on her waist and stood, getting up in one smooth motion and then drew her close. His erection probed at her flesh insistently but when she moved her hand seeking him out he pulled back and gripped her wrist just enough to stop her. "Not now. I want you to think about what just happened and make your decision. I'll contact you tomorrow but don't contact me before then. Just think about it."

She couldn't believe it. "I know what just happened. I want more."

A slow smile curled his lips. "You want instant gratification. The American dream. Mine too once but no more. I've learned patience." His mouth tightened. "Barely. You're a wonder, Edie, a fucking wonder and I don't want you to do anything that might change it. But it's your decision. Always."

Chapter Four
80

Tempt the Cougar blog:

I met John Sung again last night and I took him home. He's the most amazing man. Girls he's ten years younger than me! Can you believe this is the first younger man I've ever dated? And by 'dated' I don't mean 'went out with' I mean got hot and heavy with. He's intense sexy—and he doesn't want me to have the surgery. Says it would be like whitewashing the Mona Lisa. Nuts. I never saw what Leonardo saw in her anyway. She could have done with a bit of lip-plumping at least.

This man is seriously hot. He made me come just by touching my nipples. Can you believe that? He asked me to call him tomorrow. I don't know. Should I? Or should I let this be just one of those ships-in-the-night things. Thing is, while I'm seeing him we're on a bet and the prize is that I don't have the surgery. I have a TV interview coming up and if I want surgery I need it soon so I can recover enough to appear. They can do wonderful things these days fast but not that fast. I'm running out of time.

An email alert flashed on her screen so Edie put up her blog post and clicked on the mail. The address meant nothing to her at first but she decided to open it and risk a virus.

Edie.

Dinner tonight? Say yes.

John.

She wrote her assent before she really thought about it. Oh yes she wanted to see him again.

She had an unfamiliar dilemma with her wardrobe before she went to meet John. She arranged to meet him at the restaurant at eight. Sure, there'd be photographers outside but they frequented every decent eating house in LA so that wasn't a problem for her. At least she told herself not. But this was the first time she'd been out on a date with a younger man and the fluttering in her stomach reminded her she was nervous.

After deciding on a tight black number, she tore it off, deciding it was too short. A green corset top went the same way even before she found a skirt to put with it. Maybe the red— *Scarlet woman* went through her mind. Shit. She picked up the phone and hit speed dial. "Cam, what do you wear for a date with a man who's ten years younger than you?"

Her friend's warm husky tones came reassuringly down the line. "You wear something that says 'look who I'm with aren't you jealous?' You relax and you wear something appropriate. Nothing that gives the finger to the gossips but nothing that plays too safe either. Chances are they'll ignore you."

"Sure they will. John's not exactly unknown. Surgeon to the stars they call him. We were lucky the other night at the art gallery. No pictures today. But they noticed. If they see me with him again they'll do more than notice."

Cam's laugh sounded like warm honey. She'd always calmed Edie down before a big show and her presence albeit at a distance soothed her now. "And you're shitting big ones because he's younger than you. Girlfriend he's gorgeous and so are you. Just for a change don't dress for the paparazzi don't dress for yourself. Dress for him, fuck-me heels and all."

"Great thought. As long as you don't mean lingerie and stockings only."

They cut the call still laughing.

On the other hand, sexy lingerie always helped her feel confident. She found a sapphire blue set, one she'd always loved. The color set off her red-gold hair to perfection. Out of a bottle these days but still only to cover the gray, not change the color.

Stockings. Not black but sheer nude silk that made her legs feel pampered and she hooked them on to the matching blue garter belt.

After that, the rest was surprisingly easy. A vivid dark blue silk dress with a draped cowl neckline, classic lines, a couple of inches above the knee. Silver jewelry a sapphire pendant on a slender chain and matching stud earrings and since the dress was sleeveless a silver bracelet watch.

She parted her hair at the side and encouraged the waves to frame her face but tossed most of it over her shoulders to lie against her back to the level of her bra. At one time, she'd had hair down to her waist but it was a sonofabitch to look after so she'd gradually had the length reduced over the years.

She had a brief panic when she couldn't locate the matching shoes to the dress but she unearthed a pair of silver stilettos she hadn't worn yet that would do just as well. She surveyed her walk-in closet desperately trying to forget the last time she'd stood in front of this mirror. She had too many clothes she should really sort it all out. It was a symptom of her growing dissatisfaction about her looks or her condition or something. Restlessness since her last divorce and a growing belated sense of insecurity and lack of confidence. God knew where it came from. She'd never felt that way before.

She grabbed a silver purse and shoved her keys, change, a few bills and a credit card inside. When the concierge called up to say her taxi had arrived, she was ready. Except for the butterflies going batshit crazy in her stomach.

Edie had eaten at this place a time or two but it seemed particularly busy tonight. And the figure lounging outside, the only one she had eyes for seemed at home here. He stepped forward to help her out of her car, and cameras flashed. He leaned forward to kiss her cheek and took the opportunity to murmur, "Next time I pick you up, no arguments." She hadn't wanted him to do that tonight knowing they wouldn't have gotten as far as the restaurant. Despite his desire to take it slowly she would have hauled him inside thrown him to the floor and fucked him crazy. But part of the dare on the blog was to be seen with her guy. At least it was for her. She wanted to go all the way. Sex in private was good but she wanted more.

Though she wasn't sure what that was.

Seeing John again sent warmth through her, one she recognized. Taking a new lover was always like that. If she felt the same after a week, three weeks maybe then she'd consider herself caught. Or not. This time she knew she could walk away if she wanted to. This time. Did every woman think like that?

He led her through the doors opened for them by two men in uniform. "Why didn't you wait for me indoors?"

"I wanted to see your arrival and know it was for me." He laughed. "Stupid eh?"

"No." Some of her pleasure was the photos and the questions she'd heard shouted as they'd entered the sanctuary of the restaurant. *Je Suis* it was called. Aptly named because it gathered all the egos in LA into one place. "It seems a bit busy tonight. I don't kid myself. I don't get that kind of crowd anymore. Thank God," she added fervently and meant it.

"Clooney brought his new squeeze to dinner," John said. "They're waiting for them to come out."

She laughed. "In their dreams. If he wants to, he will, otherwise he'll go out the back way. He's a savvy guy, he'll have scoped that out long before he brought anyone here. But let's hope he does go out the front because he's a good distraction for us."

He glanced outside, the smoked glass windows adding a dreamlike quality to the crowds gathered on the street. "Nevertheless we've been seen and they've noted."

"Do you mind?"

He laughed. "Are you crazy? I'm proud of it. I know some much quieter places but you seemed okay with this and for a trendy restaurant they do some damn fine food."

She gave him the look, straight up straight down. "So the fat kid eats?"

"Hell yeah. As soon as I came out from behind the computer and started to live a little, the weight fell away. Together with some exercise." He winked at her and she laughed.

The maitre d' approached them and led them to a table near a window where they could see but not be seen as the glass was of the one-way variety. Cars hurtled by, chrome trim gleaming in the sunshine. LA didn't have much nighttime at this time of year but the June night dropped hard and fast when it finally came. It wouldn't for another couple of hours yet.

He leaned back in his chair and regarded her from half-closed eyelids. "You look fucking gorgeous but I bet you know that already. It must be second nature to you."

"No not anymore. I reared two kids and I spent most of my off-runway time in jeans."

He raised a brow. "Where are your kids now?"

"One's at college doing a doctorate, the other is working in Seattle." For once, it didn't make her feel old.

"I didn't notice any stretch marks." The professional speaking. "Not that it would have put me off." A glimmer of desire flashed from his eyes. She felt herself flushing. The curse of the redhead, that responsive skin.

"I was lucky." And it *was* luck. "I was working then. I would definitely have had surgery to correct stretch marks."

"It can't always be corrected although there are ways of disguising the marks." He glanced up as the waiter approached. "Do you know what you want or do you need the menu?"

She shook her head. "I've eaten here before."

They let the waiter outline the specials and they sounded interesting so she took a chance and ordered those. Mussels in white wine sauce followed by spring lamb with creamed potatoes. John ordered a salad and fish.

She grinned at him. "Anyone would think you were watching your weight." He laughed. Right then she decided she wanted to hear more laughter from John Sung.

Then the sommelier came to their table and Edie loved that he consulted her about the wine. They settled on a crisp dry white, a Moselle.

John didn't choose her meal for her or insist she try something because "I know you'll like it", he didn't decide on the wine without consulting her and she loved it. Her previous husbands had all done that, the first because she was young and needed to learn, the second because he was the possessive type and the third because he was an insecure controlling fuckwit.

Enough. All gone now two friends and a man she tried to ignore the existence of.

The meal came and they chatted their way through the first course getting to know each other a bit more but under all the pleasant conversation ran an undercurrent like the thrum of electricity, ready to snap to life when something connected with something else. Her pussy his cock, please God.

The main course arrived. John asked her if she preferred red wine but she said no and he topped up her wineglass with the white, which was perfect for a late spring evening. So were the conversation and the venue. For a fashionable restaurant *Je*

Suis was a haven of quiet content, at least tonight. The food was served on fine white china the lighting was discreet but not too low and classical music played quietly in the background. She savored a mouthful of tender lamb before she spoke, taking her time.

"The in crowd, the busy people will move on soon. This place will be too boring for them."

He smiled and twirled his glass to make the wine surge and eddy inside. "But the management here is very clever because some of us will remember and return. I certainly will. And I can't wait for the others to move on. *Je Suis* will have enough regular customers to survive. Those of us who don't crave the limelight." He looked up. "You don't. Did you ever?"

She shook her head. "It was part of the job that's all. I took my God-given looks and did something with them. I was someone else—Sunset, Adelaide, but not Edie. She stayed inside watching and noting. That was why I found it so easy to write everything down when it came to write my autobiography. The ghostwriter said I was articulate but I don't kid myself. She made my dry memories into readable exciting prose." She laughed. "I gave her a chunk of royalties. Her agent never even negotiated them for her."

"So you're generous too."

"I give credit where it's due. I always have. It makes for good karma."

He watched her for several seconds before he turned his attention back to his plate. That fraught few moments said nothing about their conversation everything about his intentions after they'd eaten. But she knew she'd have to agree. He wouldn't take unless she gave first. "Karma or not you have relatively few enemies for someone who is spectacularly beautiful and worked for years in one of the most cut-throat industries in the world." He glanced up. "Another being medicine."

That broke the tension but only temporarily. When he looked at her again she was waiting. How could anyone become addicted to a gaze? But she feared she was.

He leaned back in his chair and picked up his glass. She followed suit and lifted hers, toasting him before she drank. "Usually when I make my mind up I follow through no matter what. I did research on cosmetic surgery, decided what I wanted done and I had my timetable worked out. How can you be so sure I won't have it done? I have my first TV interview at the end of next month. They want names and dates and as far as I'm concerned, I'm giving them. But I wanted myself invulnerable. I wanted perfection. It's my first line of defense and you're asking me to give it up."

He regarded her steadily his eyes grave. She knew he was listening, really listening to what she said. "So the crap will hit the fan at that interview? Why would you do that?"

"Because my third and last husband was a shit of the stinkiest most repulsive kind. He's gorgeous, good in bed, wealthy and influential. Nothing can touch him."

"So what is he? A child molester, a murderer?"

She shook her head. "Nothing like that. Nothing illegal, just immoral. He's a user, a charmer, a seducer. He does it in his job and he does it in his private life too. I've seen him take young enthusiastic trainees and wring them dry. He'll work them until he has no more use for them then he'll discard them. While we were married, he took mistresses serially. After the first three I threatened to throw him out but he didn't believe me. I refused to have sex with him but he seduced me." She gave a wry grin. "He's very good. But I learned to resist him in time."

He finished his wine. "So he used you too?"

"We used each other." Her lips thinned. "Yes he did. He tried to push my children away too, so I had nobody else but him. But my first husband, my kids' father, didn't allow it. That started the first rift when Zach used to visit to see the kids but after we divorced we'd agreed to make sure the children came first. We stayed friends."

He nodded and the tense lines around his mouth relaxed. "So you get on with your other husbands."

She knew what he was thinking. That she was the user not Peter. "You know who they were, you said you'd looked me up."

"I know *who* they are but not *what* they are. Tell me."

Why did it seem natural to talk about her previous husbands with a man who might become her next lover? It didn't seem right but it worked for her. "My first husband was Zach Atoya, the head of his own fashion house. He was twice my age when we married but since I was eighteen that wasn't as bad as it sounded. He was my mentor and my friend. I had the twins at twenty and it could have been a disaster for my career but he supported me even designed a maternity line." She bit her lip forcing back her smile. "We divorced because we grew out of each other, wanted different things but we parted friends. My second husband was Bobby Demaris the lawyer. He's still my lawyer, which should tell you something. He was a controlling man, alpha to the max and he wanted all of me. I couldn't give it so he found someone who could. But I understood why he wanted what he did. He found himself a wife who suited him better in the bedroom. And yes I'm friends with her as well as him."

"So you don't want all women to forge their own careers and make their own lives?"

She laughed. "No why should I?"

He smiled back and his face lost the sternness she realized meant he was concentrating. Not that he couldn't concentrate when he was smiling. "I prefer a woman who knows her own mind, who has an opinion. My male ego isn't insulted when a woman disagrees with me, just when she tries to fuck with me by playing idiot games or railroad me into something I don't want to do. And I've been with women who have done both."

He met her eyes. "Shall I tell you what I want to do with you? To you? Do you want to know what I want you to do to me?"

She caught her breath. She hadn't expected that, not here. "People will hear you."

"No they won't. The people at the next table are too busy trying to get other people to look at them to bother about eavesdropping and nobody else is close enough." He leaned forward pushing his plate aside. "I promise."

The waiter arrived and took away their plates, leaving them with a dessert menu. He didn't look at it. "Maybe you'd like dessert at my place. Or yours. Wherever you're most comfortable. I have some interesting playthings." He crooked a dark brow and gave her a quizzical smile.

"Toys?" She liked toys.

"Oh yes. One or two."

"You're into…" A pang of disappointment went through her. She didn't want him to be into BDSM because she wasn't. She'd tried it from both sides and it only made her laugh at herself.

"No I'm not. I'm into mutual play and exploration. I'm into breaking boundaries whether you know they're there or not. I'm into letting go and doing what feels right whatever anyone else thinks about it. Only we matter in this, Edie. Nobody else."

Intriguing and fascinating. But he wasn't done.

"I want to fuck you, sure I do. But I want to do it in different ways. Then I want to watch while you fuck me and while you masturbate. That's one of the most beautiful sights in the world, watching a woman giving herself pleasure. I want to watch you explore yourself. I want to watch you explore me. And I'll do whatever you want me to as long as it feels good."

She couldn't breathe. He'd said it with such intensity she knew she'd met her match, the man she wanted. How this could have happened and how it happened now she was still struggling with.

He watched her and she knew he could see everything she was thinking. She just knew it. It didn't make her feel embarrassed or uncomfortable. It made her feel good. Just as he'd said.

"I want to remind you why your lips and your breasts shouldn't be subjected to the knife and I want to know what other work you wanted doing so I can persuade you against it. All I ask is honesty. So one question remains. Your place or mine?"

Outside the day was still bright but a slight freshness invaded the air, one that hadn't been there before. Cameras flashed and popped, more of them than before. Instinctively she moved closer to John and he curved his arm around her waist also, it seemed, instinctively. But she didn't shrink close to him. She knew better than that. She drew up to her full height five foot ten plus the three-inch heels she had on and pasted on the Sunset smile. She'd worn her hair loose tonight for him but now she could shake it back and remind them why she'd gotten that nickname within six months of her first picture appearing in the teen magazine that had given her the first break of her career.

More cameras flashed and she moved toward the car drawn up by the curb. She had no idea if it was theirs or not. It wouldn't be the first time she'd gotten into the wrong limo and got out a block later. Premieres and society events were packed with such eventualities. All for the sake of appearances.

But it seemed that this was his car because he took the keys from the boy holding them out to him and opened the door on the passenger side.

"Are you a couple, Sunset? How long have you and Dr. Sung been seeing each other?"

John saw her into the car and closed the door but she opened the window and listened to his reply. At first, she thought he wouldn't say anything but then he paused and tossed the car keys in his hand as if weighing his answer. He walked around to the driver's side and paused. "Yes we're a couple. For now."

He got into the car, started it up and drove away.

Chapter Five
ಬಿ

"What made you say that?"

He glanced at her and grinned. He drove like he conducted his life, competently and without fuss. "Either because I want us to be or because we are. They'll say it anyway. Clooney must have gone out the back way because the paparazzi out there are slavering for a story so we've given them one. It'll be all over the blogs by now, the gossip mags in the morning but what do we fucking care?"

She grimaced. "I know a few people who might."

"My place then," he said, correctly interpreting her distaste.

She loved Bobby dearly but she wouldn't bet against there being a phone call or an email from him when she got home. Still protective, especially since he'd handled her divorce from Peter and knew how hard that had hit her. Reminded of him, she dug inside her purse and found her phone. It had begun to vibrate when she switched it off. "Definitely your place."

He lived in the Hills, but not the flashier part. He drove into a gated community and slowed down outside a two-story villa. She liked the understated design the clean shapes of the plastered walls and the way the large windows gleamed in the light of the setting sun. Edie found herself hoping this was his place.

It was. A garage door slid up and he parked the Mercedes inside before exiting the car and coming around to her side to open the door for her. She had her hand on the door handle but she liked that little touch. It made her feel cherished. Little courtesies that meant so much and John did them when nobody was around as well as when people were looking. Unusual for this town.

However when she got out of the car he didn't step back. Instead, he placed his hands on her waist and drew her close. She lifted her head for his kiss and when their lips met she was reminded of the sensation she'd felt when he'd kissed her before. Togetherness.

Their mouths moved in harmony and anticipation built low in her stomach fizzing up to tighten her throat and send tingles through her limbs. Her nipples tightened against his chest and although he probably couldn't feel them underneath his suit jacket and shirt, he hummed into her mouth and gave a low growl of approval.

He withdrew slowly with a series of nips and licks before he leaned back and gazed at her. "I've been torturing myself all day wondering if you really tasted that good. It's better than I remember."

She smiled up at him pleasantly hazy. "You have a gift for kissing."

"It's the first time anyone's told me that. Come inside and let's see if there's anything else I'm good at."

He led her into a spacious living room and past the comfortable dark-hued sofa set to a staircase at the far end. She looked up the steps. "Clear glass. Just as well I'm not afraid of heights."

"I knew that. I saw the picture of you in *Vogue* where you posed at the top of the Empire State Building. You lay on the rails."

"There wasn't much danger. They tethered me down and then airbrushed the straps out. But it really was the top of the Empire State and I was really, really cold. They brushed out the goose bumps too." She shivered and curled her arms around her body, clasping them hard as if she were still up there. "That was a looong shoot. At the time I was so cold I thought I was going to die. I spent the next four hours in a hot bath."

He frowned. "I don't like to think about you in that position. I know modeling isn't glamorous a lot of the time but that verges on fucking torture." He reached out and drew her close just holding her.

"We earn too much for people to feel sorry for us. And there are glamorous times along with the hard work and the discomfort. I'm still here aren't I?" Unfolding her arms, she enjoyed his warmth. Although he didn't keep his air conditioning on freeze like a lot of LA residents, she felt the long-ago chill when she'd been seriously worried she'd developed hypothermia. The hours on top of the Empire State in March had left her cold right through her model-skinny body, literally chilled to the bone. It had been a long time since she'd thought about that shoot and she usually laughed the discomfort off since it had resulted in one of the iconic photographs of her career. John had seen straight through to the truth.

"I'm sorry," he said after a moment. "I didn't realize I'd be bringing such traumatic memories back to you. Do you want a drink?"

"No I'm fine." She lifted her chin. "I'm here with you and we're fine."

"So we are." He dropped a kiss on her nose and drew back but reached for her hand. "Am I rushing you? Do you want to sit and talk?"

"No. I want to get naked."

He pulled her toward the stairs laughing, the sadness dispelled. In the process of climbing the stairs, he paused and looked back at her. "But you remember our bet right? You'll give me a chance to persuade you not to have the surgery."

She owed him the truth. "I don't know if I can promise that. Dr. Roubiere suggested an extensive program but I won't have it all done at once."

He bared his teeth. "Fucking bastard," he said but without heat. "The trouble is he's good at what he does. What he does he'll do well. You can still say no." He played with the fingers of her hand.

"When you're paying?" She gave him a roguish smile. "Now why would I do that?"

His laughter sounded around the quiet room. "I'm sure we can think of something else to do with the money. Barbados maybe?"

Her brow arched. "Hey aren't we getting a bit ahead of ourselves here?"

He turned to climb the stairs. "I don't think so."

She followed him, taking her time to enjoy the way the hidden lights gleamed through the glass steps, hitting highlights that drew rainbows. The stair rail next to the wall was cool to the touch and on the other side the stairs were open hanging over the floor below as if by magic. Hers were railed in. She liked the open format.

He waited for her at the top of the stairs. He took her hand and kissed it old-style but the gesture wasn't cheesy, it was heartfelt. She loved it.

His bedroom contained a huge platform bed and a row of closets, all of them mirror fronted. She walked across the deeply carpeted floor to strike a pose, arm above her head, hip thrust forward, an exaggerated sultriness making the gesture comic rather than sexy. At least she thought so until she saw his face as he walked up behind her. She saw intensity behind the black-framed spectacles, burning heat that could keep her warm for a long time. His lips were slightly parted, giving her a glimpse of gleaming teeth. A predator heading for the kill.

She shivered when he put his hands on her shoulders. He didn't comment on it though he must have felt it. "What other work are you considering?"

"The works, everything, the full Monty," she said wildly. Really, she didn't give a flying fuck. He cared more than she did right now. If he'd known he only had to ask, he'd have the advantage. She'd make him work for it.

She'd been born with the genes that made her body. Apart from taking care of it, she had just been lucky. She'd learned how to make the best of what she had, how to stand, how to pose. It came naturally to her even now, years after she'd joyfully tossed her modeling career in the crapper. "This is my raw material." She passed her hands down her body smoothing it over her hips and thighs, enjoying the feel of expensive silk. "It was my job, my living and if it doesn't sound too pretentious, my way of expressing myself."

"Not pretentious at all." He moved his hand so he could kiss the skin left bare by her dress. "Well maybe a little bit."

She couldn't believe she hadn't had sex with this man many times, because she felt so natural with him but at the same time a frisson of anticipation ran up and down her spine making her want to squirm under his hands and beg him to touch every inch of her.

His hands left her shoulders and he walked past her to touch a closet door. It popped open and her eyes widened when she saw what was inside.

Jesus fucking Christ. When he'd talked about toys she'd imagined floggers, handcuffs, leather but she saw nothing like that.

Instead a row of glass dildos faced her, each slightly different as if modeled from life. The insides were far from realistic made stunningly beautiful with twists of colored glass and air bubble spirals. He'd ranged them according to the colors of the rainbow.

Drawers were set underneath, each with a crystal handle, but she couldn't work up the curiosity to wonder what they held right now. She'd never seen such beautiful sex toys before.

He pulled out a drawer. "I have pearls. If you were thinking of an ass lift, we might explore that area. Let's see."

He turned his back on his toy cupboard and studied her instead. Her breasts rose and fell as she took a couple of quick breaths. "Only what you want, my lovely. I want to seduce you with pleasure, fuck you to joy."

She caught her breath. "I'm not exactly inexperienced."

"If anything I do doesn't thrill you, you have to tell me. You hear?"

"Oh yes. I hear. So no blindfolds or handcuffs?"

His mouth twisted. "It's not really my thing. But I'm willing to experiment. With you."

She shook her head. Her second husband Bobby was into BDSM. He was a part-time lifestyler but she hadn't enjoyed it, although she'd tried to for his sake. She could only assume his current wife found it more to her taste. Bobby had never scared her, always went slowly and she played along for him but her heart had never been in it. Now for the first time she wondered if a new partner would make a difference to her. John Sung to be precise.

She reached out to touch one of the dildos, the green one. It felt cool and smooth. "Pick it up," he said.

It had a heft to it that could make it a lethal weapon.

When he spoke next, his voice sounded choked. "How did you know that was mine?"

"I didn't. I just liked the look of it." She spun it in her hand and watched the green spiral twist curling in her hand. It felt so different to the real thing but seductive in its own way. "What do you mean 'mine'?"

He reached past her to take up the one with tiny red droplets scattered through it, more like rubies than blood. "In the sixties and seventies some groupies were known as the Plaster Casters. They used to make casts of famous stars' dicks. The trick was to keep them erect during the time it took the plaster to harden. Either they didn't have the fast-curing stuff we use today or they chose not to use it." He grinned. "It was fun. They had a shitload of volunteers."

"I bet."

"These were taken from the original casts but being glass they're idealized. This one is Jimi Hendrix's dick. The one you're holding is mine." He held his hand under hers but she didn't drop it only held it tighter and stared in fascination. "I didn't have the pleasure of the services of the Plaster Casters but as I said we have faster setting plaster and I used it. Do you know how hard it is to masturbate for twenty minutes without coming?" She snorted with laughter. "I was a med student living at home. It scandalized my mom who opened the parcel when it arrived. She never opened another one of my letters or parcels."

She stroked the tip of the dildo. It was realistic enough for her and if this was a cast of his cock, she could hardly wait. "So you had a glass replica made? Do you use it much?"

He put the red one precisely back into place. "No. But I want to use it now. With you." He touched his lips to the side of her neck, a place that made her shiver. "So tell me where you were thinking of having more procedures. Then I'll try to persuade you against it."

"Will you give me your honest opinion?" She put the green dildo down next to the red one, not as precisely as he had done.

He smiled against her neck the slight movement sending another shudder through her. "As a man yes. As a doctor no." With a last kiss, he lifted his head and turned her to him his hands on her shoulders. "The color of your dress makes you look untouchable but I was always one to go against the rules." He bent and took her lips in a deep kiss.

He kissed like an angel—or a devil, his marauding tongue taking her, invading her. Making her feel—owned. She'd felt like that before but not now when she knew who she was and what she wanted. She wasn't even sure he knew what he was doing. And when his tongue swept over hers and stroked it, inviting her to share, she stopped caring.

He smoothed his hands over her dress and after a moment, she realized what he was looking for. The zipper. She broke away and after he'd pursued her and stolen a couple more gentle kisses as if he couldn't bear to leave her, he grinned. "Okay I give in. How do you get out of this thing?"

She took a step back. "Now that is more sensible. I wouldn't have liked you to rip it. Have you ever heard of bias cutting?"

He spread his hands and shrugged in an intensely masculine gesture.

Chuckling she reached for the hem of the dress and lifted it over her head. She dropped the silk to the carpet where it fell with a gentle susurration of surrender.

"Fuck, oh fuck, you're beautiful." The gleam in his eyes was unmistakable. His gaze roved over her form and she helped him, sliding her hands over her body from her breasts down over the curve of her waist to her hip and down to her thighs. Then she glided them up her body at the front ending just under her breasts. She cupped the silk-encased mounds and spread her fingers. When she grazed a nipple, a shiver passed through her. From his hot gaze she knew she'd turned him on but he wasn't the only one. She'd sensitized her skin, made herself ready for him.

Without taking his gaze away from her, he dragged off his jacket and as she had done with her dress dropped it to the floor. He unfastened his shirt, flicking the buttons undone one by one and took a second to undo his gold cufflinks and drop them on his coat. But he didn't take the shirt off. No smile softened the harsh, chiseled features or crinkled the dark eyes at the corners. His concentration was absolute. On her. She reached behind her to the bra clasp but he took the step that brought him right up against her and his hand covered hers. They undid the clasp together and then he held the bra closed when her hand fell away.

She touched him held his waist and gazed up at him. "Don't you want me to take it off?"

"I want to know. Have I won? What have I won?"

"You mean what have I agreed not to have done?" He nodded a sharp jerk of his head that revealed his tension. She'd thought it a game, after all why should he care what she did to her body? He liked her body enough to become her date instead of her doctor but that was all. This could only ever be a transient enjoyable affair.

It didn't feel like it now with his gaze boring into her as if he could see everything she was. Right into her innermost secrets. She had to give him something. "My lips. I won't have my lips done."

"Even temporary treatment?"

"Even that." She hadn't been sure about that procedure anyway she told herself but deep down she knew he'd won the right fair and square, and made her lips feel wonderful.

Just as he did now. His kiss wasn't a taking, it was a celebration. He touched her lips, licked them before he settled his mouth over hers and drew her flush against his body. He released her bra strap and the elastic sprang back, releasing the tension that held her breasts up and tight. She didn't want reminding about how they'd drooped with age.

He pressed tender kisses against her lips and brought his hand up to cup and caress her right breast. He tugged at the nipple, drew it into a stiff peak and stroked before he moved to the other to give it the same treatment. "I want these to stay just as they are," he said kissing her between each word. "They are so lovely and so responsive. Remember how I made you come just touching them and sucking them? You could lose sensitivity if you have implants. I don't want you to let anyone interfere with them. Except maybe me."

"I'm almost tempted." She gasped as he tweaked her nipple, loving the way it sent shards of sensation to her spine and along it to the rest of her body.

"I'll enjoy persuading you."

"You're so sure?"

"No. But I know what I want. I won't railroad you, Edie, only persuade." In a sudden movement, he bent and swept her into his arms. She giggled. When had she last giggled? She had no idea but it felt like a lifetime since she'd felt so lighthearted and downright happy with a man. He glanced back at the shelf. "Would you like to take Jimi with us?"

She smiled up at him. "I'd rather have you."

He laughed and swept up the green glass dildo, carrying her and it over to the wide bed. He bent and laid her carefully on it and placed the dildo on the night table with his glasses. "I don't think that color's quite you."

It wasn't—the cover was yellow silk, which clashed badly with her auburn-sunset hair. She lifted a brow. "Does it bother you?"

"I'd like to see you laid out on green or blue. And I will. I'll order a new cover tomorrow. Velvet soft and rich. Like you."

She laid a hand on her stomach and grimaced. "Don't remind me."

"It's good. I love it." His hands went to his pants and he flipped open the button. She watched avidly and he groaned. "Don't do that. It makes me close to coming."

"We have all night. Have a free one on me."

He threw back his head and laughed.

Now that he'd mentioned the cover it did bother her. She had enough vanity left to want him to see her at her best. She stripped it off to reveal a white duvet and bed linen. Much better.

By that time, he'd undone the buttons on his fly and now it gaped open, revealing a pair of tight white boxers that barely held the bulge of his erection. A damp patch marked where he'd leaked drops of his precious fluid. It empowered her, made her feel wanted and she hadn't felt that way for a while.

People wanted her, sure. Her children wanted her, her friends enjoyed her company, at least they came back for more, and her business associates wanted her for obvious reasons. She made money for them. But she hadn't felt wild hunger course through her body for years and it felt fucking wonderful.

He stared down at her. "I'm stripping for action tonight. I don't want anything in the way of us. So tell me now. Where do you think you need work?"

She swallowed her throat dry. "A tummy tuck?"

He gave a derisory laugh low in his throat. "More."

"Maybe liposuction on my thighs? They don't seem as thin as they used to be. And my ass—I've never been entirely happy with that. My agent used to say that if she had to pick anything, that was the worst flaw I had."

His lip curled. "Your stomach is beautifully rounded. Made as a pillow for my head I'd say so I can watch while I touch and tweak that gorgeous pussy." He pushed his pants past his hips and they fell to the floor with a soft thump. No hiding his cock now. His underwear stood clear of his taut stomach where the plump head pushed up, demanding its freedom.

He gave it by hooking his thumbs in the top of his boxers and sliding them down. She watched as he spoke, licked her lips. "I want to examine your ass in greater detail. I have to be sure don't I?"

Edie didn't want to take her avid gaze off his beautiful cock but she turned over. His soft groan came sweetly to her ears. "Perfect. It's perfect."

And then he touched her, leaned forward and cupped the curves of her backside in his hands. He weighed them stroked them through her barely there panties and all she knew was she wanted them both naked. He eased his hands over her thighs enough to pull the silk down and free her to his gaze. She didn't know where her panties landed. She didn't care. Turning her head, she watched him.

That sight of John Sung naked, proud and beautiful fed her addiction. She wanted him so badly moisture trickled between her thighs when she turned.

He wasn't touching her but she felt his presence as if he were, as if his eyes had the power to caress her. What did he find wanting? She couldn't bear it, that fraught silence. "Are my arms okay from the back?"

"Every way I look at you I see perfection." He sounded husky. He cleared his throat. "Your ass is an invitation a boy's wet dream. And I'm no boy."

"I noticed that."

"My cock isn't the only part of my body desperate for a taste of you. My mouth, my hands—God I thought those photos of you were touched up but they weren't."

"They were." Once her third husband had shoved her and left a bruise. He didn't go in for crude physical abuse usually but that night he'd had too much to drink and she'd been particularly accurate in her description of him. They'd had to airbrush that bruise out after the shoot the next day. Nobody asked about the mark. Strange that Bobby, the husband who was into BDSM rarely left a mark on her and never without her permission.

She wouldn't tell that to John. It was none of his business. He wanted her body although they had enjoyed themselves earlier at dinner, found a few things they had in common. And she liked his house. The spaciousness and airiness appealed to her.

All that raced through her mind while she was trying not to come just from him looking at her. She knew he'd be watching her with the deep intensity of a man who concentrated on the things that mattered to him. Right now she did.

So enjoy right now. They could fuck like bunnies and she'd leave smiling in the morning.

Chapter Six
ಬ

She sighed into the soft pillow under her head and at that moment, he touched her. Curved his hand over her ass then his other hand over the other cheek. The contact felt like she'd been waiting her whole life for him to do that. Then he pulled the cheeks apart not hard but firmly and he groaned. "Everything about you is gorgeous. Turn back again, Edie, before I forget myself and do it all to you. But you said you wanted an ass lift. I'm going to find out if all you need is an ass job."

Nervousness tightened her throat and she swallowed. None of her husbands had been into that, not even Bobby. She was panicking again, trying to think herself out of the wild intensity that suffused every pore of her body.

She turned around not knowing how to arrange her body, how to appear before him. The raw honest hunger in John's face almost destroyed her. It stripped away any attempt she might have had at subterfuge or trying to keep this light. They'd laughed during dinner but no laughter remained on his face now.

Stark want delineated every feature from the sharply defined cheekbones straining against his skin to the taut mouth. And those dark eyes so intense, clear of everything except lust. Honest lust.

She took her cue from him and lay back, legs slightly apart, arms by her sides, trying not to think of posing. Here she was, Edie, that was all, the girl who had come from England to LA with such hopes and become one of America's sweethearts. Or America's sex symbol anyway.

"Why the smile?"

"I didn't know I was smiling. But I can see plenty to smile about."

He gave her a wry grin. "Thanks for that."

At last he moved, coming down and resting one knee on the bed by her feet. He ran his hand up her leg. "So smooth." He turned his head sharply when he heard her intake of breath. "No don't tell me the effort it takes to get there, don't tell me how it's done. Right now, I don't care. Let me admire you."

That was something she was used to. Maybe not as intimately, but this she enjoyed. She'd had lovers before who when she got them into bed turned out to want Sunset or even Adelaide, not Edie, so that was what she'd given them. Posed, preened, acted as egotistically as they'd expected, given nothing away and then she'd gotten them out of her front door as fast as she could.

But John wanted to *appreciate* her. She could do that, admire her body as if it were a separate entity to herself, to the Edie stuck inside the fabulous exterior. She'd been gifted her body, the long limbs, the slender figure and all she'd done was take care of it. Now it was time for payback. All those hours of smoothing, massages, exercise, toning, now she wanted something for herself.

Much, much too soon for her to call it love but it was coming perilously close. Sex yes. John was moving his hand slowly up her leg, massaging the calf with careful fingers, moving on to her thigh. No cellulite yet.

Stop it, Edie. He'd asked her to drop the criticism of herself. She'd try to for him if not for herself. Years of objective assessment had forced her to divorce the body that had made her fortune from the person inside but it was time surely it was time for that to change. For her to get back in touch with who she was, what she wanted and solder the two into a complete if imperfect whole.

Perhaps that was why she needed this so badly. Perhaps John had realized what she needed. Who knew?

Those soft caresses and the sight of the lithe tanned body before her moved her libido level up slowly but inevitably. John glanced up as he shaped her thigh with his hands. "I know what you're thinking. Your mind works twenty-four/seven doesn't it?"

Yes it did.

"Concentrate on the way my hands feel on you. Look at your legs. Long, luscious gorgeous. That light tan is just enough to enhance them not enough to damage your skin. And it's a real tan isn't it?" He didn't wait for her to answer. "No cellulite but I wouldn't care if there were. And this..." He slid his hand under her and cupped her ass. "So inviting. So good."

He looked and it was so not the gaze of a professional medical man, his eyes so hot she thought he might melt her on the spot. And it was cool in this room. She let her legs remain slightly open, felt her lust oil her pussy, liquid bathing the tops of her thighs.

"You can have all kinds of things done to your cunt you know."

She gave a sharp laugh. "Is that a medical term? Cunt?"

He looked up at her face, smiling. "Who cares?" He returned her attention to her cleft. "You can have the hood of the clit removed or even extended. You can have collagen injected in the labia to plump them up. You won't feel them for a while, but who cares, they look good."

Her blood ran cold until she saw the smile and realized what he meant. She licked her lips to moisten them. Her mouth was running dry while her pussy was dampening. "I could have that done couldn't I?" It was the best she could manage. Because if she didn't say she wanted to change that part of her body, he might not touch it. And she'd die if he didn't.

"But if I show you the sensation you might lose, you could give it to me couldn't you? Give me another part of your body you won't allow the knife to touch." He laid one finger on her just above the line of her pubic hair. "You could shave if you wanted to."

"Would you like that?"

He gave another smile. "Maybe I would. So we'll exempt that part shall we? You might even allow me to do it for you."

"I used to shave there, I had to. I still trim."

He ran his finger between her legs along the bikini line. "So you do."

Without warning, he bent and licked her slit front to back. Her legs were only slightly open so he couldn't reach all the way but as she shuddered in reaction, he gripped her thigh and urged her legs apart. His low groan vibrated along her cleft, peaked at her opening. She panted sharp and fast and he purred against her skin, a low rumble that flowed through her body and amplified her arousal. Her body tingled with awareness, with wanting. His low words, his reassurances all served to lull her to stop her thinking.

So she just felt. His tongue curled along her cleft and then tickled her clit. She gripped the sheet under her, felt the smooth fine cotton scrunch in her hands, added it to the sensations she was feeling. She felt every movement of his talented tongue as he curled it around her clit like a guardian, a protector and then he sucked it in like a marauder, owning it.

The combination sent her up into a cycle she dimly recognized as pre-orgasm when every sense tingled in response to his touch.

He traced patterns on her thigh with his fingers, intricately weaving sensation into a rich tapestry of delight. Every time he touched her, she soared higher. He sucked, pulled her into his mouth and made a sound that he might make for the richest chocolate or the finest wine.

Lynne Connolly

He changed his angle, lifted up on one hand, his other still tracing patterns and he devoured her. Ate her. And she couldn't hold back any longer. She arched her back and screamed as the climax hit her with the intensity of a tropical storm, rocking every inch of her. "Oh fuck me, don't stop, keep going—oh God!"

Her pussy pulsed and she realized he'd pushed his finger—fingers—inside her. He didn't stop licking and sucking although she squirmed to get away, the sensitivity too much but he kept a hand on her thigh, holding her in place for his invading tongue.

She cried out, begged for him to fuck her now but he ignored her until he'd lapped up every drop of her essence. No man had ever done that to her before, not eaten her out as if he couldn't get enough of her.

Finally he pulled away and rested his forehead on her mound. He breathed deeply as if he'd sprinted a hundred yards at Olympic speed.

"I could do this all night." His voice sounded muffled. "You taste glorious." He lifted his head. His mouth glistened, his chin was damp. "So good, honey, so good."

She stared at him enthralled. Gorgeous, hot and for tonight all hers. "I could let you. But we have other places to go don't we?"

"Oh yes. Plenty of other places." With a sudden movement, he pushed himself up on all fours. His cock thrust up aggressively close to her pussy. Not close enough. He eased himself up the bed until he crouched over her but he wasn't touching her although she could feel his heat and the way he wanted her. She swallowed. She could smell herself on him. The scent turned her on with a power that was new to her. At least this way. He vibrated enjoyment. He stared down at her, his gaze molten lava. "I need a moment or I'll come all over you right now. And I want in."

"How do you do it?"

"Do what?" His voice purred over her like velvet against her skin.

"Be this—this intense."

"I live in the moment. It's hard to do." He smiled down at her, bent for a gentle kiss. She licked her lips, savoring her taste on his lips and he watched avidly. "But it's a skill you can learn. Ten years ago, I was going nuts, literally. My nerves were shot to hell. I was a clever kid and my parents pushed me. My dad especially, the Chinese ethic to achieve kicking in. So I graduated early, set up the business and nearly had a breakdown. I went to classes and I learned not to agonize so much. Want me to teach you?"

She shook her head. "I'm doing okay. You stop the world for me."

He kissed her a lingering closed-mouth caress. "Now that is the best thing anyone's said to me."

She laughed. "Ever?"

"Ever." He bent again and he breathed in deep through his nose, a sexy sound that added to her enjoyment of him.

John took her mouth, explored it, tasted it and then lowered his body so it lay over hers, his cock between her legs caressing her pussy. Right now she didn't care about protection. He could do what he wanted.

But he finished the kiss and drew away, his attention going to the nightstand. He reached inside the drawer and found a condom before he leaned back, sitting on his heels while he slid the protection over his cock with a deliberation that she now knew meant he was appreciating every stroke, every easy glide. She should have put it on for him. She wanted to but after that wonderful orgasm she was still floating in a warm tide of aftermath.

He stretched over her again, smiling into her eyes. "Ready?"

"Oh yes." She smiled back. He'd made her more aware of her body, she realized. Ready for him, her pussy so wet her juices trickled in the cleft between her buttocks but assured by the promise in his eyes, she reached for him and opened her hands wide over the skin of his back. "Fuck me, John. Fuck me good."

His muscles flexed and she felt them stretch as he lowered his body to hers and inexorably entered her.

Despite her openness, he was still a tight fit. The head worked through her opening into the welcome he'd helped her prepare for him. He pushed, and more slid in. All the time they kept their eyes open and watched each other, neither of them speaking or breaking the moment as if this was something sacred.

In a way it was. It felt so different so new. Not virginal new but a new kind of sex a new kind of awareness. Was he a magician or some kind of hypnotist?

No. He'd talked to her and he'd listened. Listened to her body as it sang for him. When he'd gone down on her, he'd felt the way she responded, listened to the sounds she made and reacted accordingly. Did what she wanted although she hadn't realized she'd wanted until he did it to her.

And now he was doing it again. Easing into her, letting her feel every inch of him as he slid his cock inside her pussy. She sighed, her breath catching in the back of her throat. "How big are you? Do you know?"

"How big does it feel?"

"Fucking huge."

He laughed. "Very flattering, sweetheart. Thank you. I never measured it. It always seemed adequate. So how do I compare?"

"You're bigger than average but you're not scary."

"Scary?"

"Big isn't always better."

He laughed. "I'm not even going there. This is us, me and you, and if we fit that's good enough."

She arched up to him. "Oh yes, we fit all right." She let her eyes half close and felt the hardness sliding so easily now deep inside her. Every touch, every moment, every inch. Until his balls nestled softly against her ass. He came to rest. "Me and you. Me in you. Never so good, Edie. Never."

She believed him because it was the same for her. But before she could tell him, he pulled out and pushed back in. Slowly. His control awed her. He must have amazing physical strength to fuck her with such controlled slowness.

He kept up a rhythm like the constant but deliberate motions of Tai Chi, easing in and out, the liquid sounds providing an accompaniment she knew she'd never forget or ever want to.

With blinding recognition, she realized what he meant. This time was all that mattered. Whatever came next, whatever had happened before, they had this and if they appreciated it, if they lived and enjoyed it now they'd never regret it.

"We'll never lose this will we?"

His slow smile warmed her. "No we never will." He bent his head for another kiss and she reached up eagerly to share it with him. He never stopped moving in and out of her and with every glide he touched her sweet spot, caressed it and withdrew only to caress it again. Her arousal rose almost without her being aware of it. It just was.

They reached the high points, passed through them and went higher. Everything outside their bodies ceased to matter until they could have been the only people in the world.

And then she exploded but not like the fourth of July. More like underwater fireworks if there was any such thing, the shimmering, magnificent climax drenching them in a mist of fire.

Edie didn't know if she cried out, didn't care, but she heard his voice crying out to her, calling her name. She didn't realize how closely she held him until she breathed deep and found it more difficult than it should be.

John rolled to one side, taking her with him, his eyes closed, his mouth slightly open breathing deeply. She rested her head on his sweat-sheened chest and licked his skin, the salty taste a tribute to their efforts.

"You," he said slowly, his voice deeper than usual, "are a miracle, Edie Howard."

He called her Edie. She'd lived as Sunset for the last thirty years. Now it was Edie's turn.

Chapter Seven

ഇ

John wondered if love at first sight existed. This sublime sensation unlike anything he'd felt before could be because he'd tried harder with Edie. She needed it, he'd thought, sensing the lost soul under the sophisticated beauty but it had turned out that he needed it too. Maybe he was as lost as she was. And maybe she was bringing him back to life.

He opened his eyes, saw her watching him and lifted his hand to caress her cheek and cup it before he kissed her. She invited touch, that soft skin begging him to worship. It had been a long time since he'd thought about the mess he'd been ten years ago but something in her had brought it out, reminded him of what he'd been. On the surface a raging success, underneath a pathetic fuck-up, his nerves shot, his ambition and self-confidence out of control.

Now she needed help too but he was afraid that in bringing it to her he'd reopen old wounds. With horror he recalled that helpless feeling of being dragged along by a tide he couldn't stop. He wouldn't let that happen to Edie.

Slowly he withdrew from her, his body protesting at the separation as if they already belonged together. He pulled away to discard the used condom. Already he wanted her again, his cock swelling once more, so he found the task more difficult than it should have been.

One taste and he feared he was addicted to Sunset. No, to Edie. The woman behind the sophisticated ex-model fascinated him much more, the real woman behind the elegant polished façade. And never for a moment did he forget how lucky he was that she'd allowed him in. Edie was adept at keeping people at a distance, he'd seen her do it on TV interviews. That had been the first time she'd intrigued him rather than elicited his imagination as a symbol of perfection when he'd had a glimpse of how she worked.

Now here she was in his bed, the focus of his loving.

He rose up over her and took her lips once more, explored her mouth with leisurely thoroughness. She opened for him, accepted him and gave back. He drew away slowly. "Are you still thinking about surgery?"

"What's that?" She smiled up at him.

"How about an ass lift?" His voice suddenly became hoarse as he remembered the sight of that elegant curve. His cock completed its expansion.

The witch snuggled close and purred. "Possibly. Is it the thought of the surgery that makes you so—interested?"

He laughed. Her honesty in bed enchanted him. He curved his arm around her and cupped those delectable curves, deliberately allowing his longest finger to slip between her buttocks down to her labia and just inside. Damp still, and when he touched fresh juice flowed from her onto him. He wanted to taste it again, but to do that he'd have to take his hand away and he didn't want to. So he curled his finger in a little, increased the pressure on her ass. "You can't want to do anything to this. It's beautiful, tempting. You could end up with a small scar here." He traced a line in the lower crease with his forefinger but he didn't remove his middle finger from her cleft. He doubted that he could right now. Her heat scorched him and all he wanted was to burn. "It would be a sin to mar such lovely flesh. And where you have a scar the nerve endings are damaged or destroyed and you'll lose feeling there."

He kissed her forehead, let his lips linger on her fabulous skin and felt her answering kiss on his chest.

She lifted her head. "You're pretty delicious yourself you know."

"Not like you."

"Exactly like me." She stroked her cheek against his skin, sending sensation skittering down his body. "You made yourself. You told me you were overweight as a child."

"Derided for it." He recalled how he'd felt but it was a distant memory now as if it had happened to someone else. "I was a clever fat kid. A clever, fat Chinese kid. That gave them plenty of ammunition. I pretended not to care."

"But you did."

"Fuck, yes I cared. I cared enough to lose weight and work so hard at my studies that I graduated early. I met Henry Roubiere. He was like me, a misfit but for different reasons. We set up the partnership, his money, my expertise until it was our money and our expertise." He stopped abruptly.

"Then you had a breakdown."

He smoothed his hand over her hair and forked his fingers through the waves, wild now. "Pretty much."

She wriggled against him, working his cock with her body. He groaned. "And you became the sex symbol you are today."

He laughed and enjoyed the freedom of the moment as he'd been taught, as came naturally to him these days. "That's you."

"Don't be modest. You've appeared on enough screens and been at enough premieres for the media to know your face. 'Sexydoc', I've seen you described as. More than once."

"Oho, so you noticed me before did you?"

She primmed her mouth. "I googled you when I was thinking about the surgery. I had an interesting afternoon investigating you."

"Hmm surgery. That reminds me." He wriggled his finger, still nestled in the cleft of her ass. "I have more persuading to do don't I?"

She hummed, more in appreciation of what he was doing than agreement or cogent argument. At least he hoped so.

He rolled up on his knees, taking her with him so she was on all fours. Only then did he take his hand away and admire the beautiful sight. She kept her legs spread and her glorious hair, the hair that had gained her the nickname she'd had for most of her life spread over the upper part of her back, gleaming autumn gold in the subdued light of his bedroom.

John would never forget that moment. This woman embodied all his dreams, was the epitome of the perfection that he'd sought for in his early years, the perfection he now knew was better flawed.

He saw tiny marks airbrushed or unseen by the camera. A scar from, he guessed from its age, a childhood incident and a slightly darker patch on one side. It marked this back as belonging to Edie and no other. The blemishes made the sight dearer to him, not less.

He spread his hand over her back, savored the contrast between her pale skin and his olive tones, loved the sensation. He breathed deep, scenting their previous lovemaking, knowing that it would soon be renewed. He watched her pussy dampen for him, the tops of her thighs glistening with her arousal and he just managed not to bend and taste it, lick it off. He had a use for it. Her rosebud tempted him, the tight furl of her anus beautiful, far too tempting for him to refuse to accept.

Then he reached for the dildo and lube.

Edie gasped. He put them on the sheet beside him where she could see them and curved his hands over her waist. "I'm trying to give you pleasure, Edie, only good feelings. A pinch of pain can add to the pleasure. You know that don't you?" If she said no now he'd die. But he had to make sure.

"Sometimes." Cautious but she was still with him.

"Trust me?"

"Okay."

He massaged her skin, keeping his motions smooth and gentle. No sudden movements. He saw her muscles tighten slightly with the increased tension. "You say stop, I stop. All I ask is that you give it a chance. Has anyone taken you in the ass before?"

"Someone tried."

She sounded subdued. He hated that. He wouldn't destroy the trust building between them. "I really want to. I want to show you how good it can be. But those other times, you didn't like them did you?"

She shook her head, her hair moving against the pillow, falling over her face. He leaned forward to smooth it back and tuck it behind her ears so he could see her. "Did he force you?"

"A bit. Not rape, never think that but..." She bit her lip. He wanted to bite it too just a nip.

"But you didn't like it. If you don't like what I'm doing, say so. Just give it a chance to feel good."

He picked up the dildo and rolled it over her buttocks. The coolness raised goose bumps. "Even a subtle sensation like this might not feel right after the procedures. You'll have dead spots in your body where a continuous feeling would be halted. Most times it won't matter, you'll hardly notice." He rolled the phallus down over the crest of her buttock to the top of her thigh, the flanged head pointing to her pussy and ass. "But you'd notice if I did that. Like a blind spot in your eye, you'd have a break." He stopped, lifted the dildo to the other side and repeated the action with his other hand. "Does that feel good?" He retrieved the lube and popped the tube open with one hand without her seeing. She was looking at the dildo. It showed his cock right down to his balls, the smooth glass skimming over any wrinkles or creases in the original. He moved so his cock bobbed up to lie over the crease between her buttocks and he placed the dildo next to it. "They did a good job. But I have more fun with the real thing." He twisted the glass, twirled it against her skin.

Leaning forward he pressed his cock into her buttock crease so the head nudged over the top. She felt so good he could come from working it there. He took a moment to kiss her shoulder blades, waiting for the peak to die down.

He squeezed the lube, letting the clear gel flow over his fingers before he dropped the tube on the sheet. He leaned back and slid his glistening fingers into the crease where his cock had just discovered intimations of glory.

Working the liquid over and over, he slid past her rosebud opening, not attempting to enter. She liked that, liked him to massage her there. Allowed it. So he slipped the tip of his forefinger inside. Just the tip, although it killed him not to take her, fuck her deep inside and feel the beauty of that hot velvet sheath.

He thought he'd learned patience in the last ten years. He'd been wrong.

Moving the dildo to the front of her body, he slid the smooth glass head over her clit and felt her shiver. A drop of her honey slid down her thigh and he watched its glistening progress, knowing he'd driven it out of her.

The sight enthralled him. He caught his breath until the drop was lost in the sheet under her knee.

And still he worked her, rubbed the phallus over her clit down to her cunt until it slid in almost of its own volition because by then she was so wet she could have accepted the dildo and his cock together. Except that the dildo *was* him in a way. Strange how she'd picked that one even before she'd seen him naked.

He took a couple of deep breaths. Her soft moans drove him higher still and he knew he wouldn't last much longer without fucking her. He wanted to be inside her body so badly he could taste it. Moaning, he dragged his mind away from the prospect.

He pushed one finger inside her anus and waited. Just to the first joint to let her feel it. She didn't object; if anything her moans increased. She clutched the sheet under her hands, fisting and releasing the crumpled fabric. He wanted it to be his cock but he couldn't be everywhere. He added another finger.

Working his fingers inside her softly he managed to get them further inside, then began to introduce a third finger. With the dildo pushed inside her cunt, working her slowly, she melted over him, soft as butter while he was hard as iron.

He leaned against her ass until she got the message and lowered her body so the dildo could remain lodged inside her while he leaned over to get the condom he'd left on the nightstand. He dropped a kiss on her shoulder, stopped to suckle and taste her skin.

Almost as far gone as she was, John managed to get the condom on one-handed before he replaced his hand on the dildo and urged her back up. He needed her completely open so he wouldn't hurt her. And he wouldn't force it much, though the demon that resided deep inside him told him to. *Just push, fuck, shove inside her as far as you can go. The real ecstasy is the deepest heart of her. Tear her apart.*

Edie could hardly believe it. A few instances excepted, and they'd been a long time ago, the last time she'd allowed herself to be so vulnerable with a man was Bobby. Her sex was usually done with her on her back or on top, both enjoying themselves with the intensity of a tennis game on a summer afternoon, or rather, the lack of intensity. Not this.

His fingers inside her where she'd only allowed tentative attempts before, his cock sliding inside her cunt. Another word she rarely used, but here, emotions and needs stripped raw, it was right.

And she wanted him now. Now. Urgency sent need ripping through her. When he removed his fingers from her ass, she felt bereft but only for a moment because smooth hard heat touched her. He slid the very tip inside, barely opening her. "Here we go, sweetheart. Breathe out for me." His hand on her waist was shaking. He wanted her as much as she wanted—needed—him.

She took a deep breath and released it slowly as he ied in. He got the head in and a little of the shaft she thought from the way it felt. *So good.* He moaned a long drawn-out sound of appreciation. The hand holding the dildo inside her trembled.

He gripped her upper thigh, drawing it back. "God I wish you could see this! My cock as it slowly, so slowly, slides inside your body. Fuck."

"John!" She lifted her head and saw them reflected in the mirrored closets opposite. His golden olive-toned body behind hers, her leaning forward on her elbows, her breasts nearly grazing the rumpled sheet below them. The expression of ecstasy on his face surpassed anything she'd seen before on a lover and nearly made her come on the spot.

The blue outer rims of her eyes had almost disappeared, swallowed by the dark pupils that displayed her arousal. John's sexy dark eyes showed raw blatant need. He watched his lips drawn back over his teeth as he pushed home.

Perspiration was breaking out all over his body. And he drew back and drove in again. At the same time, he pulled out the dildo and pushed it home. "Can you come up here, sweetheart, to me?"

She'd never felt so full. She moved gingerly, wondering if it would hurt but it didn't. Instead, she felt full. Full of him, cunt and ass both, his cock in both holes. And she wanted to see that area between her thighs, her view blocked by her breasts and deep shadow. But he wanted a part of this. He didn't just want to do it to her, he wanted her close to him, moving with him. He kept still as she straightened her arms and pushed up on all fours.

He looped his free hand around her waist and pulled her up the rest of the way. "I've got you."

She cried out as she moved against him and her back made contact with his chest. He cupped a breast and she reveled in the feel of her hardened nipple against his palm, sensitivity cubed.

Inside her like this, double fucking her with the dildo and his cock, she felt complete. Coming home never felt so good before and here with him buried in her body she *was* home.

She tilted her head so her cheek rubbed his shoulder and murmured his name against his neck. He tasted so fucking sexy. Then she lifted her head so he could hear her next words. "They're both you." He was driving her insane.

The dildo and his cock. "Yes, yes they are. Yessss." He thrust again, withdrew and thrust and gritted his teeth. The phallus glistened with her juices, her thighs wet with them, mingled with lube and sheer desire.

Then she tensed as everything went into overdrive, sending her higher than she'd ever been before. She finally knew what the phrase "screaming orgasm" meant. Her muscles clutched him, held him tight, released, clenched. Her ass fisted around his cock. She cried out, her body stiff against his and that was enough. No more holding back.

She came in agonizingly ecstatic waves, feeling his explosion, hearing him crying her name.

Chapter Eight

ᔓ

Tempt the Cougar blog:

Do I get my toaster now? We did it. But I'm in deeper than I meant to be. He's great in bed and out and his invention in bed is amazing. I thought I was experienced. I am, but while I might have done the things we do before, I haven't done them with him, felt the perfection of being with him. What is happening to me?

Cam—You sound like a teenager with her first crush. Be careful because at our age we're vulnerable. Think about what you want, what you really want. Younger men are good for a fling but keep your head straight.

Rachel—I know you well enough now to know you have sense, that you'll hold back. Just go for it but never forget to keep at least one toe on the ground. Younger men are fun but most of them don't have staying power. So don't expect it to last forever.

Edie grimaced as she read the responses to her blog. She still felt good. The euphoria after their first night had taken her completely by surprise. But three days after that first night she still felt it. She could fall in love with this man and that would be a big mistake. Nothing more pathetic than an older woman falling for a younger man and failing to know when it was over.

So she wouldn't tell him. From the way John called her, connected with her, she knew he wanted to be a couple but she hadn't gone that far.

She clicked the tab on her web browser and brought up the gossip columnist Patrick Sheraton. Bitchy and gay, Patrick was an essential guest at every party and he lived in LA, where else?

She and John had made it onto Sheraton's fucking column for two nights out of the last three. Their first meal out together the comments had been snarky but suggestive, and Patrick seemed more interested in the possibility that she was seducing him for free cosmetic surgery although he ameliorated it by saying, "Mind you, peeps, if all plastic surgeons looked like John Sung there'd be a lot more paying in kind. I know I would. Look at this man and say you wouldn't!"

Their second appearance had been last night when she'd picked up John after work and they'd gone back to her apartment. Someone had done a candid snap of them getting out of her car and even caught the way John grabbed her hand and dragged her inside, too intent on getting her to bed to exercise any caution. At least he hadn't picked her up and carried her, although once indoors he'd done that too.

The comments there were definitely more snarky. Some made her wince although she could have sworn she was immune to the little shit behind the column. She'd weathered gossip columns for years without feeling too concerned and now she felt concerned for John. Would their affair mean that she shouldn't go to Roubiere? She rather thought so. In any case, the date of her first TV interview for the book was coming uncomfortably close and she wouldn't recover in time from any major procedure.

Not that she wanted it anymore. She'd see the doctor and explain.

Except it didn't turn out quite like that.

* * * * *

John found himself on the second floor where the operating rooms were situated, looking for a missing piece of equipment. His stethoscope. He hardly ever used it these days but he'd had it since his student years and he wanted to know it was safe.

So it was that he saw an unconscious figure wheeled out of Operating Room One.

Edie, her hair bound back, no makeup but unmistakably the woman who'd promised not to have any cosmetic surgery. Only last night she'd told him, gazed up at him and said "I won't have anything done. I swear. You've persuaded me."

Disappointment reverberated through him. He stared as the nurses wheeled her past, hardly able to believe that she could lie so well.

John found his stethoscope and returned to his office. He sat at his desk, numb to his surroundings until his assistant called to let him know his next appointment had arrived. The woman he saw probably thought he'd earned his reputation as cold and clinical but he agreed to the breast implants she wanted and sent her on her way. She glanced back when she reached the door. "I thought you'd say no. My friend who recommended me said you put her through hours of counseling before you agreed to do her op. Has someone changed your mind?"

He stared at her, not seeing her but the high-cheekboned, porcelain-skinned face of Edie Howard. "I haven't changed my mind. You still have to go through the counseling."

The woman sighed. "I'll wait for your letter then. But I want it done in the next two months. I'm getting married again in October and I want to be fully healed by then."

He didn't give her any outward response. "If you're a suitable candidate we can handle that." A new husband, a new pair of boobs. Somehow, John doubted he'd be doing this one. Once when he'd started out and they needed the reputation and the money but these days he could pick and choose. Be more ethical.

She left after one short smile, tentatively, as if she expected him to pounce on her. Maybe he did, but probably not in the way she intended.

Finally he was free to go upstairs and visit the wards. One in particular.

When he entered, Edie was sitting up in bed, her hair brushed out, her eyes still bearing the blankness and confusion he saw in most patients after an operation. She wore a pretty but modest nightdress. He stared at the bandage over her nose. She looked at him as if she was looking at a stranger, her stunning blue eyes fixed on his face.

He closed the door quietly and stood with his back to it. "You did this without talking to me?"

She opened her mouth, closed it again. Nodded.

Sorrow tasted bitter he discovered. Disappointment added a sour note. "Edie, it wasn't that you had an operation, it was that you did it without talking to me. You promised me and then you had it done anyway. I can't trust you can I?"

She still stared.

"You're not the woman I thought I was falling in love with." He should never have trusted his instincts over his clinical judgment. He should have known. This woman had supreme confidence, had run her own life for so long she didn't recognize when to give way. It was no fucking good. He'd only ever be an adjunct, an extra to her, never able to compete with the wealthy, powerful men she'd married.

His lack of self-worth warred with his anger and both won out over the lurking suspicion that she was holding something out on him. But despite his fury, he was relieved to see her recovered after the procedure. Even now he cared for her well-being. He told himself it was because she was an important patient here, not because of what he'd thought they'd had.

He forced a smile. "Edie, it was fun wasn't it? You were the best fuck I ever had. I wish you all the best in the future."

He left while he still could but he went straight to Roubiere's office where he vented some of his wrath on his partner. "You could have told me, you bastard."

Roubiere lounged back in his chair. "And violate the sanctity of the doctor-patient relationship?" A smile twisted the corner of his mouth. "If Ms Howard wants you to know she'll tell you for herself or she'll give me permission to tell you. Otherwise you'll be breaking the oath you took."

John snarled. "You fucking bastard. She told you?" His sense of betrayal increased, sent fury rocketing through him. He'd been let down before too many times to count but he'd never thought Edie would do this to him. He trusted her.

"What does it matter? You told me it was an affair, something to amuse you both. It couldn't be that you thought it was something more, could it?"

Breathing deeply helped. Not thinking about how she'd fooled him didn't. So he blocked the thought and shoved it to the back of his mind. "You're right. She promised to tell me, that's all. It's not important."

He straightened up and left the office.

Roubiere watched the closed door thoughtfully before he hit the intercom that connected him to his secretary. "Jude, don't tell Dr. Sung anything about what happened here today. He'll try to find out, so encrypt the records and don't tell him a thing."

The fucker deserved to stew if he had such little confidence in his own judgment and in Edie's trust.

Edie sat in front of her laptop again. Her stay in hospital hadn't been long. She pulled up the blog page and read the entries. Not much had changed but then although her life had taken another turn she was too old to imagine that the world revolved around her.

She typed her entry with a heavy heart. Back to reality.

I promised John I wouldn't have any cosmetic surgery but I had to break that promise. However he didn't wait to find out why.

I went to tell Dr. Roubiere I'd changed my mind and tripped and fell in his office. Maybe it's time to give up four-inch stilettos but I refuse to go into flats forever.

Broke my nose. Apparently the bone shattered or something and if I hadn't had work done it could have affected my breathing. Hell, I don't know but I couldn't bear the thought of going around with a flat nose and everybody laughing at me. Okay I'm vain but I've spent my life taking care of the way I look, so I let him do some plastic work as well as the necessary surgery.

I went straight into surgery. They knocked me out for it. I'd skipped breakfast so I could take the general anesthetic. Straightened my nose and you couldn't tell. I must have been down as a rhinoplasty, or maybe John just jumped to conclusions but he decided that the immediate postoperative period when I was feeling vulnerable was a good time to yell at me. My mouth and lips were dry and I felt disconnected from everything and he thought it was the best time to vent his anger on me. He said I'd violated his trust, refused to think about anything else and stormed off in a righteous rage. Ripped me a new one.

I did think about replying but honestly, do I really want a man who can do that? So if we made our affair more permanent would I be letting myself in for more heartache?

I have to be grateful to John for bringing me back to life. I'm in my mid-forties with my kids all grown up so I don't see them every day, and with my exes getting on with their lives I was at the lowest ebb I can remember.

Hence the visit to the plastic surgeon. But the book I talked about is my autobiography and my manager thinks I'm going to do well with it.

I made a couple of other decisions. I'm not going to do an exposé on my last husband any more than is already in the book. I'd wanted to use the exposure as revenge to spite him for dropping me as soon as he found a younger clone but what the hell, he doesn't deserve it. I have to say my manager, Randy Norwood, is delighted. He said the book will do much better and, hey, why didn't I think about writing more stuff. An exposé on the fashion world, or maybe a more investigative piece. It's an interesting thought.

And the second decision? I love you girls. You have been better friends to me than I've ever had in my life. You've supported me and let me help you. I don't feel useless anymore and I don't feel alone, and that is down to you. So I'm taking another chance. My name is really Edie, like I told you. It's the name my friends use and Cam has been a friend for a long time, so I haven't been deceiving you girls. But I use my middle name in my professional career. Adelaide Howard. And I've used the moniker Sunset for most of my life too. My first husband, the designer Zach Atoya gave me that name because of the color of my hair and it stuck.

I'd hate it if it made any difference to this relationship. And if any of you are in the LA area give me a shout because I'd love to meet you for real. If you're going to Romanticon again will you let me know? This time I'll be there.

Cam: Give him time, sweetie. Even hunkilicious surgeons have their insecurities and trust is obviously one of his buttons. I'm sure he'll calm down and then feel like a real jerk (as well he should) when he finds out the truth.

Hey at least you had the balls to give the cougar thing a try. And who knows if it's really over, honey. If it is then, hey, remember the good time and move on. Don't let it weigh you down. Life's too damn short. But still…don't close the door on the possibility that it's not a done deal. Remember men really are from Mars—which makes them an alien species—and we all know how unpredictable aliens are. :)

Oh I could hug you for coming clean!! You have no idea how many times I've almost slipped up and called you Sunset. And honey you know that if there's anyone in the world who can be trusted it all us gals here. Hell, the things we know about each other could fill a book…a really naughty one at that!

Romanticon? Yeah baby! I think it's time for a reunion. Friends, drinks, books, models? Bring it on!!

Rachel: Vanity had nothing to do with your decision! What you're supposed to go through life with a broken nose and breathing problems so people won't think you had a nose job? I've seen people come in for emergency problems stemming from this sort of thing. The time to do it is when you did it, not when there's so much scar tissue that you won't look normal no matter what you try to do to fix it.

Do you think part of John's reaction stemmed from worry about not doing the work himself? Don't get me wrong he shouldn't have jumped to conclusions and attacked you at your most vulnerable. (Bet you'd like to be a fly on the wall when he finds out the truth.) I'm just wondering if he completely lost it because he was worried too, not only because he thought you'd broken your promise to him.

Oh. My. God! I just about fell off my chair when I
found out who you were! My first thought was: I've been
giving sexual encouragement to Sunset?? Me? But you
know what? It doesn't make a damn bit if difference. We
all started out in the same boat didn't we and we've done
a great job of providing each other with oars. Or were
those dildos too? <g>

Being in this group had just about saved her life.

Edie closed the laptop when her phone rang and checked
the caller. Not John. She knew a clean break was best but it
didn't stop her looking and even hoping even after his shitty
behavior to her after her operation. She still didn't know why
he was so furious, why he didn't wait for explanations even if
she'd felt like giving them after his outburst. But she wouldn't
have done that. It would have put her in the wrong. Never
ever again would she allow anyone to do that.

She thumbed the green button. "Hi Randy."

"Hey. How you doin'?"

Randy Norwood had helped her too, just by accepting
her. "Not bad. And you?"

"This ain't idle chitchat much though I enjoy that too.
Listen they want to bring your interview on the Victor
Schuman show forward a couple of weeks. Are you good to go
or do you want me to turn it down?"

"What date are we talking about?"

"The first Thursday in July. Five days. If you don't want
to do it, no problem. We'll stick to the original date. But there
are rumors about you and John Sung, and rumors that you had
surgery done. If Sung did it, he's in violation, isn't he? So that's
topical now. In the news and good for the book. In a couple of
weeks it won't be so hot."

Indignation rose within her and her temper rose. John
could survive a rumor like that because they'd been

completely ethical, but it could damage the clinic, as it survived on reputation and goodwill. She couldn't allow it.

She glanced in the mirror, turned her head one way and then the other. "I'm fine. Take the offer."

"You sure?"

"Perfectly. But I won't say if I had surgery or not. Only that John Sung never operated on me or advised me." She stopped, her senses assaulted by memories. John making love to her, sucking her nipples, asking her to promise. Intensely erotic scenes when he'd tempted her into making all those promises about no surgery. Either he cared, or he was a controlling fuck who made Peter look like a pussycat.

Either way it didn't matter anymore. John Sung was a memory, nothing else.

Chapter Nine
ജ

Victor Schuman was a smarmy, snarky middle-aged ex-standup comedian who'd made such a success of his chat show that it was now generally known as *The Victor Schuman Show* instead of its official title of *Hollywood Tonight*. His frequently unfair but often funny comments reminded Edie of Patrick Sheraton. But these were only two of the fuckwits who benefited from celebrities' avid desire for publicity and the public's delight in hearing about the affairs of other people, the sleazier the better.

Not that Edie was above all that. She enjoyed Schuman's monologue at the top of the show even though it held at least one untruth and a stack of insinuations, none of them actionable, none of them about her although she knew she'd been the butt of his jokes a week or so before. She'd been too wise to watch that edition of the program. She might have been tempted to respond.

Now she sat in the small area still referred to as the "green room" dressed in one of her most elegant dark blue pants and silk shell outfits, wearing discreet diamonds, her hair brushed to a gleaming mass to lie around her shoulders, waiting for her first interview.

Schuman finished his monologue and introduced the first guest. Edie was to replace the final guest, so she had the spot at the end. She had to wait.

She'd forgotten how boring these times could be, the wait until your spot, the interminable hours waiting for the right light or for the crew to set up the shot then another wait for more of the same. Every model had her own way of coping and it varied over time. The ones into sewing had completed whole quilts over time. She wouldn't have to do this much longer. A few TV shows, some author signing sessions and the book would be launched.

But she'd enjoyed working with the ghostwriter and had, after the initial interviews, written most of the book herself and given it to the writer to polish and perfect. She wondered if she could do it again, this time working on her own. It would be a new adventure. Thanks to John, she was ready to face new challenges. But she feared she'd have a hole in her life now.

She glanced into the monitor that showed her the shots the cameras were taking. Almost automatically she'd done that when she'd arrived, deciding how she'd sit, how she'd move, even to the tilt of her head. All those lessons so carefully taught, so well absorbed. She'd never stop being a model, not really. It was like learning to drive where learned techniques became automatic. But she didn't despise herself for it. This was her chosen profession and she'd had to decide early on to take it seriously. That meant learning her best features as well as her worst, how to pose properly so as not to waste the photographer's time, how to show off the designer creations she paraded on the runway despite the unwearability of some of them.

She didn't miss it, not one bit. Nor the press attention nor the photos in the glossies. In fact she was relieved not to have to do it anymore.

Her eyes narrowed when she saw someone she thought she knew. More monitors showed the angles other cameras were taking and she found one fixed on the audience. Anticipation fizzed inside when she realized she was looking at Cam. Her friend had come and next to her—fuck!

But yes. She recognized Rachel from a photo on the blog and then she saw others. They'd come to see her. Live, here. They cared enough about her to take the journey to support her!

Euphoria filled Edie. No other woman had ever cared enough to do that for her. With their support she'd come this far, recovered from her obsession with John and the first nights when, weakened by the surgical procedure and the accident that preceded it, she'd woken calling his name.

Fuck him. Fuck all men. She was whole and her own woman. She could do this. Her women friends had helped to set her free.

Schuman began his buildup. She began to listen properly when he started with the "beautiful" spiel and she knew what was coming. "We know that some of the world's most famous models, desperate to remain in the limelight, have gone through cosmetic surgery. My next guest hasn't just done this, she's written a book that opens the lid on her world. Married to three of the world's most desirable men, she divorced them all and recently she's been seen with one half of Hollywood's most successful plastic surgeon partnership. Did she get pro bono treatment?" A picture flashed up of her leaving the clinic, her nose still bandaged after her operation. She'd seen that picture before—it had been all over the internet the day she'd left to go home. On her own. "Has the man known as Sexydoc finally gone too far and broken his ethical code for the love of Sunset? Let's find out shall we?"

And she was on her feet, walking toward the stage, guided by a stagehand. She glanced at the man who was doing his best to leer down her cleavage, but with her height plus the four-inch heels, the little shit probably didn't have much of a view. Mindful that the camera would attempt the same thing she'd kept exposure to a minimum, sexy without being obvious.

She strode on to the set and shook hands with Schuman, drawing away when he threatened to kiss her. Too vulnerable from John's possession, she didn't want any man to get even that intimate. Not yet anyway.

Schuman asked the questions about her past, the easy ones about her relatively comfortable childhood and how she started her modeling career. So of course she had to talk about her first husband.

He had few secrets left and she'd usually chosen to use his example as one to follow. The fewer secrets she had the less the bastards who preyed on her could expose. But she was careful to skim over her second husband Bobby's sexual preferences, nobody's business but theirs and Bobby's current wife.

Schuman wasn't very interested in the first two. It was the third, Peter Henderson, he wanted to know about. The one who'd dumped her so publicly. But it didn't hurt her anymore and she told Schuman why. "Peter doesn't know any other way. He took me because I was available at the height of my career and I knew everyone. I took him because he was damn sexy." She had the audience laughing with that one. "But by the time we split five years later, if he hadn't dumped me I would have dumped him. He found someone else first."

"You know his wife is pregnant?"

She shrugged. If he'd hoped to get a rise from her, he would be disappointed. She really didn't give a fuck anymore. "I have two wonderful children by Zach. They're fine adults and I'm proud of them. I hope Peter has as much joy from his children as I have out of mine." The honest truth, and it earned her a round of applause. What she didn't say was that Peter had wanted children from her but she'd kept on taking the pills. He'd wanted possessions and trophies, not flesh and blood children. Just as he'd wanted her to become a living Barbie.

Strange that it didn't hurt anymore the way Peter had deceived her, used her and then dumped her. Fate had a way of balancing things out. She didn't have to do a thing about it. He'd get what was coming to him sooner or later. Karma.

She gave Victor Schuman her best smile, the one that told him she was the sultriest, most desirable thing on two legs. He melted, the expression in his eyes softening. She had him. "I wish Peter all that he deserves. I'm sure he'll get it."

Another round of applause with some laughter. Here lay a danger point, when things were going well and she thought she had Schuman. She'd done enough of these things to know he'd strike soon, hoping her relief and maybe a touch of adrenaline might get her to say too much.

"I understood that your new book would lift the lid off a number of things. We got the inside story on your marriages so how about the modeling world?"

"There's too much for one book. I might do that in the second."

"You're planning another book?"

"I'm thinking about it."

"And more cosmetic procedures?"

He slipped that in almost seamlessly. No wonder he had the reputation for getting secrets out of the people who appeared on his show. The camera would be zooming in for a closeup, a nice reveal of her face. But she hadn't been in front of cameras for this long without learning a few things. She froze her expression and turned it puzzled, lifting her chin so she could frown at him. "More?"

"You aren't going to deny that you're seeing cosmetic surgeon Dr. John Sung, are you?"

She shrugged. "We spent some time together."

She was close enough to see the coldness in Schuman's eyes as he settled in for the kill. "And you were seen leaving his clinic recently with your nose bandaged." No doubt the screen had flashed that picture up again.

She allowed a smile to touch her lips. "Ah, I see where you made your mistake. No, I was Dr. Roubiere's patient not Dr. Sung's. And the procedure was the result of an accident. I fell and broke my nose."

Schuman's mouth turned up in a sneer and he leaned close, so close she could see the powder congealing in the lines on his face. He was sweating, probably with excitement. She wondered if he came when he got his victims this close. Well she wouldn't be the cause of one of his orgasms. "You expect us to believe that?"

She didn't give an inch, but shrugged. "Believe what you like, it makes no difference to me. Except that Dr. Sung was never my physician in any capacity. Dr. Roubiere looked after me."

"Don't they share patients?" That got him a snigger from a few people in the audience. The double entendre was too obvious for her to find it remotely amusing.

"They share the business, not each other's lists."

She'd silenced the audience. They needed something, something to win them over to her. Oh fuck, yes, she knew just what would do it. "I saw *many* people while I spent time with Dr. Sung. Going in and out of the clinic, obviously having surgery done. As many men as women." She paused, met Schuman's eyes, smiled right into them. "I could tell you who if you like. I'm not bound by any confidentiality clause."

The audience got it. She heard the collective gasp of breath. Schuman had always declared himself totally against cosmetic surgery, some of his most vicious diatribes had been aimed their way. But this close she saw a fine line under the sweep of hair across his forehead. Victor Schuman had had a facelift.

A voice was easily heard in the sudden hush. "Go for it, Edie!"

Cam. Wonderful Cam, the woman who had helped her through ups and downs and introduced her to some of the best friends she'd ever had.

"But of course," she said, turning the conversation from sour to sweet. "Since neither of us has had a cosmetic procedure we wouldn't know about that would we?"

He leaned back. At least he had the smarts to know when he was beaten. "Of course not."

The media would crucify him. Well he shouldn't have gone for her. Bastard.

Chapter Ten
ക

Edie didn't get home until the small hours, after a raucous celebration with the women from the blog. The friendships she'd cemented tonight would last the rest of her life, she felt it to her core.

Exhausted, she stepped out of the studio car and fumbled for the key to her apartment. Ahead of her, the concierge held open the door of her building, a broad smile wreathing his features. "You really stuck it to that know-it-all Victor Schuman. About time somebody gave him some of his own back." He chattered until she was in the elevator and the doors were sliding closed, then a change crossed his face. "Ma'am, someone—"

The rest of his words were cut off as the elevator finished closing and began to rise. Edie slumped against the wall; the evening had taken more out of her than she cared to admit. She wanted a hot bath and then bed.

How much better it would have been had she had someone to pamper her and care for her. Maybe she'd find someone in time, but all that she saw when she closed her eyes was a lean tanned face with eyes that burned into her soul. Despair touched her.

She straightened up and spoke aloud to reinforce the statement. "It's only been two weeks. I'll heal." Determination filled her. She had a life, a good one and she'd do her best to live what was left of it. Without him. The hollow inside her would fill because she'd make sure it did.

The elevator doors slid open and she walked the two steps that took her to her apartment. Perhaps she'd get out of this place, buy a house, take up gardening.

She typed her combination into the keypad and glanced at the fingerprint recognizer but it didn't glow in a silent request for her print. Funny, she thought she'd turned it on when she left. Maybe not. She'd been a little absentminded recently.

She closed her eyes as she entered and took a deep breath of the potpourri she left in a large china dish on the side table. A calming mixture made especially for her. She'd thought she was finally getting over her misery. Her triumph tonight and the meeting with the ladies of the blog afterward had dispelled it but now that she was on her own again, it flooded back, the dam breached once more.

A tear trickled from beneath her closed lids and she took a moment to will the others away. Tears did no good. She'd learned that.

"Don't cry, Edie."

At first she thought the soft voice came from her imagination. She'd heard it often enough and he'd never been there.

When she was ready, she opened her eyes.

He stood there. Dressed in iconic black, his collarless shirt open at the neck, his dark eyes gleaming behind the lenses of his black-framed spectacles.

Their eyes met and tears sprang to her eyes once more. She blinked them away. "How the fuck did you get in here?"

"Your concierge let me in. Didn't he tell you?"

Slowly she shook her head and realized what the guy downstairs had tried to say. "You can leave now."

He shoved his hands in his pockets. She could see the fists as he bunched them. "I will but I wanted to say something first. Please hear me out." The slight quiver at the end of his words told her he wasn't as in control as he was trying to project. That made her feel better, because she was sure as fuck not in control of her own emotions, which were rioting out of

175

control. She felt hot, she felt sick, she felt exhilarated to be in his presence again.

"You can talk but then go."

He dropped his gaze then lifted it again, his eyes blazing. And this time he didn't hide the yearning in them or the desire that nearly set her on fire. It took all she had to hide her own need for him.

"Edie, I was wrong. So fucking wrong about so many things. When you left the clinic, I knew I'd made the biggest mistake of my life. Roubiere wouldn't tell me anything, you know, not what you had done or didn't, but I did look at the operating lists. You were down for a rhinoplasty." A bitter smile twisted his lips. "I didn't even make you promise not to have one did I?" He shrugged. "Not that it matters. I shouldn't have made you promise anything. At first it seemed like a game and a way to have you, but later I really started feeling it. You're so perfect, Edie, so very beautiful. Your experience enhances what you are and if you'd had surgery, that would have been eliminated like an eraser on a pencil drawing. It hurt me to think of you doing that." He shook his head. "But that was me. I should never have asked. Just explained how I felt and left it up to you."

"Yes, you should. It's my body, my life." And the reason she'd enforced her absence. She belonged to nobody, not anymore and she never would again. Not even this overwhelmingly sexy man.

"I know." His eyes held misery now but still that desire he seemed unable to contain. "You have to do what you want otherwise you won't be happy. And that's what matters. You have to be happy, Edie. Anyway, I came to apologize and tell you I know why you walked away. And why I stayed away. If it weren't for that, nothing would have kept me from coming to you." He rocked on his heels and then started to walk.

It took her a moment to realize he was intent on leaving. She stepped aside so he could pass her but at the last minute, when his hand was on the doorknob, she put her hand on his arm. The muscle flexed as he turned to face her. His face had paled. "I'm sorry, Edie."

"So you said. Aren't you going to kiss me?"

He swallowed but she saw the spark of hope in his eyes, the way his mouth lifted at the corners. "Do you want me to?"

"I wouldn't have said if I didn't."

The next minute he'd swept his arms around her, holding her tight, and his mouth was on hers, drinking her in like a man dying of thirst. His groan reverberated through her body, echoing hers. She opened her mouth when his tongue pressed against her lips took him inside. He swept his tongue around her mouth, reacquainting himself with her shape, her taste and she took too, her body remembering how exciting, how wonderful he felt.

He drew away slowly, ending with gentle butterfly kisses to her lips so she was tempted to follow him. His eyes opened slowly. Softer now. "God I missed you!"

"So much." They stared at each other and she slid her hands under his jacket so that only his shirt lay between her skin and his. "What are we going to do?"

"Where's your bedroom? If I don't make love to you soon I'll die."

She loved his honesty. She felt the same way. And for the first time he'd said "make love".

Her bedroom was at the end of the hall to the right. She took his hand and led him there, hitting the button by the door that dropped the drapes. They fell softly over the window the green silk falling in supple folds. She tugged him to the bed and swept back the embroidered coverlet. That wouldn't be comfortable against bare skin. Then she turned to face him. "John, I—"

He cupped her face with his free hand. "I know. You don't want commitment. I got that."

Her eyes widened. "How did you get that?"

"I can't give you everything you want."

"Don't give up." That wasn't what she was going to say at all.

A smile curved his lips. "I don't intend to. And who knows, you might want more from me one day."

She was sure of it but she didn't tell him so. It wouldn't do to give him too many ideas. They'd slept together, fucked every night for a week then spent two weeks apart miserable. Normally she'd say that wasn't enough but this time she wasn't sure. Not at all sure.

But she was sure of one thing. Her fingers went to her side zipper only to meet his already there. She smiled and moved her hand away, working on his shirt buttons instead.

The sight of his bare chest made her salivate and she went to taste and kiss. His hand cupped the back of her head. "Edie, Edie!"

She nuzzled the base of his throat and then lifted her hands to push his jacket and shirt off his shoulders. They fell to the floor and she had access to his top half.

But he had his demands too. He tugged at her shell and she lifted her arms so he could pull it off. He had her bra unclipped and off. No longer ashamed to show her flaws, she smiled up at him as he touched her nipples. His fingers were shaking. He lifted his eyes to her face and kept stroking her breasts. "I thought I'd lost this. I really did only come to say I was sorry."

A suspicion crossed her mind. "Did you see the TV show?"

He shook his head. "I knew you'd do well, but I saw your name and I needed you. Needed to be with you. I thought of coming to the studio but I didn't want to put you off so I stayed away." He gave a shaky laugh.

"So you don't know what I said?"

His gaze sharpened. "No. Does it matter?"

Beauty of Sunset

She lifted her hands to remove his glasses and put them on the night table. He wouldn't need them for a while. "I said you were never my doctor, that's all."

He touched her cheek, smoothed his finger down, trailed it over her chin and down her throat to draw an imaginary line on the slope of her breast. "That doesn't matter. We could have proved it if we'd had to." He huffed. "Roubiere took more care than he needed to. Probably for the best although I nearly punched him out when he refused to discuss you at all." He paused. "I just wanted to talk about you. If I couldn't see you, couldn't touch you, I needed something. But he wouldn't."

"It could have ruined your business if people started to gossip. You know what damage rumors can do."

"I would have left, started again somewhere else. I thought about it, just so I wouldn't have to share the same city as you." He released her breasts and drew her close. "I'm not always a nice person. I didn't want to think of you with anyone else. Couldn't bear it. There's a caveman lurking in all of us."

She pressed her lips to his chest and enjoyed his taste and his nearness. "Just keep him under wraps for me. Don't get rid of him completely, especially in the bedroom."

"Does that mean…?" He cupped her head and stroked her hair. She heard him catch his breath.

"It means we take it one day at a time. I'm still ten years older than you are. That has certain implications."

"You're still the most beautiful woman I've ever seen, still the only one I want in my life. And I'm sorry, Edie, but I want that badly."

She tilted her head up and he kissed her.

By the time the kiss ended they were lying on the bed stark naked. His rigid cock pressed against the soft flesh of her stomach and he rolled her so he was on top. He kissed her cheek, her throat and lingered at the sensitive hollow at the base. She shuddered and pushed against him.

179

"Sweetheart, I need you now." He leaned over, threatening to leave her but knowing what he wanted to find, she put a restraining hand on his shoulder.

"No, you don't have to use protection. I'm not fertile, it's the wrong time of the month. And I'm clean."

He leaned up on his elbows. "You're sure?"

She nodded.

He watched her as he lifted up and settled between her legs when she spread them for him. His cock nestled in the folds of her pussy. "I love how you left that little bit of hair there."

"It's called a Brazilian."

He smiled. "I know. But on you it's called heaven." He pushed his cock, sliding through her wet folds until it touched her vagina. "Edie!" He thrust inside her.

Her name on his lips was sweeter than any endearment, the name she'd hidden inside herself for so long, the name only a few other people used. On his lips it sounded perfect. "John!"

He stilled, buried deep inside her. "Will you call me Kwoklyn sometimes?"

He sounded younger, more vulnerable. She opened her eyes and smiled up at him. "Is that your Chinese name?"

He nodded. "Nobody uses it anymore. Not since my father died. To my mother I'm always John."

"I like it. Kwoklyn. Now shut up and fuck me."

Groaning he drove inside her, pushing deep until he touched her sweet spot. She cried out and pushed her pelvis up, trying to get him deeper. He plunged and stroked it again. She shuddered and held still while he massaged it, caressed her into a pure orgasm that reached her very heart.

Her body convulsed and she lost control, crying his name, both names, over and over until he called her name in response and she felt him gush hot and wet, so far inside her he became a part of her.

She had no idea how much time passed but when she opened her eyes, they were lying on their sides, his body still embedded in hers. Still hard. Or maybe he'd hardened again. He gazed at her and she knew what he was about to say.

"I love you, Edie Howard."

She didn't need to hesitate. "I love you too." She kissed him with such perfection she couldn't believe she'd ever kissed anyone else before. "I always did love you right from the minute I saw you. But that doesn't mean I'll always do what you want."

"I don't want you to. I'd hate that." He smiled and touched his lips to her cheek. "I'll love you even if you decide to turn into a human Barbie."

"How do you feel really about me having surgery?" She tried to keep the emotion out of her voice, not giving him clues to the answers she wanted.

He gazed at her, touched her face, trailed his fingers down to her throat in the caress she adored. "The real person Edie Howard is more beautiful than any of the other incarnations. Adelaide Howard and Sunset were, are, dreams, icons of perfection. But Edie is so much more. She's lived, she's loved and she is so strong that I catch my breath when I see her. Hey." He caught her tear on his fingers. "Just ignore me. I didn't mean to make you cry."

She watched the crystal droplet shimmer on his fingertip. "Good tears, my love. Good tears."

WINTERS' THAW

Dalton Diaz

&

Dedication

ഇ

To Ashlyn Chase, who always says, "Sure you can!"
(And for introducing Sherry.)
Huge thanks to Jeff Stewart for sharing his tattoo
expertise.
Quirky Ladies Rule! www.thequirkyladies.com

Acknowledgements

ഇ

To the ladies of the cougar club, I salute you. I'd like to thank Ciana Stone for the series premise, the invitation to join the series and the blog design. She has been the driving force behind this collaborative effort. Mari Freeman came up with the blog title, *Tempt the Cougar*, which was inspired. Mari Carr, Lynne Connolly, Desiree Holt and Samantha Kane have been a wonderful group of friends and professionals to work with. Thank you all for the opportunity and the support.

Trademarks Acknowledgement

ഇ

The author acknowledges the trademarked status and trademark owners of the following wordmarks mentioned in this work of fiction:

Band-Aid: Johnson & Johnson Corporation

Ibanez: Hoshino Gakki Ten, Inc.

Penthouse Forum: General Media Communications, Inc.

Spanx: Spanx, Inc.

Author Note

You'll find the women of *Cougar Challenge* and the *Tempt the Cougar* blog at www.temptthecougar.blogspot.com/

Chapter One
 જી

Ladies, I'm going out tonight! Another nurse mentioned that her husband plays in a band at a local bar just outside of Boston and I'm going to check it out. They're doing a Saturday night 80s theme, so at least I'll like the music. I haven't been to a bar in ages and never to meet men but it's still a good place to go, right?

Elizabeth

Elizabeth Winters sat at a table in the bar, ignoring her glass of god-awful house red, wishing she'd had time to wait for an answer to her email. Because the answer was clearly no, bars were not a good place to meet men.

People congregated in groups. Even couples who came in the door together soon met up with their group. There were a few single guys dotting the barstools but there were reasons they were alone. Like the guy who had to be approaching sixty who kept winking at a small posse of young women as he pointed to his chest. His T-shirt read, *Free Mustache Rides*. Not only was he gross, his lip was bare.

No thanks. She'd already done the clueless man thing by marrying one who didn't know what to do with his penis. This guy probably couldn't find it, let alone use it right.

Bar life was depressing and she had no desire to be a club member. This was not a good fit. Thank goodness she sat with the wives of band members, or she would have stuck out like a sore thumb.

It was bad enough standing out like a sore pinkie. The bartender hadn't carded her as he had everyone else at the table and he'd ma'amed her twice, the jerk. So what if the others had gone out "retro" shopping for the right outfit and she'd simply pulled it out of the back of her closet? She still fit into the damn miniskirt, with Spanx or without. It just happened to look better with.

As soon as the band took a break, she'd thank her coworker Sara for the invite and scoot on home where she could enjoy a better glass of wine and slip into something more comfortable. Something she could breathe in would be nice.

"They're good, aren't they," Sara gestured toward the band, shouting the statement over the music.

"Yes, they are," Elizabeth said and she meant it. They not only sounded great, the four guys had dressed for the eighties theme with tight ripped jeans and variations of puffy shirts with vests. The lead singer sported a rolled up bandana around his thigh.

Not a bad fashion effort considering she'd learned they were four engineers who worked together. They were all good-looking men but the bass player was exceptional and he had the long, hard body to carry off the look. She was too far away to determine his eye color, or the exact shade of the thick, wavy hair that fell halfway down his neck. Wait, was that actually a bolo tie around his neck?

Yum. She'd bet he looked good in anything he wore. Or in nothing at all.

Too bad. He would be the perfect man for the Cougar Challenge set forth by the ladies on the Tempt the Cougar blog. Younger, gorgeous and if he caressed a woman with the same confidence he stroked his bass guitar, great in bed.

She glanced around the table wondering which one of the women was his wife before placing her money on the cute blonde a few seats down. The only couple she could link for sure was Sara and James.

Did hot bass guy and cute blonde have a wild sex life? Now *that* was a lot of fun to contemplate! So was the fact that she intended to be in the wild sex boat soon enough. She just needed to be in the right place at the right time and it would happen for her.

But timing was everything and it wasn't going to happen tonight. For that to happen she needed eligible men around. Just one would do. Really. She wasn't greedy.

The last note of their first set still hung in the air when Kevin Springer turned to his buddy James. "What's the deal with the hottie sitting with your wife?"

"I've never met her before tonight. All I know is that she works with Sara."

"Then have Sara introduce me," Kevin said. It had been a long time since a woman had made his blood sizzle with a simple look. Longer still since he'd remained at boiling point after a few sentences were exchanged.

If that was the case with Sara's friend, he was damn well going to swear off bar pickups. It wasn't exciting or worth it anymore. Hell, he hadn't even slept with the last one and she was stalking their shows.

"It's getting to you, being the only single guy in the band, huh?" James said, taking his time unplugging and winding up the mike cord. All they needed was some drunken yahoo getting hold of the mike during their break.

"Right. Because there's nothing about married life that sucks." *Shit.* Kevin didn't need to wait for the silence to figure out that was a stupid thing to say. James had been married all of three months. He'd find out the truth soon enough.

"Sorry, man," he clapped James on the back. "I guess it is getting to me. I'll approach her on my own but it would probably make her more comfortable if I go through Sara. I'd really like to meet her."

"I'll bring you over there but then you're on your own. Sara's still not thrilled with you for hooking up with her cousin Julie after the wedding."

"What?" Kevin was floored. "We made out but she ended up getting drunk by the end of the night. I didn't sleep with her."

"You didn't call her either."

"Because she lives halfway across the country," Kevin defended himself. "How does Sara know about this anyway? You guys were long gone."

"Julie's been calling her, acting like she got dumped." James shrugged.

"Shit. That's ridiculous."

"Yeah. Look, I know the score but women see things differently and I don't want Sara upset."

Damn, there went his plans for the night. "No worries," Kevin assured his friend. Well, he was kind of pissed but not at James or Sara. It was being hit upside the head with the drama of a breakup, for a relationship that never existed.

Oh yeah. *Beware the drama queen.* That was his motto.

"You sounded great tonight."

Kevin turned around to find Glenda, his own personal stalker, at the foot of the stage. Perfect. Somebody up there had a wicked sense of humor.

"There's a coffee shop still open around the corner," she continued. "We could —"

"Glenda, look, I appreciate your coming to our shows and all but..." he trailed off as her eyes narrowed, then just as quickly filled with tears. It was surreal, like she was getting her emotions from a cue card.

He was wondering how to handle it without causing a scene when he saw Sara approaching the stage with the woman he *wanted* to meet, no doubt to introduce her to James.

He looked back at Glenda, whose chin was actually quivering. It made him feel like an ass because fake or not rejection hurt but the thought of going through this after every show was more than he could take. Hell, it was the exact reason he'd declined to spend more time with her after a few hours in her company. Unfortunately, flat out telling her he wasn't interested hadn't done the trick.

So maybe taking himself off the market would? It could backfire but what the hell. It was worth a shot.

"There you are, sweetheart!" Kevin hopped down, ignoring Glenda's sound of surprise. He met the two women halfway. "Help me here, *please*," he stage whispered to Sara's friend. "Quick, what's your name?"

"El—"

But there was no time to let her finish. Glenda was rapidly approaching with no sign of tears or quivering chin. The cue card instructed her to shoot daggers from her eyes.

Great. Now he was involving someone else in their little drama but it was too late to change course. "Elle, honey, I'd like you to meet Glenda, the band's number-one fan. Glenda, meet my girlfriend Elle. And I know you've met Sara."

"Seriously?" Glenda didn't even try to keep the disbelief from her tone. On closer exam yeah, Elle was a bit older than he'd thought but not much.

Elle looked startled but he wasn't sure if it was due to his actions or the tactless slam from Glenda. He got his answer when Elle seemed to grow a good inch as she stared Glenda down. "Excuse me?"

Kevin grew too, though not in height and significantly more than an inch. *Damn!* Everyone else faded into the background as he watched the potential drama fizzle and Glenda march away with a sound of disgust, head held high.

"Sorry, bud," Kevin said to James, who had come up behind him. "No go on the no-fly zone."

James sighed. "I figured as much."

Chapter Two
ஐ

The bass player was even more gorgeous up close, though Elizabeth still couldn't tell the color of his eyes. They were dark but they weren't brown. And yes, he really was wearing a bolo tie. She guessed his age to be about twenty-nine or thirty. His hair was brown, though not as dark as hers. There was a bit of length to it where she usually preferred the clean-cut look, but it suited him. It would definitely suit her to run her fingers through it.

He was a player. That much she knew after two minutes in his company. He also wasn't married to the cute little blonde back at the table or that whole scene would have been unnecessary. To say she was intrigued was putting it mildly.

The only damper was the warning look in Sara's eye but James whispered something in his wife's ear and before Elizabeth knew it, she was alone with the bass player. Whose name she didn't even know.

For that matter, would he keep calling her Elle? Her gut reaction was to correct him like she corrected those who called her Liz or Beth but this was different. Elle sounded slightly mysterious and it fit the moment.

He fit the moment. She had to make her decision and make it fast. Either she was a part of the Tempt the Cougar blog and ready for the Cougar Challenge, or it was time to walk away from it all, clearly not as ready as she'd thought.

What had the other ladies said when she shared her insecurities?

"Just do it. What do you have to lose?" Sage advice from Autumn.

"*Don't let the scumball ex-husband of yours dictate the next twenty years too,*" Stevie's demand echoed.

"*You deserve to lust and be lusted after. If a younger man does it for you, don't assume you don't do it for him too,*" Monica had added.

The advice was sound. She was already alone and her sexual self-esteem needed a boost. She had nothing to lose and everything to gain. If she needed proof, all she had to do was look at how well jumping in had turned out for the women on the blog who had already met the challenge.

She slowly turned back towards the younger man in question, half expecting to find him gone. He wasn't. He was watching her.

"So," she gave her new alter ego a shot, "*honey*, what's your name?"

He smiled. "It's Kevin. Kevin Springer. Do you want to go to the back hall? I'd love to talk to you and it's a little quieter there."

The crowd was thick and with the band on break, recorded music blared through the bar's speakers. It would be nice to not have to yell at each other. "Sure."

He led her down a little passageway to the left of the stage, stopping between two closed doors marked "office" and "storage". She'd assumed he meant the hallway off the bar that led to the bathrooms but this was much better. No foot traffic and no speakers.

It was a confined space and when they stopped she had her back to the wall and nothing but Kevin Springer in her vision. She had been right about his eyes. They were green. Not just any green but a deep emerald green. Wow.

The whole package was drool-worthy.

"So," she looked directly into those incredible eyes, "is this where you ask me if I come here often?"

He laughed. "Nope. Not my style."

"Really?" she countered. "How do you usually go about picking up women in bars?"

"Depends." He gave a shrug. "I could joke around about it but the truth is it's not necessary to do a whole lot when you're up on stage. There are usually a couple of women hanging around after the show and I'm the only one in the band who's not married."

"Good to know. Girlfriend? That cute blonde at the table with us?" She had to be sure. Rescuing a guy from unwanted attention was one thing, but she had no interest in being the other woman in any way, shape or form.

"Nope. She's hooking up with our sound guy. You?"

"No."

"Good to know," he shot back at her. "But how about a boyfriend, or a husband?"

"Neither of those either." She laughed. "You?"

He smiled and shook his head. Oh man, the guy had a dimple on the right side. She loved a wicked sense of humor and she was a sucker for dimples.

"Okay," Elizabeth said. "Now that that's settled, let's go back to your technique for picking up women in bars. What *do* you look for?"

He thought about it for a minute before answering. "Bar pickups are all about attraction and chemistry. The first part is easy. Let's face it, we wouldn't be standing here together if we didn't both pass."

He found her attractive! Who cares if she already knew that, hearing him say it was pretty darn sweet. "And the chemistry?"

"That remains to be seen." The side of his index finger began to stroke her bare arm. "But I have a feeling it'll rate pretty high."

He wanted to kiss her. *Holy cow!* She realized she couldn't remember the last time she'd been kissed with any passion.

The thought of doing it now, with this man, was both exciting and intimidating.

"Wanna find out?" Kevin leaned closer, looming over her by nearly half a foot.

His entire hand now stroked the skin on her upper arm and she felt surrounded by him, yet completely safe. God, he even smelled good! All earthy male with just a hint of sporty deodorant.

He waited there, hovering not six inches from her face, those green eyes staring straight into hers as he waited for some form of permission.

Elizabeth took a deep breath and slowly closed her eyes.

She expected him to move quickly, to take her mouth a bit roughly as set by the tone of the moment. He did neither. She was about to open her eyes to see what he was waiting for when she felt the first gentle brush of his mouth on hers. Then another. His lips were soft, sweet, hinting at the underlying taste of Kevin Springer.

Elizabeth wanted more.

She leaned forward at the next contact and sure enough he lingered, deepening the kiss, giving her more of what she craved but not nearly enough.

Why wasn't he giving it his all?

Edie's voice carried across the internet. *C'mon girl, what do you need? A billboard invitation?*

No but apparently he did. Wrapping her arms around his neck, she pulled him closer and slanted her mouth over his, swiping her tongue across his closed lips.

His body jolted and he finally kissed her as she craved, accepting her tongue to duel with his. When she retreated he followed with a groan, pressing her back against the wall.

Oh. My. God. This man knew how to kiss and she'd bet *he* knew what to do with his penis. No, his cock. Kevin Springer had a cock and she was going to get to know it up close and personal.

Just not standing in the hallway of a bar.

She flattened her palms on the warm leather covering his chest and gave a small push at solid muscle. He instantly backed up a step, breathing hard.

"Jesus." He steadied himself with one arm against the wall behind her. "That was off the freakin' chart. So, where have you been all my life, what's your sign and can I take you home after the show tonight?"

Oh, he was too good to be true! She reached up and traced her fingers along his jaw, then fed the urge to do the same down the muscles of his arms. His covered arms. Dammit, tanks and cropped shirts were in style back in the eighties. Why couldn't he have been wearing one of those?

He stood still, watching her face, his eyelids heavy with lust.

She hated to disappoint them both. "I can't tonight. Sara was bringing me over to meet James during your break because I have to go. It's Friday but it's late and I have to work in the morning."

"You free next weekend?"

"I don't date." She brought her hands back up to those broad shoulders and let one fingernail play up and down the side of his neck. His nostrils flared. "But I would love to have fun for a while. Are you interested?"

He looked stunned for a moment but rallied quickly. "Could you define 'fun'? I'm debating whether it even matters but I'm not going to find myself tied up in some S&M dungeon, am I?"

"What? *No!*" What had she missed out on in the past twenty years if that's the first thought that came to his mind? Tying him up had its appeal but in an S&M dungeon?

Step aside Elle, it's time for straightforward Elizabeth to make an appearance.

196

"Look, let's be upfront with each other." Elizabeth took a deep breath and went for broke. "I'm a few years past a divorce and it's been awhile for me. I'm not looking for anything lasting or kinky. I just want to feel good for however long that lasts and you seem like a safe bet. Are you interested?"

"Hmm." He frowned as though mulling it over. "Let me see if I have this straight. An incredibly hot woman who damn well knows how to kiss wants to know if I'm interested in having sex with her, no strings, no drama, for as long as we're both hot for each other? Gee, I dunno. It *is* asking a lot. How about another kiss to sway the vote?"

She barely held back a sigh of relief. "Wouldn't that be bribery?"

He shook his head. "Simple coercion."

"Okay then." She leaned forward and kissed him again and was just as happy when he took over and pressed her back against the wall. His entire body followed and there was no mistaking his arousal.

He was the one who pulled away, still breathing hard. "Next Friday night?"

It took a few seconds for Elizabeth's brain to process what he was asking. The man could kiss! She nodded. "I have next weekend off."

She heard him release his breath. "It'll be a long week," he murmured, moving in close again. "I'll need a little more coercion to get me through."

He didn't wait for her this time. Within seconds she was completely lost in the taste and feel of his mouth, his tongue, the hard muscular body under her fingertips.

"Break's over, Kevin."

It was Sara. Elizabeth would have jumped back if there were anywhere to go but she was up against the wall and Kevin didn't move. He turned his head toward the end of the hall but kept his back to Sara.

Oh, right. It wasn't his back he was trying to hide. Elizabeth felt like a teenager caught making out with the cutest guy in school and it felt wonderful.

"I'll be right there," he said to Sara.

Her friend gave her an apologetic shrug and indicated to meet up with her before leaving.

"I don't think I'm her favorite person right now," Kevin admitted.

"Don't worry about it. I have to go too," Elizabeth said, regretting it more than ever as she took one more look into those green eyes. "Let me get your info and you should know that my name is Elizabeth. But I like that you call me Elle. It makes it easier to be, well, *free* if that makes any sense."

He nodded. "It's no different from me getting up on stage and playing rock star for a couple of hours. There's no gig next weekend, by the way."

"Too bad. I think Elle really goes for the groupie thing and, dude, abalone shell bolo ties are the coolest thing, like, *ever*."

He didn't miss a beat. "*Radical*! Great outfit, by the way, and the band really appreciates the effort. You ladies must have had fun finding this stuff."

Ouch. She laughed to hide her wince. "Yeah, something like that."

A few minutes later he was up on stage playing rock star and she was on her way out the door. She wasn't alone. Sara followed her and as soon as they were in the quiet, cool night air outside the club, the other woman said what was on her mind. Surprisingly, it wasn't the age issue as Elizabeth expected.

"Please be careful with Kevin. He's a good guy but he's not into any kind of commitment. I know it's none of my business but I don't want to see you get hurt and I don't want it to get weird between us at work."

Elizabeth was touched and amazed by this young woman who had both the confidence and caring necessary to speak her mind and she deserved the same in return. There were women Elizabeth's age who weren't that mature yet.

"You and James seem right for each other but not everyone gets it right the first time, Sara. I'm one of those who got it wrong and the last thing I want at the moment is an emotional commitment with a man. I have an entire collection of baggage that comes with getting it wrong for almost twenty years and someone like Kevin is exactly what I need to help me reduce it. Does that make sense? Because if it doesn't, I won't see him. I don't want it to get weird between us either."

Sara was quiet for a moment. "No drunken phone calls in the middle of the night?"

"Not from me," Elizabeth clarified.

Sara's smile slowly grew. "Touché. That was pretty sexist of me to assume you'd be the one hurt. Go get some sleep. The schedule said you're in the OR with Dr. Frass, Chief of Ass and he's been on the warpath lately. Tomorrow won't be fun."

"Great. Whoever told him the Chief of Proctology had to actually *be* an asshole should be shot. Beats being in the OR with Dr. Ramos any day though. At least the Chief of Ass believes in deodorant."

It was nice to end the evening on a laugh. It was great to have a friend who understood the subtleties of working in a hospital but it was even greater to have a friend outside the cougar blog who wasn't going to judge her.

Elizabeth was still feeling good when she made it home and logged on to her group for a quick post.

Hey, tonight started out pretty dismal but I ended up having a great time. Not only did I meet a perfect guy for the challenge, I discovered a coworker has serious friend potential. I'm honestly not sure which one excites me more but I do know which one you all want to hear about!

His name is Kevin and he's about six-foot-one and full of muscle. Okay, now I have that song by those guys from Australia in my head. No, he doesn't come from the land down under but you can tell it really was 80s night at the bar! He has wavy, light brown hair that falls below his collar and the deepest, dark green eyes I've ever seen.

He calls me Elle. At first it made me wonder if I would be better off pretending to be someone else but it got a little weird so I came clean. He can still call me Elle though.

Oh and did I mention that he kisses like a dream? LOL! We're supposed to go out next Friday night but I'm going to save time and make something to eat here. Better yet, we'll do takeout.

Elizabeth

Chapter Three
ఐ

Kevin sat back in his chair, staring at the latest return email from Elizabeth Winters.

If you don't mind, I'd rather eat at my place. Can we do takeout?
Elle

Hot damn! He deleted his first response asking if clothing was optional and then his second one, which began as a letter to *Penthouse Forum*. Third time was a charm and it was all he could do not to wave his fist in the air and shout with excitement when her snail mail address came sailing back a few minutes later. Office cubicles didn't offer a lot of privacy.

He honestly couldn't remember the last time he was this excited about a date. Yeah, it wasn't usually a foregone conclusion that the night would end, or in this case begin between the sheets but it was more than that. Elle intrigued him. They'd been emailing back and forth since they'd met and he hadn't been able to get her off his mind. She was smart, funny and damn sexy. Now that he knew how Friday night was going to roll, he was hard and aching. Again, not a great accessory for an office cubicle.

God help him, it was only Wednesday.

Wait, Wednesday? Well there was an instant killjoy. Shit. Not only was it Wednesday, it was the sixteenth, his dad's birthday. He debated putting off the obligatory call until later that night but that would mean calling the house instead of his dad's office.

Only his dad wasn't in the office today. Kevin left a message on voicemail and considered his options before dialing again. If his dad had taken the day off, he and Esther were probably out somewhere and Kevin could get away with leaving a message asking him to call.

She answered on the third ring. Ten minutes and a dozen complaints later she finally took a breath.

He jumped at the opportunity to end the hell. "Esther, I'm calling from work. Is my dad there?"

"No. He said he wanted to play golf today even though he knows I don't play. Now I'll have to put in the effort and cook tonight instead of going out because I just know he'll be too tired. If only the phone would stop ringing. You know, *I* don't get this many calls on *my* birthday."

Ooh, double whammy. Esther was on fire today. "Please tell him I called. I have to get back to work now. Bye."

He flipped his phone shut and gave himself a minute to let the negativity roll off his back. He'd asked his dad once what he saw in Esther that made him marry her a year after Kevin's mom had died. Even at the age of thirteen, he'd understood when the answer had been, "She's nothing like your mom." Yeah, his mom had been full of love and laughter, not complaints and bitterness. He'd tried for his dad's sake, tried as both a kid and as an adult but there was no room and no kindness for anyone in Esther's universe but herself.

Every once in awhile he wondered if his dad regretted marrying her and swore his own wife would be full of love and laughter, not self-centered drama.

Beware the drama queen.

He turned to his computer screen, determined to get back to work. Elle's email with her address was still up and he couldn't help wondering if she'd dispatch Esther as quickly and easily as she had Glenda. Her confidence that night and in her emails was a total turn-on. Christ, what would she be like in bed?

Whoa! Best not to think about that until he got home.

James poked his head around his cubicle and asked if he were free for lunch. Kevin had just taken an unplanned break but what the hell. He wasn't getting any work done anyway.

"Give me a couple of minutes and I'll be ready," he said to James, hoping he wouldn't need longer to be able to stand.

* * * * *

Elizabeth had made a tactical error. Kevin wasn't due for another hour and she was completely ready. The condo was clean and she'd showered, shaved, put on her new dark lavender lacy underwear set and placed condoms on the nightstand. There were even local delivery menus on the coffee table. She'd washed three different-sized vases in case he brought flowers and had left the wine she'd bought unopened in case he brought a bottle.

Did men still bring flowers or wine to a woman? Even if they did, would he, since it wasn't a real date?

Wow. She started laughing at herself right as the phone rang and that's when she blew it again. She didn't look to see who was calling before she picked up.

"I'm going to be late with the girls' tuition, so you'll have to cover."

"Excuse me?" There'd been no greeting, no warning, no apology. Just Phil being an asshole.

"I. Can't. Pay. By. The end. Of. The month." He spoke slowly, derision in every word.

"Well, Phil. That's. Just. Tough shit," she responded in kind. "It's your turn and you have a week and a half to come up with the money."

She was met with dead silence, another ploy to make her cave. Right. Heck, she preferred the silence and considered hanging up but that wouldn't do the girls any good.

He broke first, his tone a bit more cordial. "I didn't want to have to tell you this but it's for a medical reason."

Elizabeth couldn't resist. "Oh? Did Tanya pop a boob?"

"Actually, yes, one is leaking. Look, I just need you to cover this one and I'll take the next two. Between what I have to pay you and my living expenses, I don't have any choice. Do you think I wanted to make this call?"

Oh, he was a real piece of work. She hadn't asked for alimony. The money he paid her was child support and one hundred percent went toward the girls' college expenses. He made a decent living and there was only one reason he was having trouble making ends meet. His barely legal wife took a lot of upkeep.

Wait. Come to think of it, he also had decent health insurance.

"Why isn't insurance picking this up?" she asked.

"It is."

"Then what's the problem?"

He sighed, irritated again. "They're only paying to repair the leak. If they have to do the surgery anyway, we're going for an upgrade."

The seconds ticked by in silence as Elizabeth absorbed what he was saying.

Phil would have been wise to keep his mouth shut at that point but he knew he'd lost and in true asshole form, he was going to make it hurt. "Don't let your jealousy override what's best for our daughters. Bigger tits wouldn't hurt but they wouldn't help you in the sex department."

Son of a bitch! "Tuition is due in ten days, Phil. I doubt a judge would support your reason for delinquency any more than I will." She hung up but the damage was done.

There was only one place to go for a reset in such a short amount of time. She sent up a quick prayer that someone was around as she logged on to the Tempt the Cougar site.

Phil called and like an idiot I picked up the phone before I realized it was him. I swear he must have radar. Ding! Elizabeth is planning to have sex and as always, it's up to me to make sure she doesn't enjoy it. Let's see, which cut is best for the occasion…let's go with a mix of boobs and overall performance this time. You want to know what he said? Drumroll, please…

"Bigger tits wouldn't hurt but they wouldn't help you in the sex department."

Okay, I know he's an asshole. I know he's just saying these things to get to me but I've only had sex with one other guy. It was before Phil and it wasn't great either. It just kind of…was, like with Phil.

Shit. Kevin is due here in forty-five minutes. Do I really have what it takes to satisfy a man, let alone a hot younger man?

Forty-four minutes to detox from the ex…

Elizabeth

A watched pot took longer to boil and watched emails tended to poof, so Elizabeth forced herself to walk away from the computer for five whole minutes. The first stop was at the full-length mirror on the back of her closet door.

There was nothing wrong with what she saw. She wasn't vain but she wasn't ugly. She wasn't what she would call stunning either but she could still hold her own. Her shoulder-length brown hair had body and she'd added golden highlights when it was time to start covering some gray. That brought out the topaz in her brown eyes, which she considered her best feature. Good genes and careful makeup application took care of any major wrinkles, though the crow's feet and lines on her forehead were certainly more pronounced when she smiled or laughed.

Her body had held up well on the surface too. She knew how to dress to accentuate her long waist and hide those few extra pounds at her hips and thighs. For tonight she had chosen a fitted bronze blouse with buttons down the front over casual black slacks that zipped up the side. She was barefoot and jewelry free.

None of that was the problem.

Would she be as attractive in the nude, especially to a younger man? Had Kevin ever slept with a woman who'd had children? Whose breasts displayed the aftereffects of nursing and gravity?

As a nurse consistently exposed to the frailties of life, Elizabeth firmly believed one needed to be grateful for and take care of the body one was given. She'd started out her married life looking forward to having children with a loving a man who would consider the resulting stretch marks and gravity changes as part of the journey.

Unfortunately, she hadn't married such a man.

She'd thought so at first. Even in the beginning their sex life hadn't been everything she'd hoped for but it was enough. Looking back now she could recognize those first subtle digs for what they were. Nothing she did was quite right and required corrective "tutoring" from him. Once she gave birth to their second child, Phil barely touched her. Between the demands of two kids under the age of three, the house, plus her nursing career, she'd been too busy to care.

It wasn't as though she'd missed having sex. Based on her experience and Phil's comments, it had pretty much been another chore.

It wasn't until Phil was gone and the girls were off at school that she gave it much thought. Once she did, it began to consume her. Entire lifestyles and corporations were built on sex. What were people so gung-ho about?

It was a question that had her, at forty-one years of age, looking through the self-help section of a bookstore, where she saw an ad for an erotic romance writers and readers convention. It had dawned on her that if anyone knew about sex, it would be these people. A little online research confirmed her thoughts and she had signed up and bought airline tickets before she could change her mind.

The trip changed her life. Meeting a core group of woman, five there and one online later, women who understood her fears, her desires, gave her the most valuable tool to make those desires come true. She found out she wasn't alone and they confirmed there most certainly was a lot to be gung-ho about.

She just needed the courage to test the waters. It was what the group and the Cougar Challenge, was all about.

She could do this.

Ten minutes had gone by and she already felt better even though an email check didn't reveal any response. She posted another message.

Me again. You know what? I'm good! I used one of our exercises and spoke to myself rationally in front of a full-length mirror.

I forgot to mention the reason Phil was calling. He says he can't make his payment because his new wife sprung a leak and they want to upgrade her breasts while they're having it fixed. The more I think about it, the sorrier I feel for her. No matter how big or what shape she makes them, it will never be quite good enough for Phil the Asshole.

I'm going for the test drive with Kevin. My body may have some wear and tear but there's still decent mileage left. I'm signing off for now but you can bet I'll post later.

Wish me luck!

Elizabeth

Chapter Four
ॐ

Kevin was right on time.

Elizabeth let him in her front door, careful to latch the safety behind him. The girls attended the same college and it was local enough for them to pop in on the weekend without calling first. Rare, but it did happen.

She turned from the door and stopped short. The view from behind made an equally great impression. He had an incredible body and the thought of having free rein with it almost sent her into V-fib. The man could fill out a pair of jeans in all the right places, no padding necessary. Of course, that was a fun fact that needed confirmation and she was up for the challenge.

They hadn't discussed his staying through the night and he didn't have a bag with him. Or flowers. He did have a bottle of wine.

"Why don't you have a seat and take a look at the takeout menus on the coffee table," she suggested. "I'll open the wine."

"Great." He handed her the bottle. "And hi, nice to see you again."

Elizabeth laughed, immediately more at ease. God, he was even more delicious than she'd remembered, and those eyes! He was wearing a royal blue short-sleeve polo shirt and when he moved she caught sight of a tattoo winding around his right biceps. His dark jeans hugged his body, though they weren't nearly as tight as the ones he'd worn on stage. And they weren't belted halfway down his ass with his boxers sticking out, thank god.

Huh. Did he wear boxers, or briefs? Or did he go commando? The knowledge that she was soon to find out added to her excitement. She hoped it wasn't tighty whities, though with a body like that he had to look better in them than Phil had.

And why the hell was she thinking about Phil? *That damn phone call!*

Motioning Kevin toward the couch and watching him walk in front of her helped get her mind back in the gutter. She continued into the kitchen, separated from the living room by a countertop, where she opened the wine and watched as he made himself comfortable by looking around.

He paused at the pictures along one wall and then at the ones dotting her built-in bookshelves. She kept quiet and let him look his fill. He knew she was divorced and yes, there were a couple of pictures that included her ex. She'd given the girls most of them but this was still their home and he was their father.

Kevin didn't say anything until she came into the living room with two glasses of the pricey merlot he'd brought. When the first question came, it was one word.

"Family?"

Just as she'd thought, he was a very smart man. That one word left her the option to say as little or as much as she wanted. "Yes, the girls in the pictures are my daughters."

She didn't expect his wince.

"Are they off with their dad right now?" he asked quietly.

Mental head slap. Of course he didn't know how old they were and the last thing he'd want would be to get caught in bed with their mother. And *ew*, thinking like that wasn't a huge turn-on for her either.

She had two choices. She could simply say the girls wouldn't be home all weekend, or she could lay the whole truth out now and get the age thing over with. It was like ripping off a Band-Aid. Do it in degrees to try to hold off the inevitable pain for a while, or do what she advised her patients and get it over with.

She chose the quick rip.

"Let's sit down." She handed him his wineglass and walked toward the couch, away from the watchful eyes of the photos. If there was any chance of success, she couldn't think like a mother tonight.

They sat, she on one end and Kevin choosing the middle. She took it as a good sign he was still interested when he didn't leave a huge space between them.

With one bracing sip of her wine, she forced herself to look straight into those incredible green eyes, which now reflected curiosity.

His reaction mattered. She didn't need a pity fuck. She'd had enough "try it anyway" failure in the bedroom, thank you very much.

"Both girls are in college. In fact, they attend the same college. They don't know I invited you here and I don't care to find out what their reaction would be to my entertaining a thirty-year-old." She paused as another thought hit. "You *are* thirty, aren't you?"

The question made him grin.

"What?" she asked when he didn't say anything.

"I just turned thirty. Do I get to ask your age in return, or will I find myself dripping merlot on my way out the door?"

Elizabeth took a deep breath. "I'm forty-one."

She'd surprised him. She could tell that by the quirk of his brow but there wasn't anything more to it.

"Is that what you needed to get off your chest?" Kevin sat back a bit, his posture more relaxed. "You were forty-one and had kids when we kissed at the club. Knowing your age doesn't change that we were smokin' hot. As long as we're being honest here, I haven't been able to think about anything but coming here all week long."

Oh, he was so getting laid! She still needed one more bit of info from him before completely jumping his bones though, knowing it would be more relaxing if his answer was yes. "Have you ever been with a woman who's had kids?"

He slowly shook his head and slung a shot right back. "Have you been with anyone since your divorce?"

"No."

"Good." Kevin leaned forward to put his drink on the coffee table before reaching over and doing the same with her wineglass. He sat back, managing to slide closer to her in the process. "I kind of like being on even ground that way."

It was all she could do not to laugh out loud. He was worried about following Phil in the sack? He could be hung like a gherkin and do better.

But there wasn't any time to dwell on it, or to set Kevin straight. There was only time to lick her lips, an action that made his eyes flare with heat. Her heart pounded like a jackhammer, remembering exactly how *"smokin' hot"* it was the last time they kissed.

"You have the most incredible bottom lip," he murmured, right before nibbling her there. "Remembering how you felt, how you taste, has kept me hard all week."

Oh. My. God. All ability to think, to reason, to doubt, went out the window the second his mouth opened over hers.

Kevin Springer wanted her. Badly.

Christ! Something about this woman set Kevin on fire. Ten minutes and he was on her couch with his tongue in her mouth, trying to keep his hands from wandering. Not that she was protesting.

There was a hesitation in her, though. He couldn't quite put his finger on it but he felt it when they spoke and for a split second when he brushed his hand over her breast. It was why he didn't linger there or push for more right then.

He couldn't blame her. This was fast, even for him. Yeah, she'd made it clear what she wanted from him and hell yeah, he wanted that too. But the more they'd corresponded during the week, the more intrigued he'd become with her.

Finding out she hadn't been with a man in at least a couple of years added to the mix big time. It had been about a year for him and he was ready to explode. Maybe he shouldn't have let his desire build all week without jerking off but it was too late now.

God, she tasted sweet. If he came right away, he knew he'd only have to kiss her to start over again with round two. He figured he might be ready to let her rest by round five. *If* she let him stay that long.

Hot damn if not being able to read her wasn't half the excitement. She didn't need him, she wanted him. He was the one with the desire bordering on need.

Still, he could be a gentleman and wait longer than ten freakin' minutes in her presence before jumping her bones.

Pulling back was hard, hard being the operative word when he tried to sit up. He couldn't quite hold back a wince and was glad for it when she responded with a slow, sexy smile.

Oh man. He swallowed hard. Would fifteen minutes be gentlemanly enough?

He was giving that serious consideration when the takeout menus caught his eye. Dinner first would be good. They'd both need the fuel.

He leaned forward and grabbed the one right on top. "Ozzie's sounds good to me."

She sat up straighter. "Sure. You know the place?"

"Yeah. My apartment is a couple of towns over. A little closer to the city but a lot lighter on the wallet."

He'd felt a bit intimidated when he'd driven up to her building. Elle lived in a luxury condo complex, complete with guest parking. His place was twenty minutes down the road but his one-bedroom, cookie-cutter apartment was an entire universe away in class and style.

Thankfully, that feeling had disappeared the second she'd opened the door. The clothes, makeup, hair, condo, it all fit her and she wore it easily. He liked that a lot.

"It's a perk of selling off a house with equity and working longer at my career. Does it bother you?" she asked.

Man, he got off on how straightforward she was. "Nope. By the way, you're buying." He handed her the menu, pleased when she laughed. He hoped to hear that a lot. *If* she asked him to stay.

Maybe that was part of the key to reading her too. She'd probably appreciate it if he were as forthcoming as she'd been with what she felt and wanted. Shit. Did that mean he wasn't usually that way? Funny, until he met her he hadn't really thought too much about his role in the dating game. Just because he sat back and let the drama queens dictate which game was played didn't excuse him. He still played the game. Worse, he kept dating young drama queens.

"Is something wrong?" Elle interrupted his thoughts and he realized he was frowning.

He shook his head and went for it. "Why don't we go get the sandwiches instead of having them delivered? It would give us a chance to talk a bit and I can grab my bag from my car." He paused to gauge her reaction. One raised eyebrow. He did that himself when he was surprised but still listening, which wasn't a bad thing.

"I know you didn't invite me to stay the night," he continued, "but if it works out for both of us, that's what I'd like to do and I'll be prepared. Hell, if it's as good as I think it will be, I'll stick around as long as you want. Either way my bag and I are both out of here at the first word, no questions asked, no emotional outburst. Okay?"

She studied him for a moment, that perfect brow still raised as her intelligent, deep brown eyes assessed him. "Okay," she finally said. "Thanks for the honesty."

He wanted to kiss her again but he knew he wouldn't stop this time and he was determined to get to know her better. He sure as hell liked what he knew so far.

Chapter Five
ॐ

Elizabeth had to admit she was enjoying herself. She'd figured, hoped, she'd be a couple of orgasms into the evening by now and instead found herself in a sandwich shop joking around with the hottest guy in the room. Knowing she was going home with him for a night of wild monkey sex made her giddy with excitement. *Please god!*

The girl behind the counter had actually stuttered while taking Kevin's order and delivered such a look of envy when he took Elizabeth's hand that it was probably a good thing someone else was making the sandwiches.

You bet your perky boobs he's going home with me! If the thought put her at the maturity level of a schoolgirl, oh well. It felt damn good to have Kevin's attention and she was going to revel in it. And she did indeed pay for the sandwiches, though Kevin drove.

They'd talked about music on the way there and he asked her about her work on the way back. She found out he liked all types of music and playing with the band a couple of times a month was a satisfying way to have fun and relieve stress. The gigs were part of the reason he drove a pickup, which made it easier to haul equipment.

She hadn't mentioned it to him but letting someone else drive for the first time was always a little nerve-racking for her. It was a control issue that had developed over the time she'd spent as a nurse in the ER, where a large percentage of their patients were brought in following car accidents.

But Kevin kept his hands firmly on the wheel and his eyes on the road even when they were talking. It only took a couple of blocks for her to relax. He was also interesting and he truly listened when she spoke. There wasn't much time to delve into anything deep but she enjoyed telling him some of the lighter side to being a nurse.

By the time they pulled up to her building, she was more curious about him than ever. She was also more excited than nervous when he reached into the extended cab for his bag.

"Do you like being an engineer?" she asked, determined to keep those nerves at bay.

"Yes." He shouldered the bag and reached for the sack of sandwiches she carried, leaving her hands free to get them inside. Their fingers brushed and his hand lingered a second before he alarmed the truck and pocketed the key. "I like puzzles and at the end of every project there's a tangible item that I helped build. Depending what the contract is for, sometimes those items have an important role in people's lives. It's a good feeling, knowing I was at least partially responsible for its creation."

"I can understand that," Elizabeth said. She got her door open and latched the safety behind them.

"Bad neighborhood?" He joked.

"Unpredictable visitors." She stepped out of her flats and left them by the door.

"Ah." He paused to kick off his sneakers, leaving them next to his bag just off the entryway. He could have kept them on. She was simply more comfortable without shoes but she liked that he paid attention. "We're not talking ex-husband with a grudge here, are we?"

Elizabeth put her purse down and went to the kitchen to grab plates, napkins and the open bottle of wine. "No. I don't think his wife would appreciate that."

He watched her as she set the stuff down on the coffee table. If he was looking for any pain behind her disclosure, he was barking up the wrong tree.

"Your daughters, then," he said, coming to the right conclusion. "So suggesting we eat this in our underwear is out of the question?"

She laughed. The question should have made her nervous again but the pure eagerness in his voice and the heat in his eyes were exciting. Then she thought, *why not*? She'd have her bra and panties on and she'd get to lay eyes on him too. It wouldn't be a bad start and they would be a dozen steps closer to the ultimate goal.

Her hands went to the buttons on her blouse and she had two undone before she dared to look at him.

He sat so still she wasn't sure he was breathing. If she thought she'd heard eagerness in his tone before, the visual put that to shame. The fire in his eyes made them shine like emeralds.

She didn't look away and he didn't move until she had the blouse completely undone. When it dropped to the floor, he took a shaky breath and let it out in a rush as her hands went to the zipper at the side of her slacks.

God, was she really doing this?

"Don't stop now." He sat up farther.

Elizabeth took her own deep breath and lowered the zipper. This was it. She'd waited long enough to see what it was all about.

The material slid down and she lifted her foot to step out of them one leg at a time. Only she didn't realize that when she switched feet, she caught part of her pant leg with her other heel.

One moment she was pure grace, the next the carpet was coming at her in a rush. Strong arms wrapped around her at the last second and she landed atop a hard, hot body. Definitely a softer landing for her but his giant *"Ooph"* didn't bode well for her rescuer.

Not that she was lifting her head anytime soon to see if he was okay. No, the nurse in her was going to have to stand back. She was staying right where she was, red face buried in his chest. Forever.

"Just shoot me now," she groaned.

The chest beneath her began to shake before she heard his laughter. Great. Her big moment and she goes ass over teakettle in her underwear. Oh wait, she was still technically wearing her pants. They were wrapped around one ankle.

Kevin, of course, was fully dressed.

"Damn. I suppose I should be glad you have good reflexes," she grumbled. "Hate to show up in the ER where I work having to explain that one."

That got his laughter going all over again. "You okay?"

She couldn't look at him. "I'm fine. I should be the one asking if you're okay."

"Oh yeah. I'm right where I want to be."

That was not a third hipbone poking her lower belly. He was still aroused and while that had been the intention before her little acrobatic feat, the mood was broken for her. She wanted nothing more than to inconspicuously get up, get her clothes back on and rebuild her confidence.

Her moving was obviously not what Kevin wanted. His heart thundered beneath her ear as his hands began a sensuous slide down her lower back to curve over her cheeks. Prickles of heat instantly radiated from his palms through the thin silk of her panties.

His chest vibrated again, this time due to the groan that rumbled from his throat when he ground his cock against her.

She dared to lift her head to look at him for the first time since making a fool of herself.

"Sorry." He closed his eyes and let his let his head fall back. His Adam's apple took a hard bob. "You seem hesitant and I'm trying to hold off to give you what you need but you feel so damn good," he admitted.

Okay, so maybe she could leave her clothes off and rebuild her confidence right here where she sat.

He wanted to give her what she needed. For some reason, he thought that meant waiting to have sex even though that was what he was there for but it was still really sweet.

She didn't want sweet. She *wanted* what he was holding back from her, that all-consuming passion she'd never felt or driven a man to feel. Until now.

For the first time in her life she had the overwhelming urge to make a man come. To see him, touch him, taste him to her satisfaction and she wasn't going to waste another second before making her wish come true.

Kevin had to get hold of himself. He literally couldn't see straight. Apparently it wasn't jerking off that could make a guy go blind, it was *not* doing it that caused the problem. The thought would be funny but shit he was close.

Maybe if he opened his eyes and stopped caressing her ass...

Yeah, his fingers curved as he ground her against his cock again, *that was going to happen.*

Christ, it hadn't been *that* long since he'd had sex. A year, tops. What the hell was happening here? His body wanted in her, *now!*

He knew he hadn't said that out loud but she sat up, tearing another groan from him when she settled that sweet ass over his aching cock, his hands still molded to her curves between them. He felt her undo his belt and slowly unzip his jeans, before she lifted off him to drag them down his thighs. The boxers came along too.

His palms slapped to the carpet as her fingers wrapped around him and all movement stopped. He needed a few steadying breaths before he finally opened his eyes.

Elle was looking at his cock through half-shuttered lids, that mouth with its lush lower lip slowly closing the gap between her and his already leaking slit. Her tongue poked out at the last second.

Oh fuck! "I'll come," he managed to gasp.

"I'd like that."

The first swipe of her tongue was tentative. Watching as she did it again, feeling that wet heat and seeing her tongue retreat, taste and come back for more made him forget how to breathe. Within a minute he went from wondering if she was experienced to wondering why she'd held back when she so clearly knew how to drive a man mad with her mouth.

Her other hand scraped down his stomach, his thigh and her fingertips began to explore his balls as she concentrated slow licks and nibbles to the sensitive crown of his cock.

Holy shit!

He hoped to god she really did want him to come because he had about ten seconds until detonation. His shaft pulsed a warning against her hand and the last thing he saw was her smile so carnal it needed a warning label. Then she engulfed his entire cock in the soft wet heat of her mouth and sucked.

He went off like a rocket. Heat suffused him from head to toe as his entire body stiffened and it was all he could do to try to dig his fingers into the carpet fibers as he jerked with each pulse of release.

She didn't stop. And there was no warm splash on his stomach, no mess.

"Jesus, Elle! Stop! *Stop!*"

She took him deeper and he came again, every muscle in his body tightening so hard it actually hurt but *fuckin' A, it hurt so good.*

It took a long, long time to relax his body, one muscle at a time, when she did let go. She didn't go far. He could feel her watching him and when he opened his eyes, he saw her intense scrutiny in double vision.

He'd been treated to blowjobs before, great ones but he'd never had his mind blown along with it and he'd never come twice like that. Until now.

"Fuckin' A," he grunted. He'd meant to say it but his voice was too hoarse, making him wonder just how loud he'd been.

"Fuckin' beautiful," Elle murmured.

He jackknifed to a sitting position when it looked like she was going to reach for him again. Hell no! It wouldn't do either of them any good if he passed out. Besides, it was her turn. Christ, it was her day, week, month and year.

Just as soon as he could breathe right again.

But Elle stood up and then *damn*! She left the living room and came back a minute later wearing a black silk robe. It was sexy but her message was clear, especially when she sat on the couch.

Playtime was over for the moment.

Kevin very carefully slid his boxers and jeans up and fastened them. He pulled the belt free and tossed it near his bag. Getting up to sit with her on the couch took a lot more effort with his muscles feeling like jelly but he made it. And he wasn't letting her get away with a nonverbal delivery. They'd started things off on honest, open footing and he liked it that way. He liked it a lot.

"Do I get to return the favor after we eat?" he asked as casually as he could, considering he sounded like he'd just sung backup for a death metal gig.

"I don't know," Elle admitted in that straightforward manner he appreciated. "I really like how I feel right now and I don't want it to go away."

"You like how *you* feel right now? Did we just have the same encounter? Because I'm remembering something pretty one-sided. Don't get me wrong, it was amazing but only one of us got the prize. Twice."

She shook her head and reached for her wine. "I don't know if I can explain it but I won too. I've never done that before. I mean, I've done *that* before, just not with the same results." He watched her take a healthy swallow of her drink, knowing there was more to what she wanted to say. "I wasn't sure I was capable of making you lose control and I want to savor my victory."

The admission surprised him enough into saying the first thing that popped into his head. "Your ex is a fool."

Shit. He was about to apologize for bringing it up again, let alone in a sexual context, when she smiled that little smile that made him wish he were back on the carpet for round three.

"Yes." She handed him his sandwich and began to unwrap her own. "I'm truly beginning to understand that."

Chapter Six
∾

It was kind of nice having Kevin around for dinner. Elizabeth generally made large portions whenever she cooked something, then froze the leftovers in single servings so she didn't have to cook every night. It was quick and efficient. It also made for lonely mealtimes.

She knew she'd get used to it over time but it was her younger daughter's freshman year at college. It hadn't been too long since she'd had someone there to share their day and those meals had been completely different. She highly doubted Kevin was going to bubble over with who was dating whom, which college his friends had chosen and which boys may have caught his eye. Likewise, she wouldn't be asking him if he had enough money for the night and to make sure he was home by curfew.

So what should she discuss with a guy she'd just been remarkably intimate with? *Never thought I'd say this but you taste good. That's a turkey club you're eating, right? Care to share your diet with the rest of the male population?*

Right. Best save that one for after dinner. Or never.

Kevin lifted his sandwich and the tattoo peeked out from under his sleeve. It banded around his biceps and had some red in it but she couldn't tell much else from what was showing. She was curious and hey…

She frowned at him. "You never took off your shirt."

Thankfully she caught him after he'd swallowed his food because he gave a bark of laughter. "I lost my underwear while you kept yours on," he pointed out. "But I'm willing to play again. I'll lose the shirt if you'll lose the robe."

That was a no-brainer. "Pants too," she said, then added, "and no, I don't have to take the bra off," when he opened his mouth to speak. "It's underwear."

"So much for equality," he grumbled.

"You could have worn a bra."

"Nah, my lacy one was in the wash." He grinned as he reached up and over to fist his shirt from the back.

Yum. She'd always loved it when guys yanked off their shirts that way. Very sexy.

"You sure I can't convince you to lose the bra?" he asked as he tossed his shirt over the back of the couch.

Huh? Oh, right, she was supposed to be taking off her robe. Damn, his chest was fine. How could she have left it covered earlier?

His skin was smooth and golden, the muscles on his chest and arms pronounced but not overly so. Just enough to form mounds and ridges and to know he'd be hard to the touch. He wasn't hairy. A fine line ran up the middle and scattered across his chest, so light a brown it was barely visible. It got heavier and darker farther down, where it traced to his bellybutton and lower, before disappearing into the waistband of his jeans.

"Elle," he said softly. "You were going to take off your bra?"

Right. She slowly got up, slid the robe off her shoulders and reached for the front clasp, still taking in his perfection before she realized what he'd said.

"Hey!" She sat back down, bra still on.

He shrugged and offered no apology, those green eyes dancing with humor as he finished off his sandwich. The full tattoo caught her attention as he leaned forward to pour them more wine.

Elizabeth reached out and traced the ink with her finger. It didn't band around his arm as she'd originally thought but stretched across about three inches long and two and a half inches wide. It was a black cross, quite a simple one, with a vine bearing red rosebuds climbing up the vertical post and one red rose in bloom at the cross. To the left of the open rose on the horizontal was the number nineteen, to the right the number fifty-four. Odds were the numbers combined to form a year.

She'd seen a lot of tattoos as a nurse and while this was well-done and cared for, it was not new.

"It's beautiful," she told him. "Is this your only tattoo?"

He nodded and sat back again, leaving his drink on the table. He was trying to appear relaxed but she could feel the tension in him. He didn't want her to ask what the tattoo stood for.

It made her more curious. Instinct told her the explanation was a huge part of what made him tick and it was surprising how much she wanted to know his secrets. Besides, she'd been more than forthcoming about a few things she'd rather have kept to herself.

"You don't want to tell me what it means," she said. It wasn't a question. She put the rest of her sandwich on the coffee table to give him her full attention.

"It's not something I usually talk about," he admitted. "And it's been awhile since anyone has asked."

"Yet you display it for all to see."

"You're not going to let this go." He looked at her for a pregnant moment and then sighed. "Okay, yes, at first that was the idea. My mom died of cancer when I was twelve. I got the tattoo in her honor the day I turned eighteen."

There was more to it than that. It wasn't instinct guiding Elizabeth this time, it was years of seeing patients and their families deal with terminal illness. There was a whole world of pain behind his three simple sentences.

"Was she sick for a long time?" she asked.

Again, she got the flat answer. "No, it was pretty quick. About four months from the time she was diagnosed."

"I'm sorry you didn't get more time with her before she died. I'm sure she wanted more time with you."

That obviously wasn't what he expected to hear and she doubted he realized he'd given himself away by crossing his arms and stroking the tattoo with his thumb. "Thanks. Yeah, I do know it was better that she went quickly but at the time it felt like she was there one day and gone the next."

"I'm sorry," Elizabeth repeated more softly. "You created a beautiful tribute. Did you design it?"

He nodded. She didn't think he was going to say anything more but he surprised her. "I didn't do it for the right reasons. I wish I had but I didn't. I began designing it a year after she died, the day my father married my stepmother. If I legally could have, I would have had it tattooed up the side of my face right then and there. Thankfully, by the time I was old enough to get it done I had mellowed to putting it on my arm."

"Oh, Kevin." She had no trouble picturing him then, one hundred percent hurt little boy.

"I got what I wanted. It drove Esther crazy every time she saw the drawings in my room and it really drove her nuts when I got the actual tattoo."

"Until you left for college and Esther wasn't around anymore."

"Yeah." He looked at her in wonder. "Not too many people would get it but you do, don't you?"

Elizabeth nodded. "You were left with a reminder of your spite for your stepmother instead of your love for your mother."

"Shit. This is a real mood killer, you know that?" He made a sound that would have been a laugh but it held no humor. "The one smart move I made was to put my mom's date of birth instead of the date she died. I wanted to celebrate her life, not mourn her death."

"I'm sure she would have appreciated that."

"Yeah, well my stepmother sure didn't. Ironically, that's the part she hated most."

Elizabeth put her hand over his thumb that stroked the tattoo. "Sometimes we see things that aren't there, especially as children. I'll bet she's forgiven you."

This time he did laugh but she didn't get the joke. "She, as in Esther? Sorry but no. Her first rule was that my mom was never to be mentioned in what was now 'her' house. I don't give a flying fuck what Esther thinks."

It was Elizabeth's turn to be shocked. She could live to be one hundred and never understand the motivation behind cruel behavior, especially toward children. "Then again, sometimes children see more than adults do," she said, reversing herself. "Sounds like you had her pegged from the start."

"Damn. Are you sure you're not a therapist?"

"I've learned to read people. It helps with my job," she shrugged, trying to lighten up. If she was reading him right, he really had dealt with what he'd told her.

"Just so you know, we're not doing the one-sided thing again," he warned her. "By my estimate, you now owe me three questions in the red zone and another three in green or orange for everything I divulged. Possibly more."

Oh god. He wasn't going to ask her if she'd had oatmeal for breakfast. He was an astute man and she didn't doubt he'd know exactly where to delve. That could be a good thing, considering her issues had to do with feeling like a sexual failure. When they had sex, she'd find out if the cruel things her ex had said were true. She wouldn't believe them for a second if her one attempt before Phil hadn't been dismal too.

Wouldn't it be great to not give a "flying fuck" what Phil thought?

227

Kevin, on the other hand, was a great guy and being closer to him before sex could only help. She braced herself for the roller coaster ride and looked straight into Kevin's gorgeous emerald eyes.

"What is it you want to know?"

* * * * *

Kevin needed to regroup. He had friends he'd met in college who didn't know about his parents and he'd met Elle a week ago. *What the hell?*

He should be running for the door.

Fuck that. Less than an hour ago he'd come twice in her amazing mouth, yet he was ready, willing and able to come again. They were sitting in their underwear. He should be stripping off that underwear and coming inside her anywhere she'd let him enter, not spilling his guts.

If he did either of those things, he'd never learn her secrets. There was still that hesitation he hadn't been able to put his finger on and he'd bet his prized Ibanez bass that it was every bit as deep and personal as what he'd told her.

It was a piece of her puzzle he craved.

He took her hand, surprised to find how comforting it was. Those caramel brown eyes of hers, filled with curiosity and genuine concern, had already pulled at him to say more than he'd intended. Even though she did understand, it was all old news. He'd found his own way after college, hooking up with the right therapist at the right time. It had taken a while but he'd laid his anger to rest. It was what it was.

"You sure you wouldn't like to lose the bra first? I could be easily distracted before you open yourself up to everything, right down to your first make-out session."

"Nice try. Wayne Collins when I was about eight. He was a couple of years older and we were neighbors. He stuck his tongue in my mouth and I told him that it was wet and gross.

228

For some reason he never kissed me again. That counts as your first question, by the way."

Kevin couldn't help laughing, only to be instantly captivated by her return smile. What the hell were they doing talking about this crap when they could be indulging in their own make-out session?

"Seriously? Eight years old?" He leaned forward to kiss her before swiping his tongue across her closed lips. "His loss. He should have waited a few years when wet could be hot."

Her murmur of agreement, which parted her lips, was all the encouragement he needed. Within seconds he was the one with his tongue in her mouth and she wasn't complaining.

But she did hesitate when he tried to unclasp her bra.

She tried to hide it right away but he sat back, not willing to let her get away with it this time. Forcing herself to do something she didn't want to do was a distinct *no* in his book.

"Elle?" He used his finger to trace the lacy edging at her cleavage until she opened her eyes to look at him. "Question two. Why are you so afraid to lose the bra?"

Okay, she could do this.

"I'm not afraid, exactly," Elizabeth said. "I just know I'm...different from what you're used to."

Kevin's eyes dropped to her chest and he stared as though he had X-ray vision. "Do you have an extra nipple or something?"

If anything, he looked more intrigued. "That's not as uncommon as you think but no."

"Do you *have* nipples? I mean, the bumps I see could be stick-on."

Great. Now he was just messing with her, which oddly gave her more courage to set him straight. "Eyes up here, bud. There are two of everything and only two of everything. I'm talking about gravity. I'm not only older than you're used to, I've nursed two kids."

"If you'd had three, that extra nipple would have been useful."

"Kevin!"

"What do you want me to say?" He caught his finger in the front clasp of her bra and gave a little tug. "I like real breasts. Doesn't matter what size, what shape, pierced or not pierced. I've dated women with implants and I don't find it attractive."

She wasn't buying it for a minute. "Isn't that every man's fantasy? Legs to the armpits and breasts to the eyebrows?"

"Are we still on the blunt honesty kick?" he asked.

"Of course."

"I slept with one of them and it was like trying to balance on two handballs. I don't think it was all that comfortable for her either. The sex was okay but there wasn't a repeat." He traced the swells of her breast with the back of his finger. "A woman's skin is so soft. I like to feel as much of it against me as I can."

It would have been better not to laugh at that moment but she couldn't help it. All she could see was Phil fruitlessly thrusting away at Tanya, only to be bounced off like a trampoline. Hey, maybe that was how she'd sprung a leak!

"Did I say something wrong?" Kevin asked.

"No, the complete opposite," she assured him. "Thank you. You have no idea."

His fingers came to rest on the clasp again. "So enlighten me."

She focused on the pulse point in his neck and nodded. What was it Rachel had said on the blog? *"Take a deep breath, throw back your shoulders and go for it."*

There was a quick tug and the sides relaxed. She felt his fingers grasp the edges and peel the cups away.

A heartbeat later the tip of his finger traced her nipple. "Definitely not stick on," he confirmed. "Elle, you're beautiful."

It was hard not to believe him. His voice was deeper, raspier and his finger wasn't one hundred percent steady. She slowly raised her eyes to find him looking not at her breasts but at her face.

"I have stretch marks," she choked out the words. It shouldn't matter but dammit it did! This man had never seen her breasts before gravity took its inevitable toll, hadn't shared in the joyous reason she had stretch marks.

"I see them," he dropped his gaze and trailed his finger along a particularly deep one. "You're beautiful," he repeated.

The heat in his eyes didn't diminish. He leaned forward and her nipple was engulfed in liquid fire. "*Oh!*" She caught her breath. "That feels amazing."

His answer was to groan, then treat her other nipple to the same pleasure. The next thing she knew he had her horizontal on the couch, his big hands caressing her breasts, her neck, her belly while he sucked and licked her sensitive nipples.

It was good. Better than good. It was everything she'd fantasized about for years. She could feel the heated pull all the way to her toes when he drew at her nipple, felt the throb between her legs when he licked and nuzzled. She lost track of time and everything but that incredible mouth until he nudged her legs apart and settled between them.

"Let's go to the bedroom," he groaned.

Her nerves hiccupped and she took a mental gulp before she reined them in. The man and the moment weren't going to get more perfect, dammit! Why couldn't he have kissed her a bit longer?

She instantly felt guilty. It wasn't his fault she'd choked and he hadn't gone far. He was kissing her neck, her ear, working his way to her mouth while his fingers did wicked things to her nipples. Things which seconds ago had threatened to bring her to orgasm.

By the time he reached her mouth, he knew something was wrong.

"Elle..."

She winced. His tone was filled with frustration and a hint of warning as he spoke the name of the woman he thought he'd met. The woman Elizabeth so wanted to be at that moment.

She completely understood his frustration. He may have started off by receiving a hell of a blowjob but he'd just spent a good half an hour talking her out of her bra and now she was holding back again when the whole purpose of his being there was to have sex.

Chapter Seven

** හ**

"Believe me, I'm just as disappointed as you are." Elle sat up and Kevin watched as she refastened her bra, *dammit*. He slumped against the back of the couch and closed his eyes, trying to figure out where the fuck he'd gone wrong.

"I won't be angry if it's time for you and your bag to be out of here, no questions asked," she said.

His eyes shot open and pinned her with disbelief. "Are you *asking* me to leave?"

She shook her head. "Not at all. I figured you'd want to go."

"I'm debating it," he was frustrated enough to admit.

She winced and truth or not he felt like an ass even before she asked, "What's stopping you?"

"You're not doing it to be coy." He reached for her hand. "Bottom line, I like being with you. So what's it going to take to get you to tell me what this is about? Obviously something was said and or done to make you feel insecure about sex. You're confident in every other way that I've seen."

She shook her head again. "It's not one thing, it's twenty-plus years of mediocre sex. The only way around that is for us to have great sex."

Kevin wasn't buying it. It had to have been her ex. He was also smart enough to know that asking, *What the fuck did that asshole do to you?* wasn't going to help.

"Forging ahead isn't working for you," he said quietly. "And if you're looking for me to do it anyway, that's not going to happen."

She didn't say anything. She still didn't look at him. She also didn't start crying or snap on him. Or offer to blow him off again, which he would have found insulting.

If he'd needed proof, he had it. Elle Winters was not a drama queen.

She wanted him to stay. She *wanted* to sleep with him. He wanted to stay and he damn well wanted to sleep with her.

They knew what wasn't going to work. Maybe what they needed was a different jump off point.

It was definitely worth a try.

"Elle?" He squeezed her hand until she turned to look at him and he knew he was doing the right thing. "How about if I trade my last red zone question for spending the night together, naked, in your bed. We can talk, play around if we feel like it but if the rest doesn't happen it's okay. I have a feeling we'll have a great night anyway."

Hope instantly changed her expression. "But having sex would still be the goal?" she asked.

He gave a slow nod. "Seems to me we both want that to happen. What do you think? Fair trade?"

"More than fair."

He grinned. "I want it noted that I remembered to include not just the bra but *both* pieces of underwear."

"Duly noted," she smiled right back. "So what are we waiting for?"

She was back. The woman he'd met last Friday night, the one who'd kept him hard all week, rocked him twice and had him willing to work for more. Oh yeah. This was going to be one helluva night. It already was.

* * * * *

Elizabeth Winters had a naked man in her bedroom. She wished she could freeze time to go post that fact to the girls on the cougar site. Not to gloat but to seal the moment with her keyboard so she could savor it later. Unfortunately that would mean leaving the room, which meant leaving the gorgeous naked man all alone.

The man who now expected her to get very naked too.

It was a brilliant plan on his part to get her most uncomfortable aspect over with. She could do this. According to his visible gauge, she turned him on. A lot. The question was how to go about it. If she wanted to stand up straight and throw back her shoulders for the whole bra removal thing that meant the panties had to come off first.

Kevin's lips parted in surprise when she hooked her fingers in the silk at her hips and slid her panties down her legs. His cock had doubled in size by the time she got her bra off and tossed it aside. She slid under the covers onto her back, sheets pulled up to her armpits.

Hot damn, Edie was right about that too! Her breasts looked nice and full squeezed in from the sides by her arms.

Kevin didn't appear to be shy. Then again, there was nothing to be shy about that she could see. He climbed onto the other side of the bed and came up on one elbow over her.

"I like your room," he commented as if they were sitting in a public place. "It's very you."

"Thank you," she automatically replied, then bit her lip to keep from smiling. It felt so odd saying the normal niceties while lying naked together.

"Being naked in your bed together was a trade for the red zone question. You still owe me three in green or orange."

"Oh really?" Elizabeth couldn't help noticing that his biceps were within reach of her fingers. Couldn't help noticing, or taking advantage of the opportunity. "Who gets to decide if a question crosses the line into red?"

"Hmm." He acted like he was seriously considering the answer but his eyes twinkled with humor. "You do. But I'll get to ask a different question."

"All right, I'm game. Go for it."

"Do you ever want to get married again?"

That one was easy. "Probably not but I reserve the right to change my mind."

His fingers touched her side under the covers and came to rest on her hip. "Was there a lover before your ex?"

"Yes but just one. That was orange, by the way."

His eyebrows rose and he gave her hip a gentle squeeze. "Sorry, that only pertains to questions."

"I was talking about the question."

"*That* was orange? Huh." His fingers went on the move. It would have been really hard to protest since hers explored him too, as much as she could reach while keeping her elbows by her sides.

His chest was amazing, so strong and nicely sculpted. He worked out and it showed. Felt pretty damn good too.

"How old were you when you lost your virginity?" he asked.

"Seventeen. How old were you?"

"Sixteen and that question is now a draw. I have one left and I'm going to make it count."

Elizabeth nodded but no new question came. He was breathing harder, no doubt because her index finger had found his nipple and teased it in a swirling pattern. She flicked the hard nub from below and he jerked in response.

The next thing she knew he was over her with his legs outside of hers, his palms skimming up her sides until he was the one bracketing her breasts.

Every inch of his hard, hot cock branded her just above the knees. She felt a brief second of panic before he began to inch down her legs not up, leaving a blazing trail with his mouth and his leaking cock.

"Your pussy looked so pretty before you hid under the covers." His voice was thick with lust. "Did you prepare yourself for me?"

Oh god, his fingers had found one nipple, his tongue the other. "Yes!" she cried out, both to answer his question and to get him to keep going. She arched against him, her clit scraping his hair-roughened belly. The sensations were incredible and they didn't stop. Another scrape and she realized it wasn't just her movements. He was migrating down her body.

He stopped to tongue her bellybutton. "I'm exercising my option for another question. You have an incredibly talented mouth, Elle. Did either lover ever bring you to orgasm with their tongue?"

Oh! Was he saying he *wanted* to do that? From the look on his face, he sure did. She couldn't quite get her "talented" tongue to work, so she shook her head no. He made a strangled sound, as though cutting off a groan.

She had brought up her frustration with oral sex on the blog and the other women had convinced her it was all in the technique. In other words, her lovers had sucked at it. One of them literally and not in a good way.

This was something she felt good about trying, especially with Kevin. She had a feeling he knew what he was doing.

Oh god, it was finally going to happen for her!

Except he didn't ease between her legs as she expected. When she felt his hot breath *right there* it was because he had simply kept going down her body, taking the covers with him until he had his legs neatly wrapped around hers. She couldn't spread her legs for him if she wanted to.

The first probe of his warm wet tongue barely penetrated her pussy, followed by a quick retreat. She held her breath for it to come back but he only licked and nipped at the tops of her closed thighs. It was nice but—

With no warning he buried his mouth deep in the vee he'd created, using his tongue to lap and retreat, over and over until she thought she'd go mad.

He tasted and savored, leaving no question that he liked what he discovered. She tried to lift her hips, wanted to spread her legs to give him better access but he held her steady with his big hands.

The second she cried out he changed his technique. Now there were deep probing French kisses along with long slow licks that studiously avoided her clit. His mouth was a caress of molten silk, his tongue following to stroke everywhere he touched. It was the most incredible, yet the most frustrating thing she'd ever felt.

"Kevin, please!" She needed that focus on her clit. Dammit, she was so close.

"Will you come for me?" he growled.

"Yes! Please!"

He didn't release her. She nearly screamed her frustration when his arms wrapped completely around her hips, tightening like a vise.

She opened her mouth to beg again, sure he didn't understand how close she was.

Pure liquid heat engulfed her clit. The only sound she managed was a surprised, "*Oh!*" and then her world spun like a vortex. Her hands flew between her legs to clutch his head, her fingers buried in his hair.

That soft probing tongue abruptly became direct and relentless, flicking her clit so rapidly she couldn't catch her breath. Her belly convulsed and a tidal wave of pleasure swept through her body.

The sounds that tore from her throat still echoed in the room when another convulsion hit, even harder than the first. *"Oh my god!"*

He didn't let go of her, didn't ease up on her clit. Each flick of his tongue made her spasm and come so hard the bed shook from her efforts to move and his to hold her still.

At last he released her clit, though he still held her hips. His blissful groan mixed with her harsh gasps for breath as he went back to long licks and probing laps between her thighs.

The urge to curl up in a ball had passed by the time he unwound himself from her body. Kevin was moving around but she didn't have the energy to open her eyes to see what he was up to. Her body felt so hot and heavy and god help her, if there were even the slightest breeze in the room she'd come again. No wonder empires were built and lost on this stuff.

She didn't even care what kind of picture she presented at the moment, lying on her back with her arms flung wide. She felt like one very satisfied throbbing block of pure lead.

Orgasms ruled!

"Don't fall asleep on me, Elle. Christ, not now."

Oh yum, he was doing that sexy voice thing again. All deep and husky and full of arousal. The bed dipped with his weight and the next thing she knew he had spread her legs. She pried her eyes open to tell him no way, that she needed more time before going through *that* again. Like maybe a week.

Only it wasn't his mouth returning to the scene of satisfaction. He came down over her at the same time there was a giant blunt pressure between her legs. He paused, nostrils flaring, arms trembling with restraint.

"Say the word," he growled. He started to say something else but it quickly turned to a sound of desperation as the tremors spread to the rest of his body.

She was ready. Even if she froze again, she'd have this moment for her mental scrapbook. "Yes."

There was instant fullness as his cock slid deep.

"Oh fuck!" he roared.

He was…they were…*it felt so good*! But… "*Condom!*" She cried out the word in a panic, sure he'd forgotten.

"It's on. Elle, *son of a bitch*, don't move or I'll come."

She could see the restraint on his face, hear it in the tightly spoken words, in the way his muscles bulged and quivered. He was beautiful.

It was obvious he didn't want to come without her. Not again. What he didn't understand was that his loss of control at this moment was a gift. For the first time, the voices of sexual doubt were completely silenced. This wasn't a time to think, it was a time to feel.

She focused on each glorious inch pressed deep and throbbing inside her, every pulse creating a lightning bolt that shot straight to her recently awakened and already greedy clit.

Oh sweet heaven, she couldn't —

She could. With his first thrust her entire body locked and burst forward with the power of a roller coaster ride. The last thing she saw was the look of sheer pleasure on Kevin's face as he lurched into the freefall with her, groaning her name. His thrusts found a rhythm, deep surges that buffeted her again and again, the movements of a man not completely in control. Every time she found release the pressure would build again and every time she clenched his cock, his thrusts grew harder and deeper.

She knew the second he came. His cock grew and pulsed and he cried out but it was more than that. Right before he came something nonphysical picked her up and plunged her headlong into the vortex with him. For a few brief seconds she felt the tingle in his spine, the enveloping heat of her body, his overwhelming desire to feel her soft skin against him.

The fireball explosion that followed was so intense she almost didn't hear his astonished gasp, wouldn't have known he felt the same awareness of what was happening to her both inside and out.

When they slowed to a crawl, he was the one looking at her with shock. "What the fuck was that?"

Not the most romantic thing to say but it was perfect. She knew exactly what he meant. She'd heard about this kind of connection with a lover but had seriously doubted its existence. She'd literally laughed at the description so often used in books about not knowing where one person ended and the other began.

It was real. Not only had she experienced it but her lover had too.

She'd taken the challenge and aced it. Great. But more than that, she'd accomplished the underlying goal for accepting the challenge in the first place.

Any and all doubts about her sexuality were forever silenced.

The feelings coursing through her were overwhelming but she didn't realize she was crying until she watched Kevin's expression turn to panic.

Shit. Kevin slowly pulled his cock free and started to climb off the bed to take care of the condom. He never knew what to say or do when it came to waterworks and it was a damn uncomfortable feeling.

"Hey," Elle stopped him before his feet hit the floor. "Why are you so freaked out?"

"Me?" He turned back to look at her. "I'm not the one crying."

"I wouldn't be a jerk about it if you were. That was physically and emotionally earth-shattering and I can cry about it if I want to."

Damn. She was right on both counts. He'd never felt anything like that in his life and he was being a jerk. He took a deep breath and slowly released it. "Okay," he said softly, then repeated it before leaning over to wipe one of her tears with his thumb.

He kissed her, then kissed her some more until he wasn't sure how much time passed but the tears had stopped.

"I'll be right back," he told her.

She nodded and he grabbed one more kiss before going into the bathroom. He knew she couldn't see him from her angle on the bed so he took a good hard look at himself in the mirror after turfing the condom.

He looked the same way he felt. Satisfied and…happy.

The satisfied part was easy to pin and he supposed he could say the great sex made him happy too. The guy in the mirror wasn't fooled.

The happiness was being with Elle. He could see himself falling in love with her. Hell, no joke, he was more than halfway there.

Even her drama was undramatic, yet he wasn't anywhere near bored. She kept him on his toes and as hard as a rock. He'd come three times tonight and it wouldn't take much on her part to get him going again. God willing he would make it last longer this time.

He wondered if she was sore from the pounding he'd given her. She'd been right there with him though, literally in his head. Instead of freaking him out, he wanted more.

Taking a little extra time in the bathroom to really think about getting involved with her didn't change his mind. He wanted to see how far this thing between them could go. It wasn't just the sex, though *fuckin' A,* that would do it. He really liked being with her.

It wasn't a proud moment to realize he'd had relationships based on far less.

He knew what he wanted. Now it was up to Elle.

Elizabeth had to work hard to keep her shock from showing. Kevin had come back from the bathroom with a warm wet washcloth and he'd insisted on using it to clean her up. It was more than that though. He was so gentle, so loving that she felt something she'd never felt in sexual terms. Cherished.

In an evening full of firsts, this one was right up there with the orgasms.

When he was done, he turned her on her side and told her not to move while he returned the washcloth to the bathroom. Then he climbed into the bed and drew her back against him.

"Comfy?" he asked.

Their heads shared a pillow, so she nodded. Despite her history with Phil, a history Kevin was about to know, she wasn't alarmed. She knew what was coming. Kevin pulled them into this spooning position on purpose, to offer her comfort and make it easier for her to talk.

It amazed her that she already knew him so well.

She must have made some sort of noise. He smoothed her hair behind her ear and traced the shell with his finger. "What?"

"I feel like I know you. I mean, better than I should at this point," she admitted.

"You do. I've told you things I haven't talked about in years. I want you to trust me like that too."

"It really does seem ridiculous now. It's nowhere near as devastating as what you told me."

"Why don't you let me be the judge of that? I'm assuming it was your ex. Was it something he said? Did?"

"Both." She paused, letting the warmth and strength from his body, of *him*, envelop her. "It was a culmination of stuff but a couple of things really stuck. Sex was never great. You asked me if a lover had ever brought me to orgasm with his mouth. The truth is, tonight was my first orgasm not by my own hand."

"Really? Wow."

"Pretty pathetic, huh?" she asked.

"No. Sad, yes. You were married for a long time, right?"

She nodded again. "Over twenty years. The one guy I was with before my marriage wasn't much different. I just figured I wasn't a sensual person and let it go at that. You can't miss what you never had. I was raising two kids, working and running a household. Who the hell had time for sex and like I said, I didn't exactly miss it. Bottom line, I didn't care."

"So what changed? What finally ended the marriage?"

She turned to face him. "Kevin, no offense but why in the world would you want to hear this crap?"

He shrugged. "It's part of what makes you tick and I like you. Your marriage shaped your life for over twenty years just like my tattoo shaped mine for over a decade."

He had a point there and it was kind of nice snuggled up with him like this. What had the cougars called it? *Post-coital bliss with the cub.* "Okay but the thing is there's not much more to tell. He didn't miss sex and instead of working on it together it became all about what I could do for him."

"Ahh."

That was the only sound he made but she knew Kevin was thinking about the blowjob she'd delivered. She couldn't let him think she'd felt obligated. "I meant what I said before. Doing that with you was a victory. It was on my terms and the first time I truly enjoyed it. I hope you'll let me do it again sometime."

His soft green eyes sparkled. "No worries there, believe me. And now that you mention it, I'd like for there to be an again. For *all* of it."

"No worries there either." Like she was going to turn that down!

"One more question." He reached up and brushed several strands of hair behind her ear. "What brought you here to this point with me and why were you so hesitant?"

"That's two questions. It'll cost you one in return." At his nod, she summed it up for him. "It wasn't until after the divorce that I had time to wonder if I was missing out on something good. I tried to date but Phil's hurtful comments over the years bubbled to the surface. The same thing happened a couple of times tonight but it was like it was automatic. I didn't feel hesitant in my gut."

He'd asked for the truth and even though she'd tried to soften it, there was disappointment in his eyes.

"You told me the night we met that you don't date," he admitted. "That part of it makes more sense now. You thought if you went through with having sex somewhat anonymously, you'd at least know if the stuff your ex said was true or not."

She nodded. "I wanted to make sure I didn't mislead you. I told you exactly what I was looking for."

He didn't say anything for a minute. "Do you still feel that way?" he finally asked. "I know we haven't known each other long but I could really fall for you."

Her heart thudded hard against her rib cage. "Me too. This is crazy. We haven't even been on a real date yet."

That made his eyes twinkle in the way she was starting to crave. "Best non-date I've ever had."

"I mean it," she insisted. "You're talking about taking it to the next level and there are so many factors to think about."

"Like what?"

"Our age difference, for one thing."

He shook his head. "Not an issue for me. Even if it doesn't work out between us, I'm done with younger women. I can't take the drama."

There were plenty of younger mature women but she'd be a fool to point that out. "I'm not just older, I'm beyond important milestones. You should know I've had my tubes tied."

His brows shot up and Elizabeth braced herself. Been there, done that, blessed with two beautiful girls for the effort. God love the women who had the energy to do it all over again at her age or older. She was not one of them.

But Kevin once again surprised her.

"*Fuckin' A*, we don't need a condom?"

Kevin had one hard and fast rule about sex. Always use a condom. At that moment he wanted nothing more than to slide into Elle's sweet pussy without one.

He eased her to her back and came over her on his forearms, so intent on his mission it almost didn't register when she flattened her palms to his chest.

"I appreciate the enthusiasm," she gave him a rueful smile, "but I brought up an important roadblock. There are also other reasons for wearing a condom."

He couldn't get the words out fast enough. "Given my family medical history, there's no roadblock. Rugrats are cute enough when they're someone else's and I'm clean. I haven't been with anyone in a year, I give blood every six months at work and I had a physical a couple of months ago. How about you?"

She smiled. "I'm safe. I needed peace of mind after I found out Phil had cheated."

"Shit, he did that too?"

The look she gave him spoke volumes. Yeah, that had been a stupid question. Still, being married to that asshole for over twenty years must have been like a form of water torture, slowly and insidiously leeching her sexuality.

He bracketed her face with his palms and held her gaze. "Hell, I could have made it all better by simply speaking the truth. Do you want to hear it?"

She swallowed hard before giving a barely perceptible nod. She had no way of knowing what he intended to say or do but she offered her trust.

"You lost your virginity to an idiot and you married a jackass. You need to have sex with a man who doesn't have shit-for-brains or a pencil dick."

She blinked. He waited for his words to sink in and was rewarded with a smile that lit her up from within. "I thought I just did."

Her smile lit him up too, like a powder keg. It was his turn to swallow hard. "I recommend more than one round. Elle, I've never had sex without a condom. Never even considered it. I want that so badly with you but if you need medical proof I'm clean first, I'll slap one on."

Chapter Eight
&

It was unspoken but they both knew that agreeing to make love with Kevin sans condom meant agreeing to try a relationship with him outside the bedroom.

Somehow in the span of a few hours Elizabeth had met a challenge to sleep with a younger man, tried to slay all of her sexual demons with his mighty sword and leapt toward a relationship with a man who already held enough power to squeeze her heart.

Mighty a sword as Kevin wielded, she knew her sexual demons were not all gone. Wiping out years of self-doubt with a single fuck worked well in theory but reality prevailed. It was going to take awhile to get there and until she did, her first instinct was to protect her heart.

So was she ready to take an emotional chance with Kevin? It was a terrifying proposition. The only thing scarier was the idea of letting him go without at least trying.

Which was, in essence, her answer.

"How about a kiss to sway the vote?" she asked him. It was what he'd said to her the night they'd met. *God, had that only been a week ago?*

The thought was cut short when his lips lowered to hers, his kiss slow and thorough, yet so carnal her arousal pulsed to life. It grew hard to stay still and her hands skimmed his back, his arms, the sides of his neck where his pulse pounded wildly.

His kiss remained calm. Centered. Focused on what was important. Their connection.

When he pulled back they were both breathing hard and she could feel his erection hot and heavy at her thighs. She knew with absolute clarity what she wanted.

She slowly spread her legs.

Kevin froze above her, making a strangled sound when the crown of his cock made contact with her pussy. Without a latex barrier, he felt hot and silky against her slit. The look on his face told her how incredible she felt to him.

He wasn't even inside her yet.

She wanted that first thrust, that ultimate connection, with a desperation that bordered on insanity. When he started nibbling kisses along her jaw and shifted to continue down her body, she stopped him with a hand to his cheek.

"Kiss me. Kiss me and come inside me," she said.

Lifting her head, she drew him to her mouth, slowly pressing her tongue deep as he followed her back to the pillow. He groaned against her lips, shuddering as his cock probed between her legs and penetrated that first inch.

The heat of him was astonishing. She released his mouth with a gasp, his response more a snarl as he recaptured her lips. His tongue thrust in her mouth as he plunged hard between her legs, a searing arrow right on target.

She exploded around him. There was no warning, no further buildup, just a giant spasm that tightened her body and crashed pleasure through her. There was nothing slow or civilized to his rhythm, or in the sounds that tore from him with each deep drive of his cock. She swallowed it all and craved more.

She lost count of how many times she came. The orgasms had mellowed, rolling through her in gentle waves as she floated in the unique taste of his mouth, the joy of his hard, aroused body.

She almost protested when his mouth left hers but when he groaned her name and stiffened, she let him go to watch him climax.

249

Only to get slammed by the energy of it and taken right along with him.

His eyes flew open and met hers as her name again tore from him, awe filling his gaze and his voice. Their coming together as one wasn't a fluke, it was happening again. She watched him for as long as she could, seeing his eyes glaze, hearing his groans, feeling the energy fireball through him and burst inside her.

Smaller bursts followed and the tendrils of heat stretched farther with each jerk of his body and responding spasm from her. It didn't stop until long after he collapsed with a groan on top of her.

Elizabeth stroked his damp skin, smiling with pure satisfaction when scraping her nails down his low back made him twitch and growl in protest.

"I can't move. I've hit my limit," he admitted, sounding like he'd swallowed gravel.

"Me too," she assured him. "But you're a bit heavy."

It took him two tries to plant his forearms and lift his chest. "Better?" At her nod, he added, "Are you going to let me stay? With some rest I may be able to last longer by the tenth time or so."

She was horrified to feel her eyes fill with tears and she quickly closed them even as she gave him a smile she felt start at her toes. Damn, was she going to do that every time they made love? That would freak anyone out.

"Make that a few hundred times. You have a smile that lights up a room."

Her gaze flew back to his and her breath caught in her throat. He was looking at her with compassion and, if she wasn't mistaken, a sheen of moisture in his eyes too.

"It's okay," he said. "I'm kinda feeling the happy relief thing myself right now." He wiped her cheek with his thumb. "And for the record, you're the most sensuous woman I've ever met."

Oh, that wasn't fair! "Are you *trying* to make me cry?"

He laughed and before she could protest he'd rolled them over so she was on top with him still inside her. She savored the position for a moment, the steady beat of his heart in her ear, the strong hands gently stroking her back.

It was almost funny to think these were the nuances she'd leave out when she reported to the cougar blog. These moments were theirs and theirs alone.

"Kevin?"

"Mmm."

She could hear his struggle to remain awake but she didn't want to think she'd given the wrong impression. "You still owe me a question. You do know we're going to have to take this slowly, right?"

"One day at a time, if that's what you need."

"I've thought about it and a week will do. Let's reassess every Friday night with the same rules. If either one wants out, tonight's rules apply. No questions asked, no emotional outburst."

"Mm-hmm. Perfect. It'll never happen. Plus it's after midnight, so we can't talk about it until next Friday."

She smiled and kissed his chest. *Perfect.*

* * * * *

Elizabeth got up before Kevin the next morning, managing to get out of bed without waking him. She started the coffee and sat down to scan the responses to her panic posts from Friday night, after Phil's phone call. That felt like it had happened a hundred years ago.

His new wife clearly has a brain leak. Let her have him. You have a young stud who is hot for you coming over in a few minutes. Forget detox. Get drunk on life in his arms! In your bed! Immediately! If I hear from you before Sunday, I will make you regret it. I'm going to go make prank calls to Phil now.

Monica

I saw you shaking that booty on the dance floor at RomantiCon. I have the utmost confidence that Kevin will be a very happy young man.

Stevie

Hell, sweetie, I've seen you and you could do at least twelve cross-country trips with your mileage. You're beautiful! Screw Phil. Actually, that's wrong. Screw Kevin and tell Phil to go take a flying leap...preferably off a tall building!

Rachel

1. Honey you REALLY have to start checking your caller ID and when the rat bastard calls exercise your option to NOT ANSWER. Or barring that, use what you get from those conversations to fuel your fire to pick up the pace with Kevin.

2. Okay, babe, time to get your groove on—and yes, you DO still have one!! Personally, I hope it's LATE Sunday afternoon before we hear anything.

Cam (living vicariously through the sex lives of others)

You should commiserate with him on his cock size. Tell him it did impact on his performance and didn't he think it weird that a woman every other man describes as hot didn't feel anything with him? Sweetie, we've all had men like that. My last husband was a bastard of the first order. Dropped me for the younger model. I think I came out of that one best and believe me, you are better off without him.

Edie

You bet you do, honey. That asshole Phil wouldn't know a good orgasm if it fell on him. Reel in that man and ride him hard.

Autumn

Wow, talk about being dead-on. How right they all were. Warmth filled her as she acknowledged how much these wonderful ladies had given her.

At the risk of their wrath for posting before Sunday, Elizabeth took the time to send two words that said it all.

Thank you

Elizabeth

Also by Samantha Kane

ꜱꝋ

eBooks:

A Lady In Waiting

Brothers In Arms 1: The Courage to Love

Brothers In Arms 2: Love Under Siege

Brothers In Arms 3: Love's Strategy

Brothers In Arms 4: At Love's Command

Brothers In Arms 5: Retreat From Love

Brothers In Arms 6: Love in Exile

Brothers In Arms 7: Love's Fortress

Ellora's Cavemen: Jewels of the Nile II (*anthology*)

Play It Again, Sam

Tomorrow

Islands

Print Books:

Aged to Perfection (*anthology*)

Brothers In Arms 1: The Courage to Love

Brothers In Arms 2: Love Under Siege

Brothers In Arms 4: At Love's Command

Brothers In Arms 5: Retreat From Love

Brothers In Arms 6: Love in Exile

Ellora's Cavemen: Jewels of the Nile II (*anthology*)

Hunters for Hire: Tomorrow

About the Author

ରେ

Samantha has a Master's Degree in History, and is a full time writer and mother. She lives in North Carolina with her husband and three children.

Samantha welcomes comments from readers. You can find her website and email address on her author bio page at www.ellorascave.com.

Tell Us What You Think

We appreciate hearing reader opinions about our books. You can email us at Comments@EllorasCave.com.

Also by Lynne Connolly

ℰℭ

eBooks:

Beauty of Sunset

Pure Wildfire 1: Sunfire

Pure Wildfire 2: Icefire

Pure Wildfire 3: Moonfire

Pure Wildfire 4: Thunderfire

Red Alert

Red Heat

Red Inferno

Red Shadow

Seychelles Sunset

Print Books:

Pure Wildfire 1: Sunfire

About the Author

ഌ

Lynne Connolly has been published for 5 years and in that time has won two Eppies and a number of other awards, Recommended Reads and other acknowledgements for her paranormal romances and her historicals.

While these are very gratifying, that isn't why she writes. She wants to bring the stories in her head to life and share them with others, in the hope that then she might get some peace.

Writing is what she was doing while she was working, bearing children and doing the other boring things that constitute living. Her favorite writer's motto is "I can use that."

She lives in the UK with her husband, children and cats, and her doll's houses. Creating worlds, miniature or otherwise, seems to be Lynne's specialty!

Lynne welcomes comments from readers. You can find her website and email address on her author bio page at www.ellorascave.com.

Tell Us What You Think

We appreciate hearing reader opinions about our books. You can email us at Comments@EllorasCave.com.

Also by Dalton Diaz

༄

eBooks:
Illegal Moves *(with Samantha Cayto)*
Love Cuffs *(with Ashlyn Chase)*
Stray Lovers
Winters' Thaw

Print Books:
Illegal Moves *(with Samantha Cayto)*
Love Cuffs *(with Ashlyn Chase)*

About the Author

ை

If a story doesn't have romance, it isn't worth it. If there's hot sex, it's extra worth it.

Let's face it, fantasy is usually a lot more fun than reality. Not always, but usually. As a writer, one can be anything, do anything, say anything that comes to mind. There are a thousand and one ways to make things happen, each one more exciting than the last.

This is the best job in the world.

Dalton welcomes comments from readers. You can find her website and email address on her author bio page at www.ellorascave.com.

Tell Us What You Think

We appreciate hearing reader opinions about our books. You can email us at Comments@EllorasCave.com.

Why an electronic book?

We live in the Information Age—an exciting time in the history of human civilization, in which technology rules supreme and continues to progress in leaps and bounds every minute of every day. For a multitude of reasons, more and more avid literary fans are opting to purchase e-books instead of paper books. The question from those not yet initiated into the world of electronic reading is simply: *Why?*

1. *Price.* An electronic title at Ellora's Cave Publishing and Cerridwen Press runs anywhere from 40% to 75% less than the cover price of the exact same title in paperback format. Why? Basic mathematics and cost. It is less expensive to publish an e-book (no paper and printing, no warehousing and shipping) than it is to publish a paperback, so the savings are passed along to the consumer.

2. *Space.* Running out of room in your house for your books? That is one worry you will never have with electronic books. For a low one-time cost, you can purchase a handheld device specifically designed for e-reading. Many e-readers have large, convenient screens for viewing. Better yet, hundreds of titles can be stored within your new library—on a single microchip. There are a variety of e-readers from different manufacturers. You can also read e-books on your PC or laptop computer. (Please note that Ellora's Cave does not endorse any specific brands.

You can check our websites at www.ellorascave.com or www.cerridwenpress.com for information we make available to new consumers.)

3. *Mobility.* Because your new e-library consists of only a microchip within a small, easily transportable e-reader, your entire cache of books can be taken with you wherever you go.

4. ***Personal Viewing Preferences.*** Are the words you are currently reading too small? Too large? Too… ANNOYING? Paperback books cannot be modified according to personal preferences, but e-books can.

5. *Instant Gratification.* Is it the middle of the night and all the bookstores near you are closed? Are you tired of waiting days, sometimes weeks, for bookstores to ship the novels you bought? Ellora's Cave Publishing sells instantaneous downloads twenty-four hours a day, seven days a week, every day of the year. Our webstore is never closed. Our e-book delivery system is 100% automated, meaning your order is filled as soon as you pay for it.

Those are a few of the top reasons why electronic books are replacing paperbacks for many avid readers.

As always, Ellora's Cave and Cerridwen Press welcome your questions and comments. We invite you to email us at Comments@ellorascave.com or write to us directly at Ellora's Cave Publishing Inc., 1056 Home Avenue, Akron, OH 44310-3502.

COMING TO A BOOKSTORE NEAR YOU!

ELLORA'S CAVE

Bestselling Authors Tour

UPDATES AVAILABLE AT

WWW.ELLORASCAVE.COM

ELLORA'S CAVE

Romanticon

Annual convention
for women who
refuse to behave

COLUMBUS DAY WEEKEND

www.JasmineJade.com/Romanticon
For additional info contact: conventions@ellorascave.com

Discover for yourself why readers can't get enough of the multiple award-winning publisher Ellora's Cave.

Whether you prefer e-books or paperbacks, be sure to visit EC on the web at www.ellorascave.com

for an erotic reading experience that will leave you breathless.

LaVergne, TN USA
01 November 2010
203081LV00002B/177/P